JIM ELDRIDGE

COURAGEOUS
FIRST WORLD WAR
STORIES

SCHOLASTIC

Scholastic Children's Books
Euston House, 24 Eversholt Street,
London, NW1 1DB, UK
A division of Scholastic Ltd

London ~ New York ~ Toronto ~ Sydney ~ Auckland
Mexico City ~ New Delhi ~ Hong Kong

The stories in this book were originally published as part of the
My Story and *My True Story* series, published by Scholastic Ltd.
My Story, Flying Ace first published in the UK 2003;
My True Story, Standing Alone first published in the UK 2011;
My Story, Trenches first published in the UK 2002.

This collected edition first published in the UK by Scholastic Ltd, 2014

ISBN 978 1407 14734 5

For Jack, Albert & Lila
with love from Grandad Jim

Contents

FLYING ACE

11TH NOVEMBER 1918

My name is Jack Fairfax. Twenty-one years old. Formerly of the Royal Flying Corps. Actually, I'm Lord Fairfax, but that's something I'm still taking time to get used to. Today the bells of our village church are ringing out to tell everyone that the armistice has been signed. The Germans have surrendered. The War is over. I'm at home here in Oxfordshire on this day, rather than with my former comrades in France, because two months ago my fighter plane was shot down while battling the Hun. I was invalided out of the Corps and sent back to England with a broken leg and a broken arm. I had got off lightly – unlike so many of my friends. Particularly my best pal, Alan Dixon. But to get the whole story, we have to go back to 1915, and our last days at school...

21st July 1915

The wind whistled as Alan Dixon and I clung on to the roof with our fingernails. Because it was dark we couldn't see the ground below, but we both knew it was a long, long way down.

It had seemed such a good idea at the time. The last day but one at school for me and Alan, my best friend, called for something special to celebrate it. The curtain was coming down on long years of self-important prefects, bullying masters, and four centuries of "school traditions" rammed down our throats at every opportunity. The occasion merited more than just attending the final assembly, singing the school song, and shaking hands with masters and housemasters we'd come to loathe before we went on our way.

That's when I'd suggested hanging a pair of trousers from the steeple at the top of the school chapel. Many years before when my grandfather, who was also called Jack Fairfax, had been at this school, he'd done the same sort of thing, using one of the master's mortarboards.

"If we do it at night no one will see so no one will know it was us," I said.

Alan laughed. "Of course they'll know it was us," he replied with a grin.

"You know how this school operates," he said. "Gossip and sneaking."

I shrugged. "So what if they do know," I said. "It's our last day here. What can they do? Expel us? Anyway, this place deserves something to liven it up."

And so I'd sneaked into the laundry room and snaffled a pair of trousers belonging to our housemaster, Mr Stokes, a short, balding, humourless man and my personal enemy during most of my years at school.

Now, at eleven o'clock at night, Alan and I were on the last leg of our climb, and I, for one, was starting to have second thoughts about it.

The first part had been easy – up to the top of the chapel, and out through a skylight on to the roof. The second part was more difficult – climbing up the slippery slates towards the steeple. Luckily Alan had thought to bring a couple of screwdrivers he'd picked up from somewhere, and we used these to dig into the slates to get some kind of leverage. As it was, it took us about twenty minutes just to get to the ridge at the top of the roof.

We were working our way along the ridge, me sitting astride it as if I was riding a horse, Alan more elegantly crawling along it on hands and knees, when suddenly Alan lost his grip on the slimy tiles and slid. In the darkness I heard his hands trying to clutch at the tiles, but the speed at which he fell made getting a grip impossible. I heard a crashing sound from the bottom of the roof, and then Alan calling, "Jack! Help!"

I was already halfway down the roof, but I was taking it slow so I didn't lose my grip. Alan had gone over the edge of the roof and was hanging by his fingers from the guttering. Below him was a drop of a hundred feet. There was no way he would survive if he fell.

I put my foot into the gutter, reached down and grabbed one of Alan's arms.

"Can you kick with your feet to push yourself up?" I asked.

"There's not much to kick against," said Alan.

I steadied myself, then reached with my other hand and took a firm grip beneath Alan's armpit.

"I'm going to try and haul you up on the count of three," I said. "Ready?"

There was a terrible creaking from the guttering, and Alan said, "I'd make it 'two' if I were you."

I didn't bother to count, I just pulled with all my strength. It felt as if my arms were being wrenched out of their sockets, but then Alan gave a kick which must have connected with something out of sight, and his head and shoulders appeared over the gutter.

I hauled him in, like landing a particularly heavy fish, and Alan lay balanced on the roof, getting his breath back.

"Thanks," he said. "I thought I was a goner then."

"You can't die yet," I said. "We're supposed to go and fight the Hun together, remember?"

Alan grinned. "True," he said.

That was our plan. Finish school and then go off to the War together. We were both 17, nearly 18. Alan and I had been best pals ever since we'd met at our prep school when we were both six years old. We'd been put into the same dormitory because our names were next to each other on the school roll, Dixon and Fairfax, and somehow we'd remained close chums ever since.

We even used to swap clothes if one of us had problems with something like a rugger shirt that needed cleaning, but we'd forgotten to get it washed. It helped that we were about the same height and the same build. The only real difference between us was that Alan had dark, curly hair, while mine was a mixture of fair and reddish brown.

"It's going to be difficult getting to the top of the steeple with the slates as slimy as this," said Alan.

"Well we're not abandoning the plan now," I said, determinedly.

"Of course, it depends how we define the 'top' of the chapel," said Alan. "It doesn't have to mean the steeple or the top of the bell-tower."

"That's a very good point," I said. "In fact, it'll be even harder for Stokes to get his trousers back if we hung them from the end of the ridge than if we hung them from the steeple. After all, they can get into the bell-tower from inside."

"So, we're decided then," said Alan. "The trousers hang from the ridge."

"But at the end," I said, "so they can wave in the breeze like a flag."

I gave Alan a concerned look. "Are you sure you want to risk going up on to the ridge again?" I asked.

"Of course," said Alan indignantly. "I can hardly fall off again a second time. What sort of idiot do you think I am?"

"The sort of idiot who comes up here in the first place," I replied.

We began to clamber up the greasy slates again, only this time taking more care, moving more slowly. Finally we made it to the ridge of the roof, and I pulled Stokes's trousers from where I'd loosely fixed them around my waist, and Alan and I tied them firmly into position.

"There!" I said triumphantly. "We are flying the flag of freedom!"

The summons came next morning. Alan and I were in the rooms we shared, packing our things ready to go home, when there was a knock at our door. It was Padwith, one of the school servants.

"Good morning, Mr Fairfax, Mr Dixon," he said. "Mr Stokes says he wishes to see you in his study."

"Very well, Padwith," I said. "Tell Mr Stokes we're on our way."

"Looks like they've noticed the trousers," said Alan ruefully. "I think we're going to get a beating."

"It won't be the first one," I said. "I might as well leave this school keeping up my tradition of being beaten at least once a month."

Alan hadn't been beaten as much as I had during his time at school, and he gave me a quizzical look.

"Don't you mind being beaten all the time?" he asked. "Frankly, I hate it. That cane cutting into the flesh of one's behind. It hurts like hell."

"I think of it as preparing me for life outside school," I said. "Dealing with pain without showing it hurts. When I'm over there, fighting the Hun, and they take me prisoner and start torturing me, I shall just look them straight in the eye and say, 'Do your worst! Nothing you can do can ever be as painful as my years at school!'"

Alan laughed. "We could always refuse to go and see Stokes," he suggested. "After all, it is our last day at school. What can he do if we don't turn up, but just leave?"

"Nothing," I replied. "But I won't give him the satisfaction of telling other people I was a coward because I refused to face him and take my punishment."

Alan sighed.

"I suppose you're right," he said. "It still irks me that that little bully is allowed to thrash me. In a fair fight I'd knock him down with two punches."

Alan and I finished our packing, strapped up our trunks, and then walked slowly together across the quad to Stokes's study in the masters' block. I knocked on his door.

"Come in!" called Stokes.

I opened the door and Alan and I stepped in.

I was very familiar with Stokes's study, having been summoned to it pretty often during my time at school, usually to be told off, and to be beaten. It had a smell I thought I would always remember: the strong tobacco from Stokes's pipe hung everywhere – in the curtains, in the books, in Stokes's clothes. Then there were the dusty bookshelves. I'm sure that Stokes sometimes took a book from his shelves to read, but most of the books seemed to have a fine film of dust over them. The only clean smell came from the scent of polish on Stokes's desk. His servant spent hours polishing and waxing the top of it.

Stokes was sitting behind his desk, and he stood up as Alan and

I came in. His face was creased with distaste, as if he was suffering from a stomach upset.

"Fairfax and Dixon!" he scowled.

"Sir," we responded.

Stokes came round from his desk and stood in front of us, glaring. I suppose it was meant to intimidate us, but as he was shorter than both Alan and myself, it wasn't very successful.

"I understand that you two were responsible for that dangerous and stupid prank last night, involving climbing the roof of the chapel," he began.

"It wasn't really dangerous –" I began, but Stokes cut me short.

"Silence, Fairfax!" he snapped. Turning to Alan, he said in an angry tone, "Fairfax's action I can understand, to a degree. He has been ill-disciplined and a troublemaker almost from the first day he came to this school. But you, Dixon. You have a fine academic record. Your behaviour is usually a credit to the school, and to your family. Why, Dixon?"

"It was my fault, sir," I said. "I led Dixon astray in this matter. The responsibility is totally mine."

Stokes turned to me, his little eyes boring into me.

"When it is your turn to speak I will tell you," he said. "I am talking to Dixon." Turning back to Alan, he again demanded, "Why?"

Alan hung his head.

"I am sorry, sir," he said. "I have no excuse. And it was not Fairfax's fault. I was as responsible as he was for climbing the roof. It just seemed a nice thing to do to celebrate the end of school."

Stokes said nothing, but just looked at Alan for a moment. Then he asked sarcastically, "A nice thing?"

Then Stokes turned to me.

"So, Fairfax," he said. "You have decided to end your days at this school in the same way you have spent them. With an irresponsible act and contempt for authority."

There didn't seem much point in saying anything to that, so I didn't.

"Your brother, Oswald—" Stokes began, and I gave out a silent groan. It obviously hadn't been silent enough, because Stokes glared at me.

"You have something to say, Fairfax?" Stokes demanded menacingly. "Something important enough to consider it worth interrupting me when I am addressing you?"

"No, sir," I replied.

Stokes glared at me again, and then began praising my wonderful older brother, something both he and my father did whenever I had been caught doing something I shouldn't.

"Your brother, Oswald, was a perfect pupil when he was at this school. Disciplined. Courteous. Dedicated."

Don't I know it, I thought ruefully. Everyone tells me often enough. At 19 years old, Oswald was two years older than me. At school he'd won every prize, excelled at everything, and had been head boy before he left.

"Where is your brother now?" Stokes demanded.

The question puzzled me. I couldn't see what on earth Oswald's location had to do with me about to get a beating. Especially as Stokes knew very well where Oswald was and what he was doing.

"He's with the Royal Scots Dragoon Guards, sir," I said. "On the Western Front. Fighting the Hun."

Stokes nodded. "Exactly," he said. "And what do you think he would say if he heard about this latest escapade of yours?"

I thought about that, then said, "Not a lot, to be honest. I think he'll be too busy watching out for German bombs to worry about me climbing a chapel spire."

Out of the corner of my eye I saw Alan stifle a grin. Stokes breathed in and out harshly, his face twitching, like a bull getting ready to charge.

"I suppose you think that's funny," he demanded. "No, sir..." I began, but Stokes stopped me.

"Your brother is risking his life, putting his King and Country, the good name of the school and the Empire before himself, as always, and you make a joke about it!" he stormed angrily.

"No, sir," I protested.

"Do not answer me back!" Stokes snapped. "During his time at this school Oswald was always a good example to the other boys. You, on the other hand, have been a bad example. You show disrespect for many of the masters, who are your elders and betters."

Elders, but not necessarily betters, I thought to myself, but I decided not to say anything. It was my last day at school and I was in enough trouble already. Stokes would be reporting everything I said back to my father and mother. In this situation I decided it was best just to shut up, take my punishment, and put it all behind me as soon as possible.

Stokes stood looking disapprovingly at us both for a few seconds more, then said, "It causes me great pain to beat any boy on his last day at school, but the act you perpetrated cannot go unpunished. For me to ignore such an offence would send out a wrong message to the rest of the school. The other boys here would consider it gave them licence to commit every act of folly on the last day of school, and that is not going to be the case!"

Stokes walked to the umbrella stand, where he kept his cane. He took it out, flexed it, and then returned to where we were standing.

"Dixon," he ordered, "bend over the chair."

As Alan walked over to the upright chair in the corner of the study, I spoke up.

"Sir," I said. "I think I should be beaten first. After all, I was the person most responsible."

Stokes gave me a hard look.

"I know you think you are being chivalrous, Fairfax," he said. "You believe that whoever gets beaten first will be beaten the hardest, because my arm will tire by the time I beat the second boy. I must assure you, that will not be the case. I have enough strength in my arm to beat you a hundred times if necessary, and each stroke as strong as the last."

With that he strode to where Alan had bent himself over the chair. Stokes pulled back the cane, and then launched it hard at Alan's backside. Whack! The sound of cane on cloth and flesh echoed around the room. I saw Alan bite his lip to stop himself yelling out against the pain. Whack! Whack! Six times the cane thudded into Alan, and each time he took it without uttering a sound.

After the sixth stroke, Stokes stepped back.

"You may stand now," he said.

Alan stood up and turned to face Stokes. Alan's face was white and there was a bead of sweat on his forehead. In the time-honoured school tradition after a boy had been beaten, Alan held out his hand towards Stokes.

"Thank you, sir," he said.

Stokes said nothing, just took Alan's hand and shook it.

"You may go," he said. "I will, of course, be writing to your father about this."

Alan nodded, and then – with a last sympathetic look back at me – left the study. Stokes flexed the cane between his hands, and then gestured towards the chair.

"Fairfax, take the position," he ordered.

Dutifully, I went to the upright chair and bent over it, tensing myself against the pain that I knew I was about to experience.

There was a pause, then a swishing sound as the cane cut through the air at speed, and I felt a pain like fire across my buttocks, even through the flannel of my trousers. The swine was being as true as his word – he was hitting me as hard as he'd ever hit me in all my time at school.

Swish... Whack! The second stroke bit even harder than the first, and I clenched my teeth, biting on my lip to try to offset the pain.

Swish... Whack! Three strokes. Three to go. Whack!! Whack!! Whack!!!

As the sound of the sixth stroke echoed around the study, I straightened up and turned to face Stokes, but he barked in a fury at me, "I have not given you permission to stand up, Fairfax! I have not yet finished!"

I was shocked. Six strokes of the cane was the standard punishment.

For a second I was tempted to defy him, to grab the cane from him and break it, and then set about him. But I controlled myself. I would not give him that satisfaction. Instead, I nodded as calmly as I could, turned, and bent over the chair again.

Whack! Whack! Whack! Whack! Another four blows landed on me, each one hurting more than the last as they landed on skin already beaten and cut by the previous blows.

After the tenth stroke, I waited, still bending over the chair, determined not to be caught out again by Stokes. "You may stand now," said Stokes. His voice was hoarse and contorted, and I realized at that moment that he really hated me.

I stood up and turned to face him, and, traditional as ever, held out my hand to him. Stokes glared at me, then he took my hand.

"Thank you, sir," I said, and then I began to squeeze his hand.

The look on Stokes's face became one of shock as he realized that I wasn't just shaking his hand, but grasping – hard. I felt him try to pull his hand away from mine, but my grip was too strong. I clutched harder, and now Stokes tried to squeeze back, fighting against my grip, but I was younger and fitter – stronger. Beads of sweat appeared on Stokes's forehead as he struggled to fight against the crushing pain I was sure he was feeling in his hand, but I kept a firm hold.

I don't know how long we stood like that, all the time our eyes locked on each other as we fought this silent battle. It could only have been a minute at most, but it felt like an eternity. Finally, Stokes whimpered, his eyes closed, and he croaked out hoarsely, "You're hurting my hand."

Immediately I let his hand go.

"My apologies, sir," I said.

He stood there, rubbing his crushed right hand, rocking slightly back and forth on his heels. "May I go now, sir?" I asked politely.

"Yes," he said, through clenched teeth. "Thank you, sir," I said. And with that, I left.

I spent the rest of the day going around the school, saying goodbye to my chums and making promises to meet up some time in the future. The general feeling was that we'd be meeting up next on the fields of Flanders in Belgium and France, as soon as we'd gone through Royal Military Academy at Sandhurst and become officers and joined our various regiments. Nearly everyone had someone who was out there fighting the Hun, either an elder brother – as was the case with me and Oswald – or a cousin, or an uncle.

"My father's got my commission already sorted out for the lancers," one pal, Martin Wickham, told me, adding, "I suppose you'll be joining the Greys and your brother out on the Front."

I shook my head.

"Not me," I said. "I'm going to get my wings and join the Royal Flying Corps."

Wickham looked at me, shocked.

"Flying?" he said.

"That's right," I said nodding. "That's where the future of warfare lies. Up in the skies. Alan Dixon and I are planning to go in together.

Wickham frowned.

"What does your father say about that?" he asked. "I bet he's not keen."

"I haven't told him yet," I said. "I'm going to tell him as soon as I get home."

At 3.30 p.m. on the dot, school was officially over for Alan and me, and the school servants hauled our trunks and bags down from our rooms to the lobby, where we waited for our respective drivers to take us home.

"Still up for joining the RFC?" I asked.

Alan beamed and nodded happily.

"You bet!" he said. "I'm going to start making arrangements for flying lessons as soon as I get home."

"Same here," I said. "I can't wait to get over to France and start bombing the life out of the Hun. That's what this war needs. Young people like us with new ideas. That's what's going to win it. Not treating it like it's the Hundred Years War all over again."

Just then I saw the family car coming down the drive. "Ah, here's my ride!" I said. I held out my hand and Alan and I shook hands firmly.

"I'll be in touch tomorrow, as soon as I've told Father what I'm intending to do," I said.

"Hadn't you better wait a day or two for the dust to settle?" suggested Alan. "What if he doesn't give his permission?"

"I don't need his permission to learn to fly," I said. "And if the old skinflint refuses to pay for the lessons, I've got some money of my own put by. Nothing's going to stop me, Alan, that's for certain."

Even as I said it, I knew I faced trouble over this flying business when I got home. Wickham was right about my father. He would definitely not be keen. The men of the Fairfax family had always served Britain and the Empire by joining the Greys, more properly known as the Royal Scots Dragoon Guards. Even though our family had lived in Oxfordshire for over a hundred years, we had strong Scottish connections. In fact, the family name, Fairfax, is Scottish.

Within the Fairfax family, the Greys were known as "the Regiment" and unless a male Fairfax was intended for some other profession, such as the law, medicine, or the church, that was where he went. The Regiment had been formed in 1692, and in 1693 the cavalry began riding grey horses, hence the Regiment's nickname. As you can see, it was a long tradition.

The drive back home to Bowness Hall, just outside Oxford, was quiet. Meadows, the servant who'd been sent to collect me and take me home, had been with the family for twelve years. He'd been with us since Father had become Lord Fairfax on the death of my grandfather, the previous Lord Fairfax – which had also made me the Right Honourable Jack Fairfax.

Meadows was a nice fellow of about 40 who lived with his wife and three children in a cottage on our estate. As we drove, I pumped him for information to catch up with how things were at home.

"How are my parents, Meadows?" I asked.

"Lord and Lady Fairfax are very well, Mr Jack," answered Meadows.

"And Nanna?"

"Lady Margaret is now in good health, I'm pleased to report," Meadows replied. "She had, as you may know, a touch of bronchitis three months ago, but I'm glad to say that it has cleared up. The recent dry weather seems to have been advantageous to her in that respect."

Lady Margaret, known more affectionately to me as Nanna, was my father's mother. She used to be Lady Fairfax until my grandfather died, and then, as the widow of the previous Lord Fairfax, she became known officially as the Dowager Lady Fairfax. My mother had then become the new Lady Fairfax. But, to avoid confusion, Nanna decided it would be easier all round if everyone called her Lady Margaret.

Nanna was possibly my favourite person in the whole family. She was gentle and never told people off. If a servant broke something or did something wrong and Father started to give one of his lectures (usually accompanied by a threat of dismissal "if it happens again"), Nanna would often intervene on the servant's behalf, pointing out how honest and reliable the servant usually was, and how they deserved to be given at least another chance. Nanna would sometimes even take the servant below stairs and offer them a drink of brandy or something to "help them recover from the awful experience". This annoyed my father enormously as he believed Nanna was undermining his authority and discipline when she acted in this fashion. Father was very strong on "authority and discipline".

"Any news from Oswald?" I asked Meadows. I hadn't heard directly from Oswald since he went out to the Front with the Regiment four months earlier. Not that we'd ever been that close as brothers. Oswald tended to take Father's view that I lacked discipline and was a bit too mischievous.

"Mr Oswald's most recent letter to your parents was about a month ago," said Meadows. "As I understand it, he is in good health, considering the conditions out in Flanders."

"And what are the current conditions out there?" I asked. "We've been a bit cut off from things about the War at school, to be honest. The head and the staff tell us we're winning but we have to pray for victory. When any of the boys get letters from the Front they're all marked out in black, where they've been censored. All in all, it's hard to find out what the situation is. Are we really winning the War?"

Meadows was silent for a moment, then he said, though I thought I caught a cautious note in his voice, "The newspapers and the government say we are, Mr Jack."

"Ha!" I said. "No one believes them. What do they say in the village?"

"Opinions are divided, Mr Jack," said Meadows. "There are some who say it'll all be over by Christmas. Then there are some who say it's going to be a long war. There's lots of talk about the new weapons the Germans are using. Particularly this poison gas."

I nodded. Even at school we'd heard about that. Just three months before, the Germans had launched an attack against the Allied forces at a place called Ypres in Flanders. This was the second attack they'd launched on that small town, which was right on the front line between the two armies.

In November 1914 the Germans had tried to smash through the British and French lines at Ypres. The British and French had stopped them, but at a tremendous cost to the Allies. We'd heard stories of 60,000 British and another 60,000 French dead, compared to 150,000 Germans dead. Since then there'd been a stalemate at Ypres, until this new attack in April. This time the Germans had launched a gas attack against the British, Canadian and French forces holding the town, before the actual assault. One of the boys at school, Owen Lewis, told me his uncle had been caught up in it.

"He said a blueish-white mist just came rolling towards them from the German lines," Lewis told me. "At first no one knew what it was. Thought it was just a fog of some kind." It turned out to be chlorine gas. Thousands of men choked to death as the gas hit them. Some, like Lewis's uncle, were left blind and had to be invalided back to England. The Germans, wearing gas masks, made their attack a few hours later. Seventy thousand British, French and Canadians died in that attack.

Luckily, according to another fellow at school, the Canadians, wearing makeshift gas masks made out of wet towels, counter-attacked and pushed the Germans back.

It was when I heard these kind of stories that my mind conjured up pictures of my brother and I wondered what he was doing. How was he coping with it out there? He'd obviously not been caught up in anything like that, or we would have known about it, I was sure.

As we drove the rest of the journey to Bowness Hall, I pumped Meadows for more local gossip: who was doing what in and around the village, who'd joined up in the army, who was poaching, that sort of thing.

It was about eight o'clock when we finally rolled up in front of the Hall. While Meadows unpacked my belongings from the car, I went up the steps to the house. Mother was waiting for me at the top, and from the strained expression on her face I could tell straight away that something wasn't right.

"What's wrong, Mother?" I asked. "Is it Oswald? Has there been bad news?"

Mother shook her head. "No," she said. "As far as we know, Oswald is well."

"Nanna?" I asked.

Although Meadows had told me that Nanna was in good health, there was no denying she was old and frail.

"No, Jack. Your grandmother is well."

I frowned, puzzled. "Then what has happened, Mother?" I asked.

"Your father wishes to see you in the library," she said.

The penny dropped. Stokes must have phoned Father and given his version of what had happened.

"Ah," I said.

Mother wrung her hands mournfully and said in a whisper, "Why do you always have to get into trouble, Jack? You know it upsets your father."

"I'll explain to him," I said.

As I set off for the library, I knew that it would be a waste of time trying to explain anything to Father. But, just for once, I thought I'd try. Father was pacing up and down in the library as I entered. He stopped pacing when he saw me.

"You wanted to see me, Father?" I said.

The grim expression on his face told me that this was going to be a repeat of my interview with Stokes, though without the beating at the end of it, I hoped. My bottom was sore enough already from the ten whacks Stokes had given me.

"I had a telephone call today from your house master," he said.

"Ah," I replied.

"Is that the best you can say!" he thundered angrily. "No," I said. "I tried to tell Mr Stokes I was continuing a family tradition, but he didn't want to listen."

Father gaped at me, as if he couldn't believe the words he was hearing.

"Family tradition?!" he snapped.

"Yes, Father," I nodded. "Nanna told me that when Grandfather was at school, he climbed the chapel steeple and hung one of the masters' mortar boards from it. I thought it would be fun to do what he did."

Father glared at me for a second, then turned and started pacing up and down again, as if he was having a battle inside himself about what to do next.

My father saw himself as being a pillar of respectability in his role as Lord Fairfax, a shining example to the villagers and everyone else. He didn't like to be reminded that his own father had been a bit of a practical joker, with a reputation for getting up to all sorts of mischief.

Finally, he stopped pacing and turned to me again. "I would prefer it if you discounted stories that your grandmother tells you about your grandfather. She is elderly and prone to exaggeration."

"But he did climb up the chapel steeple at school," I said. "I heard it from one of the old servants there, as well."

"Whatever your grandfather may or may not have done in his youth, he grew out of that foolishness as he grew older," said my father sternly. "You have brought shame on our family name by carrying out this particularly stupid, dangerous and irresponsible escapade on your very last evening at school. It is how you will be remembered."

I jolly well hope so, I thought. Mad Jack Fairfax, daredevil.

"I just hope that you won't embarrass Oswald in this manner when you go out to join the Regiment. Assuming, that is, that the War isn't over by the time you get your commission."

This is it, I thought. There's no time like the present.

"Actually, Father," I said, "I won't be joining the Regiment."

Father looked at me, and his mouth fell open in shock.

"What?" he said, stunned.

"Alan Dixon and I have decided to join the Royal Flying Corps. We're going to learn to fly and get our wings, and fight the Hun that way."

Father continued to gape at me as if I was talking to him in some foreign language.

"The Royal Flying Corps?" he echoed.

"Yes," I nodded. "One of the chaps at school, Chuffy Liddle, his brother's in it. Sounds awfully exciting. Lots of chances to actually meet the Hun face to face and shoot them down."

Father was opening and closing his mouth as if he was trying to breathe, then finally said, "Absolutely not! Positively out of the question! Aeroplanes! Toys! This is war, boy!"

"Exactly, Father," I agreed. "And it's going to be won or lost in the air. The side that controls the skies is going to be the one that wins this war. That's what the papers said. And that's where I'm going to be – up there!"

Father looked at me hard, then he shook his head and gave a deep groan.

"I don't know where I've gone wrong with you, Jack," he said. "Maybe it's not me. Maybe it's your mother. Or the masters at school being too soft on you."

I thought of Stokes and his cane and gave a wry smile.

Father shook his finger at me firmly.

"There's only one place for a Fairfax at a time like this, when the country's in peril, and that's in the Greys, at the forefront of the action.

Not skulking like some coward in the skies, away from the battle."

I bridled, annoyed at this.

"It's hardly away from the battle, Father," I protested. "The Hun firing at you from the ground with anti-aircraft guns. Their planes attacking you. There's nowhere to hide in a plane. There are no trenches to take cover in up in the skies."

Father said nothing at first. He simply glared at me as if the power of his stare alone would force me to change my mind. But he didn't understand me. I was no longer a little boy who could be threatened with a beating. I'd had beatings for most of my life, and they hadn't changed a thing. I was rising 18 and as tall as my father – I could look him straight in the eye and tell him how I felt and what I wanted to do. I'd left school, and I refused to be treated like a schoolboy any longer. I was my own man.

Father carried on glaring at me, but when I didn't buckle he shrugged and turned away from me.

"You may go to your room," he said. "We'll talk sensibly about this idiotic idea of yours tomorrow, and hope you will come to your senses."

As I left the library I felt a sense of pride in myself. It had been a good day. I'd been beaten for the last time by Stokes, and held my pride with him. And I'd refused to be brow-beaten by my father. Jack Fairfax was going to be making his own mark.

In fact I didn't go to my room. Instead I arranged with cook to serve me up a meal later on, and then I went to pay a visit to Nanna.

Nanna had her own quarters in the west wing of the Hall, with her own staff: her own housekeeper, Mrs Johnson, and her own maids, Milly and Dolly. It was Mrs Johnson who opened the door to Nanna's rooms when I knocked, and her face lit up when she saw me.

"Master Jack," she said smiling. "Her ladyship was hoping you'd call. She said to show you straight in when you did. Would you like tea?"

"Tea would be lovely, thank you, Mrs Johnson," I said.

Mrs Johnson went along the corridor in front of me, skirts flapping like a ship in full sail, and rapped on the door of Nanna's sitting room before going in.

"Master Jack, your ladyship," she announced.

Nanna was sitting in one of the big comfortable armchairs in her sitting room, reading a book, which she put down as soon as I came in.

"There you are!" beamed Nanna.

I hurried over to her and gave her a kiss, and then sat myself down on the settee near her.

"What's this I hear about you being a naughty boy again, Jack?" she said.

"I wasn't really naughty, Nanna," I said. "Just a bit of a daredevil. I wanted to do what Grandpa did when he was at school, so I climbed the chapel spire."

"Yes, I'm afraid you do have your grandfather's naughtiness and high spirits, but not much of his brains," said Nanna sternly, though I could see a twinkle in her eye as she said it. "Your grandfather also did well in his exams, something I understand you don't follow him in."

I gave a sigh. "That's true, Nanna. Anyway, enough about me. How are you? How's your health?"

Nanna smiled. "Not good enough for me to climb up a chapel steeple, but enough to keep me alert to what's going on," she said. "I hear that you've upset your father, and you've only been home five minutes."

"Oh well, you know Father," I shrugged.

"I know him well enough to know how upset he'd be with this idea of yours of going into the Flying Corps." I gaped at her, stunned. "Nanna, you are truly amazing!" I said. "I've only just told Father, and then I came straight here! How did you find out so soon? I swear, in the old days you'd have been burnt as a witch."

Nanna gave a small, sly smile. "Walls have ears, and I listen to them."

Of course. The servants. Our servants had obviously overheard my conversation with my father. In turn that had been passed on below stairs to other servants, and either Milly or Dolly would have picked it up and passed it on to Mrs Johnson, who would have passed it on to Nanna. And all in the space of a few minutes. In a large house, servants need to know what's going on: who's in a good mood and who's in a bad mood, or when large sums of money are owed to tradespeople. All these things affect their position. As a result, the "bush telegraph" is usually faster than any telegram.

"I take it you're serious about this flying business?" asked Nanna. "It's not just a whim to annoy your father?"

I shook my head. "I'm absolutely serious, Nanna. I know it will mean that Father won't talk to me for weeks. Maybe months. But I've heard about this war and what's happening, and the way to win it is in the air. And I'm going to be there, in a plane, fighting for our side."

Just then, Mrs Johnson came in with a tray. As she poured our tea out for us, I asked Nanna, "Do you think I'm letting the family down? After all, Grandpa was a hero of the Regiment as well."

"No, no," replied Nanna. "Your grandfather loved the Regiment, but it wasn't the be-all and end-all for him. No, it was the men of the Regiment who were most important to him. The soldiers who served under him. That's the difference between your father and him. Your father loves the history of it. My Jack loved the people in it."

She sipped at her tea, then said, "Did you ever hear about Christine Welsh?"

I frowned, puzzled. "No," I said. "Who is she?"

"Was," corrected Nanna. "She was in the Regiment." This puzzled me even more.

"What as?" I asked. "A cook? Washerwoman?" Nanna shook her head. "She was a soldier," she said. I laughed. "Oh come on, Nanna!" I said.

"It's absolutely true," said Nanna. "Your grandfather told me about it."

"Then he was having you on," I said. "Playing a joke." Again, Nanna shook her head.

"I checked," she said. "All the facts were right. You can ask your father, if you like. He won't like admitting it, but it's true."

I was intrigued. A woman fighting as a soldier in the Greys? It was impossible. Women simply weren't allowed in the Regiment.

"It was back in 1702," said Nanna. "This woman, Christine Welsh, had married a man who'd joined the Regiment and gone off to war. Unlike most women, who just stay behind and get on with their lives, Mrs Welsh set off to find her husband. She dressed herself as a man and called herself Christian Welsh, and joined up in the Regiment to look for him."

"And no one noticed?" I said, incredulous.

"Not for four years," said Nanna.

"Did she find this husband of hers?" I asked.

"Oh yes," said Nanna. "But he was killed in active duty, so she carried on serving as a soldier until she was seriously wounded in the Battle of Ramillies, I believe it was, in 1706. It was while the surgeon was fixing her up that he noticed that she was not what she appeared to be."

"Four years, and no one spotted her! It doesn't say much for the eyesight of the soldiers in the Greys."

"No, but it says a lot for Mrs Welsh's courage," said Nanna. "She broke the tradition of the Regiment, and she proved her worth as a soldier."

I looked at Nanna quizzically, still not completely sure she wasn't playing a joke on me.

"I'm sure there's a point to this story, Nanna," I said. "But, I must admit, I don't see what it is."

Nanna smiled. "It's about not thinking in straight lines," she said. "You don't have to live by everyone else's rules, but you can't just challenge them. You have to go along with them, at least part way, if you want to get what you want. Christine Welsh didn't try and join the Regiment as a woman. She wouldn't have got in."

"So how does this affect me and Father?" I asked, still puzzled.

"Your father is a good man, but he thinks in straight lines," said Nanna. "If you want him to see things differently, you have to go along those straight lines with him at first, before you start to move off and go on different roads."

"You think I ought to go into the Regiment," I said gloomily.

"No," said Nanna. "I think you ought to offer your father the chance that you will."

"But I can't do both," I said. "I can't join the Flying Corps and join the Regiment."

"You can tell him that you'd like to give the Flying Corps a try first. And, if it doesn't work out, then you promise to join the Regiment."

"He won't accept that," I said. "Father's very firm in his views."

"He might accept it if he realizes that you're going to join the Flying Corps anyway, with or without his permission. This way he doesn't lose face. As far as he's concerned, you're still going to join the Regiment. But later, once you've got this flying nonsense out of your system."

I sat there, tea cup in hand, and thought about what she said.

"You are very clever, Nanna," I said.

Nanna smiled and nodded. "I know," she said.

Next morning over breakfast I tried out Nanna's suggestion on my father. To my surprise, he agreed. He didn't agree at first, obviously, and it took some pretty hard talking on my part to persuade him. He only finally gave his begrudging agreement after I'd given him my word that, if I couldn't get into the Royal Flying Corps, or if I did and made a mess of it, I would immediately try for a commission in the Greys.

I telephoned Alan straight after breakfast and told him the news.

"Well done!" he said.

"How about you?" I asked. "Have your parents agreed?"

"No problem there," he said. Alan came from a different sort of background from me. His father and grandfather had been merchants and so he wasn't stuck with a family history of riding in cavalry ever since the horse had been invented.

"Right," I said. "Let's go and join up."

"Ah, that's not so straightforward," said Alan. "What do you mean?" I asked.

"We got in touch with the RFC yesterday, but it seems they're full up at the moment and they can't take any more people on for training."

My heart sank. All that arguing with my father, persuading him, and now it looked as if I wouldn't be able to get in to the Flying Corps after all.

"Hello?" came Alan's voice in my ear. "Jack? Are you there?"

"Sorry, Alan," I said into the phone. "It's just that you gave me a bit of a shock. I've promised my father that if I can't get into the Flying Corps I'll join the Regiment, and now you tell me they're full up."

"Only at the moment," said Alan.

"Yes, but that won't be any use when I tell my father why I'm not going straight off to join up. He'll insist I keep to my promise and go into the Greys."

"It doesn't mean we can't learn to fly," said Alan. "In fact it would be a good idea for us to get some basic training. The chap I spoke to at the RFC said it would make us more likely to be accepted into the Flying Corps when we do get the chance to apply to join, which will be in about a month's time."

"Excellent idea!" I said, cheering up immediately. "I've found a private flying school that can give us lessons," said Alan. "It's the Empire Flying School at Hendon, just north of London. They'll teach us to fly for £100 each. They reckon it'll take about three weeks for us to learn. Is that all right with you?"

"Count me in!" I chuckled happily into the phone. "Hendon, here I come!"

August 1915

Ten days later Alan and I reported for our first flying lessons at the Hendon school. Basically the school was little more than a field with a wooden shed in it, where the owner of the school, Mr Walter Mitchell, sat and filled out forms and answered the telephone. Our flying instructor was a Frenchman, Monsieur Chapelle. He was about 30 years old, a shortish, thin man with a big curly moustache with waxed ends. He told us that French planes were the best in the world, and that we were lucky to be learning in "one of the best creations ever seen, the Maurice Farman biplane".

Frankly, this machine looked just like a load of wood and cloth held together by a lot of wires. It was dual-control, which meant that both the instructor and the student pilot could control it. This struck me as a good idea. I'd heard that some people went up solo straight away, because there was no room for two people in some planes. It occurred me to me that it would be useful to have someone to take over if you had trouble with the controls and were a thousand feet up in the air. The biplane, which was known as a "Shorthorn", had two long wings – one above the pilot, one below – and was driven by a Renault engine. The instructor sat at the back, and the student sat at the front.

Alan and I tossed a coin to see which of us would go first, and I called heads and won.

Monsieur Chapelle put on his leather cap and goggles, and climbed into the rear seat behind the pilot's. I also put on my leather cap and goggles and clambered into the seat at the front.

"Those bars, where you put your feet, are the rudder bars," explained Monsieur Chapelle. "The stick in front of you is called the joystick and that controls when you go up and when you go down. Just rest your hands and feet lightly on the controls and feel when they move. Notice how they move when I operate them.

"Do not attempt to put any pressure on them yourself, just get the feeling of what they do. I shall get us off the ground this first time. Once we are in the air, I shall pass the controls over to you. Is that clear?"

"Perfectly," I said.

The school's mechanic, a giant of a man called George, had been waiting beside the plane while Monsieur Chapelle and I got in. Now George went to the large wooden propeller at the front of the plane and took hold of it in both of his huge hands.

"Ignition off!" he bellowed.

"Ignition off!" confirmed Monsieur Chapelle in a shout from behind me.

George then began to turn the propeller slowly.

"He is priming the engine from the carburettor by turning the propeller," explained Monsieur Chapelle. "When the engine is primed, he will give it one last turn to get the engine going."

George kept turning the propeller. From the sweat pouring down his face from the effort, it looked like hard work, even for a big man like him. Finally, he stopped and called out, "Contact!"

Monsieur Chapelle switched on the ignition and echoed the cry. George gave the heavy propeller one last quarter turn. Behind me I could hear a handle being turned round quickly.

"I am turning the handle of the starter magneto to boost the spark at the plugs!" shouted Monsieur Chapelle into my ear. "The magneto is the electrical motor that makes the engine spark and burn the fuel."

Suddenly I heard the sound of the engine behind us kicking into life, and then it began to rattle with an alarming coughing and chattering sound, like a car engine with hiccups.

George stepped back swiftly from the propeller and out of the path of the plane, ducking his head down to make sure he was under the wings. And then we were moving forward.

We rolled across the grass, bumping and jerking along, getting nearer and nearer all the time to the hedge at the edge of the field ... and then suddenly we were up in the air, and flying over the hedge! It was an absolutely exhilarating feeling. We were only about eight feet off the ground, but I was flying through the air!

Keeping a light touch on the controls as Monsieur Chapelle had instructed, I felt the joystick being pulled back and we began to go up. Up, up, up. Soon the ground was far below us. From my position at the front I could see for miles. Houses and buildings were tiny. People were just specks.

"I am passing the controls to you," shouted Monsieur Chapelle from behind me. "Keep a firm grip on them. If you get into difficulty, or if I tell you to, release your hold on all the controls immediately and I will take over. Is that clear?"

"Clear, Monsieur Chapelle," I replied.

"At first, just keep the plane on the course which it is already flying," instructed Monsieur Chapelle. "Hold it steady. Use the rudders."

I felt an enormous sense of excitement as the bars responded to the pressure of my feet. That feeling of resistance that let me know that I was in control. I was flying this machine. Me, Jack Fairfax.

"You are now going to take the plane up higher," shouted Monsieur Chapelle. "But gently. Slowly pull back on the joystick."

I did as instructed. Higher we went, and higher. Now I began to feel the air getting colder, a chill wind picking at the skin on my face.

"Level off!" Monsieur Chapelle called.

I levelled the joystick and flew in a straight line for a while.

"We are now at 3,500 feet," came Monsieur Chapelle's voice from behind me. "The higher you go, the colder it is. Take us back down to 2,000 feet."

I pushed the joystick forward, but unfortunately I pushed it too hard, and we suddenly dropped into a dive. I felt the joystick pulling back in my hand and the plane levelling out, and realized that Monsieur Chapelle had momentarily retaken control of the joystick.

"Gently, mon ami!" called Monsieur Chapelle. "If you dive too fast and too steeply you can go into a spin. If you go into a spin you will not come out of it easily and the next thing you will do is crash into the ground nose first, and die. I do not recommend it."

He released the joystick and I felt the pressure of it in my grip again. This time I eased it forward much more gently, and we descended into a slower dive.

"Good!" said Monsieur Chapelle. "Level her out now!"

Down at 2,000 feet that frosty feeling on my skin eased off.

"We will now do some manoeuvres, left and right," instructed Monsieur Chapelle.

For the next ten minutes I followed his shouted instructions: turning the plane to the left, then to the right, locating and following the course of a railway line, and then a river. During this I had to admit that I had lost all sense of direction and hadn't got the faintest idea where we were. From this height the countryside looked much the same, whichever way I looked.

Finally, Monsieur Chapelle said, "We will now return to the airfield. I will navigate you to the field, but on this first occasion I will carry out the landing. As before, you will just let your hands and feet rest on the controls and feel what they do. Is that clear?"

"Clear!" I called back.

To my surprise, I discovered that we weren't far from Hendon. Monsieur Chapelle had obviously been manoeuvring me so that my left and right turns were all the time heading us back in a circle towards the flying school. We were still some miles away, but I could see the field and the wooden hut in the distance. Monsieur Chapelle instructed me,

"Gently ease the joystick forward!"

I did as he ordered, and we began to go down, heading straight for the hedge that bordered the flying school field. Down, down, down, we went, until Monsieur Chapelle called out, "Level out!"

I levelled out, and Monsieur Chapelle ordered, "Release the controls to me!"

As he had instructed, I released my firm grip on them but kept my hands and feet loosely touching them, feeling their movement, the way they went up and down and moved from side to side as we flew over the hedge.

The next second the ground was rushing up towards us. There was a bump as we came down, then we lifted up again, and a second bump as we touched the ground again, and finally we were bouncing over the uneven ground, slowing down. As we coasted to a halt, I wanted to shout out loud with joy. For the very first time, I had flown!

After my lesson I sat on an old chair beside Mr Mitchell's wooden hut and watched as Monsieur Chapelle took Alan up in the Shorthorn for his first lesson. As I watched them lift off the ground and disappear into the distance, I relived the excitement of my first flight. It was a feeling like I'd never known before. It wasn't like climbing a chapel steeple or a peak in the Lake District. This was altogether different. This was being free of the ground completely.

Later that afternoon, as Alan's driver, Woodson, drove us back to Alan's place, we talked about what a completely wonderful experience it had been. Alan's place was at Radlett in Hertfordshire, which was about ten miles away from Hendon. His parents had invited me to come and stay with them while Alan and I were doing our training. It was a welcome offer and meant that I didn't have the long journey from Oxford every day, nor have to find digs locally.

"I thought Monsieur Chapelle was excellent," I said. "A damn good instructor."

"Yes," agreed Alan. "These Frenchies seem to have a talent for aeroplanes. I was talking to Mr Mitchell while you were up in the air. According to him, if it wasn't for the French there'd be no such thing as aeroplanes."

"What about the Wright Brothers?" I asked. "They were American, surely."

"Yes, but according to Mitchell they used a lot of French designs in their plane. Plus, it was the French who first used the rotary engine. In 1909, he says."

"I expect he's right," I said. "Frankly, I wouldn't know a rotary engine from a lawnmower. But then, I don't want to be a mechanic, I want to be a pilot."

When we got back to the Dixons' house I telephoned Father and told him that I had been up in a plane and had landed safely, and that everything was going well. Although I guessed that he was relieved that I hadn't killed myself and my instructor on my first flight, I detected a note of disappointment in his voice on the phone. He obviously was still hoping that I'd get over this "flying madness", as he'd put it, and join the Greys.

Every weekday for the next three weeks, Alan and I drove to Hendon for more lessons from Monsieur Chapelle. By the end of that first week we were both flying solo. Finally, on 23rd August, both Alan and I were awarded our flying certificates by the school. We were now both qualified pilots – at least as far as civilian flying was concerned. The next stage was to learn to fly military planes.

During our time at the Empire Flying School, we'd been in touch with the applications board of the Royal Flying Corps, and the day after we got our flying certificates from Mr Mitchell, Alan and I were accepted by the RFC and told to report to Farnborough.

It was with a feeling of great gratitude that I shook Monsieur Chapelle's hand as we left Hendon for the last time. He had safely taken us through every aspect of flying, and it was thanks to him that we were now both on our way to the RFC School, and eventually to the Western Front.

Alan and I spent the next month at Farnborough, carrying out more flights – some dual-control, some solo – in a variety of planes. As well as the Farman biplane, we also flew pretty ancient Caudrons, which were the devil to control in windy conditions, and Avros, which were much better to fly in my opinion.

The worst of the lot was the "Bloater". The Bloater's proper name was the BE8 and it was supposed to be an improvement on the earlier BE and BE2. Frankly, I found it to be an appalling machine. And I wasn't the only one. All the chaps had difficulty with it. It was unstable both on the ground and in the air. At the slightest touch it was prone to go into a spin, and it took all your strength and skill to get out of it. The dreadful thing had to be handled with kid gloves: too much rudder or too much bank and the thing threw itself all over the place. I suppose the reasoning behind getting us to fly these awful machines was that if we could handle a Bloater, we could handle anything.

After four weeks of this, Alan and I had both clocked up enough hours in the air and passed all our exams to qualify for our "wings" – our pilots' badges. We thought we were now ready to fly off and face the enemy, but we were in for a shock.

"Right," our flight commander, Captain Walters, told us. "You're both being posted to Upavon in Wiltshire for some advanced training."

"But, sir," I protested. "Surely we're needed at the Front, fighting the Huns. We've got our wings, after all."

"You may have got your wings, Lieutenant Fairfax," said Walters, "but the RFC needs to know that when you get out there, you won't lose us any planes. They are in short supply and we have to know you'll be able to take good care of them. So, you've got a few more weeks of very vital advanced training at the best flying school in the world. Take advantage of it. It could save your life. Some of these Huns are amazingly talented fliers, and you need to know what you're going to be up against."

And so Alan and I went off for yet more training. It was a very frustrating time for me. I was desperate to get out to France and play my part in the War. Yet here I was, with 1915 coming to an end, still stuck in England. Upavon was a dreadful place. Or maybe it was just that we were seeing it at the worst time of year, in the damp of winter. The flying school was set in the middle of Salisbury Plain and our accommodation was in wooden huts, which let in the cold and damp. However, the training we received was superb. And not just the actual flying training, but also the lectures we were given.

We were instructed that the primary task of the Royal Flying Corps was to act as aerial observers. To report enemy positions and troop movements in order that the Top Brass could take proper decisions about battle strategy and the movements of our own troops. To that effect, we were shown how to take photographs from the air using large wooden box-cameras fixed to the side of the plane. We were also taught how to locate and identify positions on maps from the air, and how to identify enemy weapons.

As "observation and reporting of the enemy" was rated the highest priority for the Flying Corps, those of us who flew single-seater planes were told that our job was to give protection to the two-seater observer planes. The two-seaters had a pilot and an observer, who also acted as a gunner, operating the plane's machine-gun. Our job was to fly with these observer planes and defend them from attack from German aircraft. In turn, if we came upon a German two-seater observation plane, or any German plane, come to that, then we were to shoot it down. So we had to know all we could about the German aircraft, and the flying abilities of the German pilots.

We were told that the most recent German fighter planes we would be coming up against were the Fokker monoplanes, single-seater fighters with deadly accurate fixed guns. According to our instructors, early on in the War pilots had just been armed with a pistol. The only way of shooting at an enemy was to point the pistol at his plane, press the trigger and hope you hit him – which, considering the way planes juddered about all the time, going up and down in the air, was pretty unlikely.

Then someone fixed a machine-gun to the edge of the cockpit of a small plane, and the fighter plane was created. The biggest problem with this, however, was that the pilot couldn't fire the machine-gun straight ahead for fear of shooting his own propeller. The French and

Germans were the first ones to come up with an answer: each invented different sorts of gears, one called an "interrupter", the other known as a "synchronizer". Both systems meant that a pilot could fire his machine-gun without his propeller being hit.

Our own side was developing new planes all the time, of course, such as the Sopwith Strutter (which was a two-seater reconnaissance machine with a synchronized Vickers gun at the front for the pilot and a Lewis machine-gun at the rear for the observer), and the Sopwith Pup (which was a single-seater version of the Strutter). But now the Germans had come up with the most fearsome advance in fighter technology yet with the Fokker E series and the Albatross monoplanes, which had accounted for many of our chaps being shot down.

"Remember, the Fokker are the best German machines, so the best German pilots make a point of taking them as soon as they appear," our instructor warned us. "The best pilots together with the best machines make a formidable combination. But they can be beaten."

To show us how they could be beaten we had instruction on tactics in air battles – and not just dry old lectures from men who'd only ever seen a plane in a picture, but gripping reports from flying aces who were actually out there fighting the Hun in the sky. They told us how to attack an enemy.

"In a battle in the sky, your biggest assets are your reflexes," one ace, Captain Harry Manners, told us. Manners was reported to have 17 kills to his name, which made him a hero in our eyes.

"Unfortunately," he continued, "reflex reactions come with practice and experience, which means you lot are going to have to make sure you stay alive long enough to develop them."

We all laughed at this, but I noticed that Manners didn't join in.

"It's very easy to get your attention stuck on something," Manners continued. "A target on the ground, say, or an enemy aircraft at a lower altitude. Because you're watching so intently you don't notice an enemy sneak up on you from behind. The first you know about it is when the bullets hit your machine. Now when that happens, just change direction. If you freeze up, even for a fraction of a second, you're a sitting target for the next burst. Move, making sure you don't fly smack into another machine, of course. Rudder, joystick, throttle forward. A steep dive, out of his gunsights. But it's all reflexes, reacting quicker than you can actually think.

"When you come up against a two-seater, remember they're heavier than you if you're in a single-seater. They can't manoeuvre as well, so you've got an advantage. However, they have one extra man who can always keep firing at you. When attacking a two-seater make your approach from below and to the rear, where the plane has got a blind spot. If you can work in pairs, so much the better. One of you comes in on a broadside attack, opening fire at a very long range. This is the decoy attacker and won't hit the target, that's not the point. The object is to distract the attention of the crew of the enemy two-seater so the real killer can come up underneath and behind.

"If you're in a single-seater attacking on your own, use the sun and clouds. Come out of the sun, so that it dazzles your opponent. If you want to hide, use a cloud as cover."

For me and Alan, the most exciting part of this training was the actual exercises. We flew in pairs, firing imaginary shells at one another and learning how to use the sun, clouds, and wind to gain a tactical advantage. We flew high in the sky, looping the loop to escape from our "opponent" who was chasing us, and then coming down behind them to get a direct line on their tail. We also practised stalling our engines in mid-air to simulate engine failure, bearing in mind the firm instruction: "In case of engine failure do not attempt to turn your machine back. Put her nose down at once and make some sort of landing ahead."

Time and time again we were told that the biggest danger to us was anti-aircraft fire, commonly called "Archie", from heavy guns on the ground.

"Learn to try to avoid flying for too long in one straight line," our instructor told us. "It will give the Hun down on the ground a chance to work out your route and get their anti-aircraft guns sighted ahead of you. You'll find yourself flying straight into flak, which is the bits of shrapnel thrown out when the shell fired by the gun explodes near you. Very nasty stuff."

"Are there any plans to issue us with parachutes, sir?" asked one of our group, Banger Wilson.

Our instructor gave Wilson a hard, disapproving look. "It is not the policy of the RFC to give people an easy way out," he said sternly. "Parachutes are only issued to observers in balloons, in case their balloon gets shot down by the enemy. They have no other way of getting down except by parachute. You men, on the other hand, have been trained to fly your machine in all circumstances."

"Yes, sir, but say our plane catches fire. There's not a lot we can do with it if that happens."

"Then your job is to aim your plane at the enemy and take as many of them with you as you can," said our instructor.

As we left the lecture hall, I went up to Banger and clapped him heartily on the shoulder.

"Well, Banger," I said. "There's your answer. Death or glory."

"I can't see why us having parachutes is such a bad thing," said Wilson. "After all, if we live it means we can get back into another plane and have another go at them."

"Ah, now you're being sensible, Banger," said Alan with a grin. "You should know by now that the Top Brass are not sensible."

Our training continued for what seemed like an eternity. Our experience of flying different planes increased. As the days turned into weeks, and the weeks turned into months, I felt that I could fly just about anything, with my particular favourites being the Vickers Gunbus and the "De Hav2", the De Havilland Scout.

Finally, at the end of February, just when I had given up hope of ever getting into the fighting before the War ended, we were told that our training was at an end. We were being sent to the Front.

Alan and I were given 48 hours' leave, and told to report back to Upavon on the Wednesday, ready to kit up and fly out to France on the Friday with the rest of our group, 32 Squadron.

We didn't want to waste any precious time telephoning our respective homes and arranging for cars to come and collect us. Instead we found a driver who was returning to London after delivering a load of supplies to the airfield, and gave him a pound to make a couple of detours on his way back: dropping me off at Bowness Hall, and Alan at Radlett. It was money well spent.

Both Mother and Nanna made admiring noises about my uniform, and the wings I was proudly displaying, but I could tell that Father was disappointed. For him, it was the wrong uniform. I should have been wearing the colours of the Royal Scots Dragoon Guards, the Greys. But he didn't dwell on the topic.

"Congratulations on getting your wings, Jack," he said. "But, if it doesn't go as you planned, remember your promise. You will always find a commission in the Greys."

"Absolutely, Father," I said.

Inwardly I thought to myself, the only way this won't go as I planned is if I get shot down. And if that happens I don't think there'll be much left of me.

I spent time with Nanna, telling her about my flying experiences, but I could see, despite her expressions of being interested, that all the technical talk was beyond her. Finally she smiled, patted me on the knee, and said, "Jack, I know you find all this mechanical talk about rudders and joysticks absolutely fascinating, but you have to remember that I am an old woman. When I was a girl, the motorcar hadn't even been invented, let alone the aeroplane. I love to hear you talk about it, but it's all gibberish to me. The horse and carriage were our means of transport. Ships used sails, not engines."

I was also able to catch up on how Oswald was doing. During his time at the Front he'd come home on leave to England only once, a couple of months earlier, just after Christmas.

"I wish you'd been able to get home too, at that same time, Jack," my mother said. "It would have been nice to have had both my boys home together."

"But I was in training, Mother," I pointed out.

"There has to be a special reason for getting leave."

"Jack's right," said my father, backing me up. "Even if it is the Flying Corps, military rules still apply. You know that, Elspeth. Remember how rarely I used to be able to make it home when I was in the Greys."

"Yes, but you were in Africa," countered Mother.

"Jack was just in Salisbury."

"Rules are rules, Mother," I said. "Anyway, how was Oswald?"

"He seems to be getting on quite well," said Mother.

"He's getting on very well," interrupted Father.

"You know he's a captain. Well, if he carries on the way he is, I'm sure he can go as high in the Regiment as he wishes. It wouldn't surprise me to see him being made a major before very long. He's as able on the Front as he was at school. Oswald is a natural commander."

The implication being that I wasn't. I didn't argue. If that was Father's opinion, then I was happy to let him go on thinking it. At least, until the time when I came back from the Front as a flying ace, laden with medals. Then we'd see what he said about me.

I fixed up for Alan's driver to collect me on his way to the airbase at Upavon. It made sense for us to return together, especially as Alan's car would almost have to pass our front door.

"How were your folks?" I asked.

"Pretty cheerful," replied Alan. "Yours?"

I gave a wry grin. "I still get the impression from my father that I'm the black sheep of the family," I said. "Because you didn't go into the Greys?"

I nodded. "He thinks this flying business is just a fad," I said. "His attitude makes me even more determined to prove him wrong. I'm going to go up and shoot down so many German planes that the War Office will give me a letter saying I've virtually won this war on my own! We'll see if he's still got this same pig-headed opinion when I show him that."

Alan laughed. "Poor old Jack," he said. "I'm glad I don't have the same family traditions to live up to."

We arrived at Upavon to find the place in a frenzy of activity. We had barely stepped out of our car when Major Govan, our flight commander, hurried up to us. "Fairfax! Dixon!" he called. "Get over to the field and get your machines sorted out. You've both drawn a De Havilland and they'll need rigging if we're to leave on time tomorrow, so jump to it."

"Yes, sir!" we chorused.

We turned to each other in delight.

"A De Hav each!" Alan chortled.

We'd both been hoping that we'd get a De Hav. The Vickers was an excellent machine, but both Alan and I considered the De Havilland to be the crème de la crème of fighter aircraft.

We hurried to our quarters just to dump our bags on our bunks and then dashed to the field, as we had been ordered, where we found our machines waiting for us.

All pilots in the RFC were given a fitter and rigger to help them fix up their machines, but it was up to the individual pilot to make sure the plane was in proper order. This made sense because a plane that wasn't in top condition could be a death trap to the pilot. Rigging meant adjusting the wires that held the wings in place on a biplane. You had to make sure the tension of the wires was just right so that the plane could carry out its manoeuvres properly, without the wings collapsing.

Our squadron spent the rest of that day preparing our machines and loading our possessions into the transport, which was setting off for France before us to establish a base for our arrival.

At 1100 hours on Friday, the 16 planes of 32 Squadron assembled on the field ready for take-off in lines of four. Each line is known as a "flight" and Alan, Banger Wilson, Monty Johnson and I were in the third flight. At the signal, we all started our engines up at the same time, and then the first four planes of first flight set off, rolling together over the green grass of the field, then rising up into the air. They were followed by the second flight, then my group in the third flight, with the fourth flight following behind us.

The first flight had been circling over the Wiltshire plain, holding position while the other flights got off the ground, and now, finally with all 16 planes in the air, we grouped and headed towards our first point of call – Folkestone on the Kent coast.

It was a glorious feeling flying together in formation. The sky was clear and blue. No cloud, no fog, no wind, perfect visibility, perfect flying weather. We all touched down safely at the airfield in Folkestone in the same sequence as before. Then we pilots went into Folkestone town for lunch at the Metropole, while the engineers refuelled and made a last check of our planes before the last leg of our journey.

Lunch was excellent. Mind, we were so full of expectation and delight that we were finally going into action, that even if we'd been served mashed potatoes and gravy, we'd have sworn it was the best meal we'd ever tasted.

After lunch, it was back to the airfield for a final check on our machines, and then the 16 of us set off across the Channel for France.

We were finally going to war.

I had only flown over land before, and I have to admit that I felt intimidated by the knowledge that beneath me there was only a vast expanse of water. If I came down in that, no one would be able to come to my assistance. But I'd been a good swimmer at school, I reflected, so I could always kick off my boots and swim for shore!

Once we'd left the Channel behind us and passed over the French coast I began wondering if we'd meet a Hun, or a squadron of Hun aircraft. But there was never a real chance of that. We were still a long way behind our own front line and, according to our experts, the Germans only made exploratory raids just a few miles into enemy territory.

We flew across the French countryside for about another hour, and landed on an airfield at a place called St Omer, which was about 20 miles behind our own front line. Even though we were a long way from the actual fighting, there was a huge military presence in the town. Military vehicles, and men in brown and blue uniforms, all hurrying to and fro as if on urgent errands. There was all the activity of war, but none of the actual battle, although we could hear the distant sound of guns firing at the Front.

All this activity wasn't confined to the airfield, but extended to the centre of St Omer itself, where we were billeted for our first night at what we were told was "the top hotel in town". The streets were filled with military vehicles and military personnel. It seemed to be a staging post for troops moving to and from the Front. The idle thought struck me that Oswald might have passed through here on his way to the Front, and I wondered if I might actually run into him.

The "top hotel" that we stayed in that night was awful. If this was the best hotel in town, I'd have hated to have stayed in the worst. We were three to a room: me, Alan and Banger sharing. The beds were comfortable enough, but the place was filthy. To have a wash meant getting water from a pump in the yard at the back of the hotel and filling a washbasin. We had been better off in our draughty wooden huts at Upavon.

Once we'd reported to the airfield the next morning and were given our orders for the day, I soon forgot about the living conditions. Four of us – me, Alan, Banger and Monty Johnson – were to fly due west to the Front in support of an observation plane, which was going to make a reconnaissance of enemy positions.

"Remember that the observation plane is the most important machine out of all of you," our new commanding officer, Major Sanders, told us. "The observer will be bringing back photographs of the enemy positions, details of weapons and troop movements. Your job is to protect the observer plane from enemy attack at all costs. If the enemy should appear, the observer plane has orders to turn and head for the safety of our own lines. You will do your best to keep the enemy from attacking it."

I felt a huge sense of excitement and anticipation as we took off on our mission. At long last I was going to see the Western Front: the heartland of where the War was actually taking place.

We left St Omer and began our journey west, climbing to 9,000 feet. Our flight path took us over the border between France and Belgium towards Ypres. We flew in a "five of spades" formation: myself and Alan at the front, Banger and Monty flying behind us, and the two-seater observation plane in the middle.

We'd travelled for about five miles when I began to make out the very different landscape ahead of us. "Very different" was an understatement. It was like nothing I had ever seen before. As far as I could see, for 20, 30, possibly 40 miles, there was not one touch of green. Not a blade of grass, not a tree, not a bush. Just a mass of grey sludge, torn and chewed up as if a giant tractor had come in and ploughed it, throwing bits of land willy-nilly.

I looked across at the pilot of the observation plane, who pointed downwards, and then took his plane down to 5,000 feet, and then to 2,000 feet. I followed him. Now I was closer I could see the trenches carved out of the grey mud. Deep, long, pitted holes running for miles, in all directions, with other trenches joining them, like a series of sunken roads. The land on top of the trenches consisted of more mud, but with rolls of barbed wire strung out across it, again for mile after mile after mile.

I had expected to find lots of shooting and explosions, but apart from the sound of the De Hav's engine the scene was strangely silent. No guns were firing. No explosions. No rifles shooting.

I looked behind me and saw that Alan had followed me down while Banger and Monty kept at about 8,000 feet.

We followed a flight path north along our front line, identified by the khaki uniforms of the men moving below us, then we turned right and headed into German territory.

As I flew I heard the sound of rifle shots coming from just ahead and below, and realized the Germans were firing at us from their trenches. I gestured upwards, and Alan followed me back up to 8,000 feet, followed by the observation plane, where we levelled out.

I was just making a turn to head back to our own lines when, out of the corner of my eye, I caught a movement in the sky about a mile away. I turned my head and saw a pack of planes heading towards us, flying in a V-shaped formation – one plane at the front, with what looked like another half a dozen planes spreading out behind it. The Huns were on to us, and we were outnumbered!

Following orders, the observer plane immediately turned to follow a course back to our own lines. While Monty and Banger turned and followed our observer plane, Alan and I went on the offensive, heading straight towards the oncoming German planes, opening up with our guns as we did so. We were too far away to actually hit any of the enemy planes, but our shooting had the desired effect, which was to disrupt their formation. The German planes scattered left and right.

From stories we had heard from other more experienced fighter pilots, we'd been told that in a situation like this the enemy would do one of three things: turn on us; ignore us and head after our observer plane; or send half of their squadron after our observer plane while the rest ganged up on us.

We didn't wait for them to make up their minds. Alan and I had already decided on our course of action if such an event occurred. As the seven German aircraft scattered from our flight path, we began a steep turn, me flying upwards, Alan flying down. This turn automatically brought us behind the German planes – me above them, Alan below.

The Germans had decided on a "half and half" strategy. Three of their planes had already begun their turns to chase after Alan and me, but our sudden turns had caught them on the hop. Alan came up fast, guns firing, and I zoomed down towards the nearest German fighter, my hand tight on the trigger, my gun blazing. I was lucky, I had caught my target plane halfway through his turn so he hadn't had time to get me in his gunsight. If it had been a two-seater, it would have nailed me with a burst from its swing-gun, but as a solo fighter on its own, this plane didn't have that luxury.

The constant stream of bullets from my gun raked along the fuselage of the German plane, tearing into it from front to rear. Then the plane began to head down in a spin, spiralling out of control. I levelled out from my dive, eyes darting left and right to see where the other German planes were, and where Alan was.

Alan had also caught his target napping with the swiftness of his turn, because I saw a second German plane spinning down to the ground below, this one enveloped in a cloud of black smoke. I saw flames licking at the side of the plane through the smoke, and then it vanished from my sight.

Alan was now higher than me and he brought his plane down

towards me, waggling his wings slightly as he did so in a victory wiggle. He passed beneath me, and we gave each other a thumbs up. Our first victories!

But the third German plane that had set out to attack us had turned again, and was now joining the rest of its squadron coming after Monty, Banger and our observer plane. Remembering our orders, that the observer plane had to be protected at all costs, Alan and I gave chase. I made the engine give all it had, determined to catch the Germans.

Ahead of us, Monty and Banger were diving and weaving in the sky behind the observer plane, criss-crossing in front of the oncoming German fighters. Monty would make a sudden turn and lunge at the German planes, firing all the time, causing them to scatter. Then he'd loop past and head back after them again. The Germans, in their turn, were showing that they were no novices at this game. Two would soar up into the sky, and then suddenly dive down, guns blazing at our aircraft, coming at us from a blind spot.

Meanwhile the observer plane at the front droned on, nearing our own lines all the time.

Alan and I were getting closer to the Germans, and I let off a burst of gunfire into the tail of one of them. I thought I'd got him, but he lifted up and went higher. I levelled him in my gunsight again, but just as I pressed the trigger he dropped like a stone and my tracer of bullets whistled harmlessly over him.

The next second he was flying beneath me, heading back the way we'd come. I guessed he was trying to come up from behind and attack me the same way I'd just attacked him. I gave the rudder a hard turn and moved sharply to the right, and then straightened my course to get in line with Banger and Monty. I was aware that Alan was now above me. All the time there was the sound of gunfire as the Germans let off burst after burst at our planes, and we replied with our own hail of bullets.

Suddenly I saw Banger's plane drop, and then start to spin wildly. Whether Banger had been hit or whether he'd just lost control, I didn't know, I just knew that his plane was spinning, spinning, spinning, heading down towards the ground.

Angry at the German who'd done this, but not knowing which one had, I started firing wildly at the enemy aircraft, letting off long bursts. But suddenly all of the German aircraft dropped out of the sky as if at a given signal. I found myself catching up with Monty, with Alan now coming down to join me. I turned my De Hav, expecting the Germans to be pulling the same trick as before of letting us get in front of them so they could shoot us from behind, but they were all heading away, back towards their own lines. My first air battle was over.

The feelings of exhilaration that I had had my first encounter with the Germans, and had not only survived but had shot one down, were tempered with feelings of loss over Banger. Actually, if I had to admit it, it wasn't really loss that I felt. Banger was a chum from the squadron, but he and I had never been that close. My overwhelming feeling was one of relief. I couldn't help thinking that could have been me, spinning down out of the sky to my death.

That evening in the mess, Alan and I refought the air battle we'd just been involved in using cutlery and tin mugs to mark our positions, and the positions of the German planes. We never mentioned Banger, except when Alan said once, "Pity about poor old Banger," and I replied, "Yes. He was a good chap."

I found it difficult to get to sleep that night. I looked across at the empty bed where, just that morning, Banger had woken up, yawned, and complained about the dampness. He would never complain about the dampness again.

The next morning Alan and I were woken up by our batman (our servant), a man called Clark, banging on the door of our room while it was still pitch dark outside. "Major Sanders' compliments, sirs," he announced as he clattered into the room, his boots making a loud noise on the creaky wooden floorboards. "You're both on dawn patrol. So here's your cocoa and biscuits to set you up for it."

He set down the tray on the table and brought me a mug of steaming hot cocoa. I sipped it, and it was delicious. It was a long way from the hot breakfasts of eggs, salmon, mushrooms, kippers, and all the other delicacies I'd imagined I'd be eating once I'd left school, but it hit the spot.

Alan and I reached the airfield and found that Monty was already there.

"Morning, chaps!" he greeted us. "Once more into the breach, eh!"

"How can you be so cheerful at this time of day, Monty?" I complained. "It's five o'clock in the morning."

"Best time of day – that's what my father says," replied Monty breezily. "Just before dawn, before the birds start stirring. It's the best time of day for good shooting."

"Let's hope the Hun don't share his opinion," said Alan.

Our mission was to protect another two-seater observation flight. This time six of us were going up: me, Alan, Monty, Reggie, Oofy and Bingo. All good chaps, as were the two in the observer plane, brothers called Walter and Ian Wilson. Both of them were very able pilots, and they took turns to act as pilot and observer. Today, Walter was in the pilot's cockpit and Ian was taking observations.

The first streaks of light were appearing in the sky as we took off. Below, the ground was still dark, which was a mixed blessing. Although it gave us protection against any enemy aircraft flying above us, because they wouldn't be able to make us out against the darkness of the land below, it meant that we couldn't spot any enemy aircraft flying below us either.

As we rose higher and higher, anti-aircraft fire began to open up from the German lines. Explosions of red flames appeared below us as the guns on the ground went off, firing the missiles high into the air. BANG!!!! The damned things exploded in mid-air, scattering debris all around.

The smell of the German Archie was foul, mainly I guessed from the black cordite explosive the Hun used. At least it told us that it was the enemy shooting at us and not our own side, as the British and French anti-aircraft shells gave off a white smoke.

We flew in a different formation this time, me and Alan at the front,

Monty and Reggie protecting the rear, and Oofy and Bingo flying on either side of the observer plane. Our orders were to fly due west to the front line, cross it, then turn left and fly north for ten miles, weaving backwards and forwards all the time to enable the Wilson brothers to take photographs and plot the German defences. Then we were to turn back and head for home.

We kept to a height of 10,000 feet to lessen the chances of being hit by the German Archie, except when the Wilson brothers decided they needed to go down lower for closer observation. We followed, keeping our eyes peeled all the time for any attacking enemy aircraft, as well as doing our best to dodge debris and missile fragments from the shells exploding around us in the sky.

We were about halfway through our mission when I was aware of Alan suddenly breaking away from the formation and dropping down to a lower altitude. He must have spotted incoming Germans. Immediately I turned my plane in the same direction and followed him.

There they were, a formation of about eight German planes, coming at us from due east, flying out of the rising sun.

Out of the corner of my eye I saw the Wilson brothers' two-seater continue its flight north. Although common sense told them to head back across into our own territory, Ian and Walter obviously felt they hadn't achieved as much on this mission as they should have. I saw Ian in the rear observer's seat working at the big wooden box camera on the side of their plane, and then I turned my attention back to the oncoming German fighter planes.

They were nearly on us now. Alan came at them from below, his guns firing, but the German planes banked and turned and twisted in the air, and his tracer of bullets went past them. Oofy and Bingo joined me as we hurtled forward after Alan's De Hav, leaving Monty and Reggie to circle round and round the Wilson brothers' plane, protecting it as they continued their northward journey. The camera clicked and the heavy photographic plates were being changed the whole time, despite the hail of gunfire going on around them.

I picked out one of the German planes nearest to me and headed straight for it. I came in from the side, guns firing just ahead of him to hit him in the engine at the front of his plane. The Hun had seen me coming because he dropped into a steep dive to get out of the way of my bullets, and then turned up again sharply. I followed him, first down, then up, keeping a watch in all other directions as best as I could, in case I was attacked by one of the rest of the enemy squadron.

The German was good. He ducked and dived in the air, and then circled fast, and suddenly he was coming straight at me from my right-hand side, his guns chatter chattering. Luckily for me I'd got the measure of my machine and I throttled back at the apex of my turn, allowing the De Hav to side-slip for just a few seconds, but long enough to take me out of the German's gunsights so I could put it into a dive.

Down I went, and now in daylight I could see the ground below – the trenches, the destruction, the mud and the mass of men – for as far as the eye could see. But only for a second, because then I banked and put the De Hav into a turn, bringing it under my German opponent. He tried to turn sharply, too, but the movement was too fast for him and his plane juddered. It was only for a second, but it was all I needed. As he recovered and began to turn away, I let him have a burst of gunfire straight into the tail of his plane, tearing it to shreds.

Without controls, the German's plane gave a sickening lurch, and then plummeted out of the sky, heading towards the ground 10,000 feet below. Meanwhile the rest of the air battle was continuing. I could see that Alan was still active, his De Hav zooming in and out between the enemy aircraft, guns firing all the time. Reggie and Bingo were also in the thick of it. It was madness up there, planes hurtling left and right, looping and turning, tracers of gunfire tearing through the sky. There was no sign of Monty's plane. Oofy was shadowing the Wilson brothers' plane, and as I glimpsed in their direction I saw the brothers' plane turn and head for our own lines. Ian must have got as many photographs of the enemy as he needed. Now I could only see six German planes in the air. As Oofy escorted the Wilsons in their observer plane over the line towards our own side, Alan, Reggie, Bingo and I gave one last flurry of gunfire at the German planes, then turned and flew after Oofy and the Wilsons.

The Germans also decided they'd had enough.

They'd chased us back to our own side of the line, so they turned and headed back to the safety of their own positions.

As I flew back with the rest of our formation towards our airfield base, I wondered what had happened to Monty. Had he been shot down? Had his plane been hit? Had he been forced to land? One thing was sure as we returned: another of us was missing.

Over the next few days I kept my ears open for any news of Monty, but there was no word. None of us had seen his plane go down, but then we'd been too busy carrying on with our own battles in the sky. Reggie thought he'd seen one of the Germans fire a burst straight at Monty, but he couldn't be sure. And so Alistair Montgomery, aged 18, went on the list as "Missing, presumed dead".

After those first two days of air battles, in which we lost Banger and then Monty, the days became a sort of blur. Each day we went up into the air, and on most occasions we encountered German fighters. Every time we came home with yet another of our pilots gone.

By some miracle Alan and I survived, coming back from mission after mission. Now and again when we landed we found our fuselage was torn and riddled with bullets, but we arrived back safely, another day older – another day alive.

Once in a while the weather was too bad for us to go up, with thick clouds forming, and on those days I was glad of the respite. It was a chance to unwind just a bit, to ease the tension that came from going up into the air, knowing that each time it could be your last hour alive.

Over the next few months, familiar faces disappeared and were replaced by new, shining young faces. Many of them, lacking the experience of us old hands who'd been battling Germans in the air for a couple of months, didn't last longer than a couple of days.

Sometimes, seeing one of the new chaps setting off, bouncing across the airfield in a way that showed he was still coming to terms with his machine, I gave thanks for all the advanced training at Upavon. At the time I'd resented the hours I'd spent there, keeping me from the Front, but now I saw that those few extra weeks of hard and repetitive training had helped to keep me alive.

Meanwhile, for the troops on the ground, the War dragged on, with the front line moving a few hundred yards one way, then a few hundred yards back. Despite the dangers we encountered every time we went up, our life in the Royal Flying Corps seemed like luxury when we heard reports about what was happening in the trenches. The Battle of Verdun had been going on since February. Six weeks later neither side had gained any ground, but there were reports that a million men had died in that battle alone. A million. It made our losses seem paltry.

I wondered how Oswald was doing. Was he even alive? Information seemed harder and harder to come by, with any questions being met with a stern look and the reply that "the enemy may have spies listening".

And so, ignorant of what was happening in the wider war, as well as not knowing which side was winning, we continued to go up and fight the enemy.

Mid-June 1916

It was some time in June that Alan and I, and a whole load of new chaps, were sent off on yet another flight, protecting an observation plane. I can't even remember the purpose of this particular mission. Each one had started to blur one into another. Every time we flew over a sea of mud and barbed wire, carved with deep trenches and huge craters where bombs had ripped the earth, sometimes 20 feet deep.

We were under attack from a group of German fighters – about six Fokkers. Only these were different from the usual German planes. Instead of the regular dull brown colour with black crosses painted on the wing, these were painted bright yellow, and one of them even had a huge grinning face painted on the propeller mounting at the front. It gave me a bit of a shock when I saw them. For a moment I wasn't even sure if they were fighter planes or if it was some kind of flying carnival. And then they opened fire.

As before, we took initial evasive action to get away from their line of fire, though at the same time making sure that the observer plane we were protecting was covered. Today it was my turn to take the rearguard position and oversee the safety of the observer plane. The problem with the two-seater planes was that they were slower than any single-seater, because of the extra weight and so more vulnerable to attack. However, the observer did have a mounted machine-gun able to move in different directions. It could shoot at planes attacking from above, the rear, or from the sides.

The yellow plane with the grinning face came hurtling out of the pack straight for our observer plane, guns blazing, obviously intent on a quick kill. Our observer plane dropped down, the observer firing upwards aiming to catch the yellow plane in its forward trajectory, while I came in fast from the left. Between the two of us I expected we would down this brightly coloured monstrosity within seconds, but just as I thought I had a sure line of fire the German pilot banked sharply and my line of tracer missed him.

The German pilot had banked so sharply that I was sure he had gone into the turn too fast and was going to go into a spin, but, to my shock, he continued the sharp turn, doubling back on himself, and I suddenly found him sharp on my right. The next second there was a RAT-A-TAT of exploding gunfire and my engine cut out, the propeller juddering to a halt. He had shot clean through my engine.

My plane began to fall out of the sky and I went into reflex action, remembering the many times I'd practised "what to do in the event of engine failure". Only this was not just a failed engine, this was a dead engine. And I was 10,000 feet above the ground in a machine that was suddenly heavier than the air I was flying in. I was fighting a losing battle against gravity. And then an even bigger horror struck me as I began to feel a stinging wetness on my clothes and on my face. The

German's bullets had cut through my fuel line and I was being sprayed with gasoline. It was every pilot's nightmare, to be trapped in a burning plane.

First rule: Don't panic.

Second rule: Put the nose of the plane down and use air currents to keep the plane as level as possible while gravity takes hold – which meant, keep going forward. But in the sudden movement of action, I'd lost my sense of direction. I didn't know whether I was heading towards our own lines, or the German positions.

Third rule: Look ahead for a flat area, such as a field, to land in. My problem was that, as far as I could see, there was no flat land, it was all mud and trenches and barbed wire. Any fields were miles away from the Front. The gasoline kept spraying out and now my clothes were soaked with it. Please, don't let it catch fire, I prayed silently.

My engine was off, which was a good thing. It only needed one spark and I knew I'd go up in a ball of flames. The danger was now my propeller. The fuel tank was at the front of the plane, close behind the propeller, so if the propeller started up and fired the magneto, the force of air generated by it would fan the flames straight at me.

Although the propeller had stopped after the engine failed, and seemed to be stuck in one position, I could see it wobbling slightly. Feverishly I hoped that the propeller had jammed. If it was still free, then it could start rotating of its on accord in the wind. As the propeller was locked in direct drive to the magneto of the engine, if the propeller began to turn, then the magneto would also turn, which would produce sparks. Then my only hope was that the magneto had also been shattered, or was jammed solid.

During all the time I was thinking this I was coming down … down … down … trying my hardest to hold the plane level as the wind buffeted the wings and body.

"Glide!" I yelled aloud at the plane, heaving back on the joystick to stop the nose of my plane from going too far down, but not too hard because that could send the plane into a spin.

Down, down I went... The ground below and in front of me was clearer now, coming up fast. So far the propeller hadn't moved. My luck was still holding. Then, to my horror, I saw the propeller shift slightly, and begin to turn.

"NO!" I yelled aloud, and waited for the sudden WHOOF of sparks from the magneto igniting the gasoline and the flames. But instead the plane just continued its descent, getting faster now as it neared the ground. The German's bullets must have smashed the magneto. At least, I hoped so. I tensed, waiting for any sound of sparks or small explosions that might signify fire. I was still too high to leap out of the plane and survive, but I'd rather die from falling than be burnt to death.

Down and down I came, and now I was aware that the trenches and the barbed wire and the mud were getting nearer and nearer … men were shouting, shouts of anger and alarm, but no one was shooting at me. I was coming down behind our own lines. Providing the magneto didn't suddenly kick into life, all I had to do was hold the plane level and hope it didn't fall apart as we hit the ground. With nowhere to land properly, it meant just bringing it down where I could.

Suddenly everything was flashing up at me and hurtling past at incredible speed – barbed wire, wooden posts, banks of mud. There was a sickening crunch as my undercarriage hit something, then my left wing smashed into something else and just collapsed, the rigging fell apart, and the whole plane began to leap up into the air, and then roll.

I held on to the controls as tightly as I could, but then the plane gave a last massive jerk and I found the controls coming away in my hand. I was flying through the air, head over heels, when suddenly I hit a pool of water and began to sink.

As the thick, foul-smelling water closed over my head, the thought went through my mind: Oh God, I survived the fall and now I'm going to drown. I pushed myself up to the surface of the water and struck out for a wall of mud at one side. My hair and eyes were so wet with sludge that I could barely see. My hands touched the wall of mud, then my feet found some kind of footing beneath the water and I began to push myself up.

"Here you are, mate!" called a voice. "I'll give you a hand!"

A soldier had appeared at the top, and held out his hand to me. I grasped it, and he hauled me upwards, out of the way. I flopped over the top and rolled down the other side into more mud.

"Are you hurt?" asked the soldier, who sounded like a Cockney.

"I don't know yet," I said. "I haven't had time to find out."

This made the soldier laugh out loud.

"Here, mates!" he called out. "This bloke don't know if he's hurt.

Says he hasn't had a chance to find out yet." At this there was even more laughter. It hadn't sounded that funny to me when I'd said it, but I suppose these chaps in the trenches didn't get much to laugh at. I struggled to get out of the mud I was stuck in and push myself upright, but as I did so I felt a terrific pain shoot up my leg from my ankle, and I fell over. "Ow!" I exclaimed. "I think I've broken my ankle."

In fact, as I discovered when they took me to the nearest casualty station, I hadn't broken my ankle, merely sprained it. This seemed to annoy the doctor on duty very much.

"Do you realize I have men coming in here with serious injuries!" he raged at me as I lay on the bed in the station. "Men who are dying. Men with limbs that need amputating. Men who are blinded. Men with holes in their stomachs that their guts poke out of, and you dare to come in here with a sprained ankle!"

"It wasn't my fault!" I protested, pretty annoyed myself. "I didn't know it was just a sprain. It hurt very much and I thought it was broken. Next time I'll ask the Germans to make sure they injure me properly before I'm brought in."

But the doctor had decided I wasn't worth arguing with and he just gave a nurse instructions to bandage my ankle and then kick me out.

Actually, I had to admit, looking round that casualty station, I felt every sympathy with him for his attitude. It was exactly as he had said, there were all manner of injuries there. Some of them were so bad that I couldn't imagine how the poor people suffering from them could survive. Then I reflected that many of them wouldn't, many of them would be dead by the morning.

Seeing the War at close quarters was a shock. I'd seen injured men, I'd seen dead men, but it was the conditions that everyone was living and working and fighting in that shocked me.

I'd also seen the mud before, but the closest I'd been was 500 feet above it. Here at ground level, the mud dominated everything. It was grey and it stank, the putrid smell filling my nostrils. It made me want to heave. But maybe it was the stench of death, not just the mud, because wherever you looked there were the remains of rotting corpses. Many of them lay out in the area called no-man's-land, which was the patch of ground between our front-line trenches and those of the Germans. No-man's-land was a tangle of rows and rows of barbed wire, aimed at preventing a sudden attack by either side, and bits of bodies and all manner of other things still hung caught on the wire.

After looking at the conditions in the trenches, I felt guilty about complaining about our quarters back at St Omer. By comparison, we were living in luxury. Again, I thought of Oswald and wondered how he was coping.

I asked one of the telegraph operators at the casualty station to wire a message to my unit, telling them that I was safe and well (except for a sprained ankle) and would be returning for action as soon as I could get there.

Fortunately for me, a truck was leaving from the casualty station and going in the general direction of St Omer. After a series of three lifts –

one on the truck, one in a battered old car, and the final part on the back of a motorcycle – I arrived back at our base two days later.

The first person I saw as I limped back into the operations hut on the airfield at St Omer was Alan, who let out a yell of joy when he saw me, and then, as he saw me limping, burst into laughter.

"That's a fine welcome back!" I complained. "What's so funny?"

"A sprained ankle!" Alan laughed. "You're shot down from 10,000 feet..."

"Not that high," I said. "Anyway, I was able to glide down."

"Your plane breaks up into pieces, and you're stuck in the middle of a ground battle between our boys and the Hun, shot and shell all around you, and all you come out of it with is a sprained ankle!"

He laughed again. "By heavens, Jack, everyone should have your luck. Lucky Jack Fairfax I'm going to call you from now on."

"I'd rather you didn't," I said. "It might be rather tempting fate."

"What I want to know is how you got out of it," put in Reggie, who came over to join us. "So I know what to do if it ever happens to me."

"The first thing to do is be shot by a gentleman," I said. "One who shoots your engine and doesn't follow it up shooting you when you're on your way down, like some of the swine. Who was he, anyway? Does anyone know? Swanning around the skies in that flying banana, someone has to know who he is."

"His name's Otto Von Klempter," replied Alan.

"But why on earth paint his plane that dreadful colour?" I asked. "And that silly face painted on his propeller mounting. It's almost as if he wants to draw attention to himself."

"He does," said Reggie. "Did you notice that all six planes were painted the same yellow? It's like having team colours. Von Klempter is their leader, so he had the face painted on his propeller mounting so that everyone will know when they've been hit by him and his team."

"What arrogance!" I snorted.

"It's more than arrogance," said Alan, "it's part of a major offensive on the part of the Hun. Those six yellow planes you saw were just the start. The day after you came down, there were fourteen of them in the sky, all painted the same yellow colour. And other groups of German flyers are doing the same, all in groups of fourteen. They're called Jastas."

"Well I call them idiots," I said. "You can paint your plane all colours of the rainbow, it doesn't make you a better flyer."

"But Von Klempter got you, Jack," Reggie pointed out. "Which makes him a pretty crack shot."

"Yes, all right, he can fly," I admitted grudgingly. "But he caught me by surprise. Next time, I'll be ready for him. Wait and see what happens tomorrow."

However the next day there was to be no flying for me. At least, not in combat.

"We're running low on machines, Lieutenant Fairfax," Major Sanders told me when I reported to him for duty. "There's a two-seater going to Farnborough tomorrow. You're to go with the pilot and pick up a new machine, and then bring it back. Think you can do that without smashing this one up?"

I ignored his sarcastic comment and saluted smartly. "Absolutely, Major," I said.

So the next day I said goodbye to Alan, Reggie and the rest of the chaps, and took the observer's seat in an old BE2C, and we set off back to England.

As we flew over the Channel I reflected about the last time I'd flown over this particular stretch of water, and how much I'd changed in so short a time. A few months ago, I'd been an eager young pilot, keen to get to grips with the Hun. I was now just four months older, but I felt years older in experience. I'd lost so many colleagues it was difficult to remember them all. You shook a young man by the hand to welcome him one day then, a day or so later, he was gone. It was even hard to remember what their names were or what they looked like. Sometimes it seemed a miracle that Alan and I were still alive.

LATE JUNE 1916

When we arrived at Farnborough I found that the plane I was due to pick up had been destroyed by a trainee pilot the day before.

"It's going to be a couple of days before the replacement arrives," the base commander informed me. "You must be due for some leave. Why don't you take a 48-hour pass. Go up to London, see some of the sights, get the War out of your system for a bit."

His suggestion seemed a very civilized idea to me, with one difference. After the chaos of the War, and the constant daily aerial combat, 48 hours of peace and quiet seemed a better prospect than the noise of London. I thought I'd take the opportunity to nip home to Bowness Hall and proudly show Father and Mother that their flyer son was in action, with a couple of victories to his credit, and a war injury – even if it was only a sprained ankle. I was also curious to find out if there was any news of Oswald.

I telephoned from Farnborough and advised Guest, our butler, that I was on my way home for a short visit, and would be with the family as soon as I'd sorted out the necessary trains.

It was about half past seven in the evening when the taxi dropped me off at the entrance to the Hall, and I limped up the steps. I have to confess that I possibly overdid the limp, just to add a touch of glamour to the image of the Flying Fighter-Pilot War Hero Returning Home.

I don't know if I expected a very warm welcome, but I didn't get one. Mother and Father weren't the most demonstrative of people at the best of times, their motto being: "Showing your feelings can be interpreted as a sign of weakness." So I received a slightly distant hug from my mother, and a formal handshake from my father.

"You're limping," my mother commented.

"Yes," I said. "But it's just a slight scratch. I was shot down, but luckily I wasn't really harmed, so I'll be able to get back in action as soon as I return to France."

I felt a bit of a cheat as I said it, so I added truthfully, "Actually, I just sprained my ankle."

Unlike Alan, neither of them laughed. Mother nodded absently and said, "You were obviously lucky."

"Dinner is ready," Father announced. "We thought you might be hungry after your journey, so we told Cook to prepare it for as soon as you arrived. Is that all right with you?"

"Unless you want to freshen up first?" suggested Mother.

"No, no," I assured them. "Food first. Believe me, after the rations I've lived on for the past months, my idea of heaven is a meal cooked by Mrs Gussett."

I expected my father to make some sort of rejoinder, like telling me how, in the Boer War, he and his troops were forced to live on hard biscuits and rainwater, but instead he just nodded and said, "I am sure

Mrs Gussett will have done you proud."

As we walked into the dining room, I thought that it was a strange sort of homecoming. Cheerless, even a sense of disappointment. I wondered if Father was still upset over the fact that I'd joined the RFC instead of the Regiment. We sat down to dinner, just the three of us. Nanna was dining in her rooms. The meal was superb. Mrs Gussett had excelled herself. Or maybe it was just that I'd been eating military rations for so long that I'd forgotten what good home-cooked food tasted like. As we ate, I talked about the War, and what life was like in the Flying Corps.

"Very different, I expect, to what poor Oswald's experiencing there. I've seen it up close and frankly I can't see how anyone can survive in it. It's just mud and barbed wire and trenches for as far as the eye can see," I chuckled. "Not at all the sort of thing that Oswald's used to. Remember how he never liked getting his shoes dirty? Well he'll be getting them dirty out there, sure enough."

There was a strange, strangled sound from my mother, which caused me to look up from my plate. My mother had her table napkin to her face, and I realized she was dabbing at her eyes. I noticed that she was even paler than usual. I looked at my father, but he seemed intent on his meal, his eyes looking firmly down at his plate. I turned back to my mother.

"What's the matter?" I asked. "What's happened to Oswald?"

Mother said nothing. It was Father who spoke.

"He's ... in hospital," he said quietly. Then he carried on eating.

I stared at him, stunned.

"In hospital?" I echoed. "Why? Where? In France? Was he wounded? Was he badly hurt?"

"Everything's in order," said Father, and continued eating, though I noticed he only took very small mouthfuls and spent a long time chewing, as if he was having difficulty swallowing what he was eating.

"How can it be in order?" I demanded. "What happened to Oswald?"

"Please, Jack, I'd prefer we didn't speak of it," said my mother in a faint voice.

"But he's my brother!" I insisted. "Surely I have a right to know what's happened to him? Is he disabled? Blind? That poison gas is dirty stuff..."

"Your mother has requested that we do not discuss this matter," snapped Father. "Can't you see that it upsets her? We do not wish to talk about Oswald. He is safe and out of harm's way. That is all you need to know. Now let that be an end of it."

With that he continued eating his meal in the same almost reluctant way as before. Mother sat, her plate untouched, her pale face set and her hands pressed together as if in silent prayer.

The rest of the meal was a disaster. The three of us ate in silence. Though when I say "ate" that's a bit of an exaggeration. Mother just pushed her food around her plate with her knife and fork. Father ate ever smaller mouthfuls, taking ages to swallow each one, but acting like a man who was forced to do so as a kind of punishment.

Question after question whirled around my head. What had happened to Oswald? How badly was he injured? Where was he – in

France or in England? What had happened to him? Had he been blown up? Shot? Gassed? When had it happened? Who had done it to him? Why hadn't anyone told me earlier?

As soon as the meal was over, I made my apologies to my parents and said I needed an early night. I could tell by their manner that they were relieved that they wouldn't be forced to spend the rest of the evening with me, with my unasked questions bubbling under the whole time, waiting to burst out and cause them even greater distress.

I hurried up to Nanna's rooms and found her sitting up in her chair, reading a book.

"Hello, Nanna," I said, greeting her with a kiss. "I'm sorry I've called so late. I hope I haven't interrupted you going to bed?"

"I rarely sleep much at nights these days," said Nanna. "I do most of my sleeping during the day. One of the least attractive aspects of getting ancient."

"Nonsense," I told her. "I'll never think of you as ancient. Just gently matured, like one of Father's best wines."

"You young flatterer," said Nanna. "So, come on, Jack. You haven't called just to pass the time of day. What's the matter?"

"What's happened to Oswald?" I blurted out.

There was a difficult silence as Nanna looked at me, as if weighing up what to tell me.

Then she said, "I take it your father and mother haven't told you?"

"They refused even to speak about him, except to say that he's in hospital," I said. "But when I asked why, I was told in no uncertain terms he is not a subject for discussion."

Again, Nanna was silent, but this time she looked away from me, studying the photographs on her mantelpiece. We were all there. Me, Father, Mother, Grandfather and Oswald.

"He's in hospital just outside London," she said at last.

"I know he's in hospital," I insisted, "but how was he injured? How bad a state is he in?"

Finally she said quietly, "The army doctor who called to see your father and mother said he was suffering from something called 'shell shock'. I believe it's a nervous disorder."

Shell shock. No wonder Father hadn't wanted to talk about it. Cowardice, some of the generals called it. Loss of nerve.

"When did it happen?" I asked. "A month ago," said Nanna.

A whole month, and no one had written anything to me about it!

"Which hospital is he in?" I asked.

"Why?" asked Nanna.

"I want to go and see him," I said. "Find out how he is."

"Do you think that's a good idea? I don't think your parents would readily give their permission," she said quietly.

"I wasn't thinking of asking them," I said.

Nanna gave a smile. "The same Jack as ever," she said. "Breaking the rules. Going against orders."

"He is my brother," I said. "Who knows, I might even be able to help him get over this ... shell shock."

I spent the next day at home, but it a was very sombre affair. The business of Oswald hung over Mother and Father like a dark cloud. Because they didn't want to talk about him we spent most of our time together in a sort of silence, talking about things like the weather. When I could I retreated to Nanna's rooms to take tea with her and talk. It was the only time I felt anything like normality.

That evening I told my parents that I was going to Farnborough the next day to report to my commanding officers, and receive further orders before returning to the Front. It was a lie, but I knew they wouldn't like to hear where I was really going. Nanna had given me the address of Oswald's hospital, which was at Palace Green near Kensington Gardens in London. Apparently it was a hospital set up by Lord Knutsford specifically for officers suffering from shell shock, or what the doctors termed "war neurosis".

I caught the train to London, and then a taxi to the hospital. It was a fine building, set in beautiful grounds overlooking Palace Gardens. The nurse on duty at reception was surprised at my arriving unannounced.

"Yes, I'm sorry," I apologized. "I've only just got back from the Front myself, and I'm due to report back for duty tomorrow, so I'm afraid there was no time for me to contact you first. But when I heard about my brother being here, I thought I really had to visit him. I hope that seeing me might even help him."

The nurse listened and then said, "I'd better have a word with his doctor first. Usually we like the patients to spend their time here on their own, coming to terms with their condition."

"I promise I won't be any bother at all," I said.

"Then if you'd just take a seat while I check with Dr Farrell," she said, indicating a chair.

I sat down and took stock of the surroundings. Although the building outside was architecturally ornate, inside it was austere. Very few things in the way of decorations. Hardly any pictures. No photographs. I wondered if the medical staff were trying to keep that sort of thing away from the patients in case it triggered off something. I was still sitting reflecting on this when the nurse returned.

"Dr Farrell says you can see your brother," she said. "But only for a few moments. He needs all the rest he can get."

"I promise I won't overstay my welcome," I said.

I followed her down a corridor. The place was eerily quiet. Now and then, as we passed a partly closed door, I heard the sound of sobbing. From one of the rooms, I heard the sounds of muffled screams, as if someone was trying to call out but had a gag stuffed in their mouth. Then I noticed that the door had a key in the lock. This whole place gave me the creeps.

The nurse stopped at a door and tapped at it, then opened it. I followed her into the room. For a moment I wondered whose room we were in. I didn't recognize the man sitting in the chair by the window. I was about to say to the nurse, "Excuse me, but I think there's some mistake. You've brought me into someone else's room," when she said gently to the man in the chair, "Your brother is here, Mr Fairfax."

The man in the chair looked up at me, and I nearly fell to the floor in shock. It was Oswald right enough, but it took me a second look to make sure.

Oswald was only two years older than me, but this man looked at least 40, with lines across his face, and white and grey streaks in his hair. Oswald had been a tall, upright boy, with a backbone stiff as a ramrod – like a soldier on parade – and prone to being a bit podgy due to a liking for too much pudding. This man was skeleton-thin, bent over, his chest sunken. His eyes were sunken, too, staring blue from black holes in a deathly white face.

The man finally forced himself to look directly at me. "Jack," he said.

His voice, too, had changed. Where before it was loud and bellowing, made so by shouting orders at the junior boys at school, now it was thin and reedy.

"I'll leave you two together," said the nurse.

I sat down on the chair opposite Oswald.

"How are you, old chap?" I asked. "I hear you've been ill."

Oswald nodded. "It's a bad business, Jack," he said. "A bad business."

With that he fell silent, his eyes going down to look at his knees. The silence continued.

I looked around the room. It was neatly, but sparsely, furnished. Clean. Orderly. Again no photographs or pictures. No flowers. None of the usual things you expected to find in a hospital room.

"So," I said, after the silence had gone on for what seemed like ages, "what happened?"

The sound of my voice seemed to remind Oswald that I was in the room with him, and he struggled back from being lost in thought into some kind of waking.

"Do you remember Father telling us about the Battle of Klips Drift?" he asked.

"Only about the first hundred times he told us," I laughed.

Oswald didn't laugh back.

"Of course," I said, in a more serious tone.

The Battle of Klips Drift had been Father's finest hour when he was fighting in the Boer War against the Afrikaners. It had taken place in 1900.

"The Boers were entrenched in a position just north of Klips Drift," said Oswald, telling me the story as if I hadn't heard it before. "Father was with the Greys, plus a squadron of the 6th Dragoons, and the Carabiniers in the 1st Brigade. Cavalry. All on horseback. They had to wait for the transport column to arrive. They waited south of Kimberley, just inside the Orange Free State border."

"I know," I said, puzzled. I wasn't sure why Oswald was telling me this. I'd heard the story from Father time after time as I'd been growing up.

"When they arrived at their objective, the Boer positions at Klips Drift, they made a cavalry charge against them. Because of the speed of the attack, and also because of the dust thrown up by the horses' hooves, they were a very difficult target for the Boer marksmen."

"I know," I said again.

"Father said it was an absolutely classic cavalry manoeuvre," said Oswald. "The front rank of each squadron armed with lances as well as swords and carbines. The Boers were overwhelmed. They left their position in the protection of the Drift and ran for it. That meant the road to Kimberley was now open, and Father and the rest of the cavalry were able to ride into Kimberley and occupy the town. It was a major victory."

"It was," I nodded. "But I don't see what it has to do with us today?"

Oswald lifted his head and looked me straight in the eyes, and now I could see tears starting to tremble on his eyelids.

"Before I went to the Front, Father told me always to use the classic manoeuvres, just as the Regiment had done at Klips Drift, and I would win my encounters with the enemy, as he had done, and my men would come home safely. But, Jack, there was no way there could be any sort of classic manoeuvre in that mud."

He was no longer looking at me, but looking into somewhere inside his own head, some awful memory. "Horses? Cavalry? Dust from their hooves?" He laughed harshly. "No horse could even move in that mud! I've seen horses and donkeys and mules stuck so deep they were nearly drowning in mud and water. I've seen shrapnel take off all four of a horse's legs in one horrifying salvo. The poor beast lay there, screaming – and don't let anyone tell you that animals don't scream. I put a bullet through its brain to put it out of its misery."

I didn't know what to say. I'd never seen Oswald as deeply upset as this before. All my life, during our time as boys at home and our school days, Oswald had been the proper respectable one, the one who did everything that should be done, and never showed his emotions.

"Father has no idea what sort of war this is, Jack. This isn't decent, civilized war. Men on horseback against other men on horseback. Rifles that only allow you or your enemy one shot, and then you have to reload. We are up against guns that fire hundreds of bullets a minute. Bombs that are so big they can destroy a small town. Poison gas. Water. Mud.

"We are treading on our own dead comrades every time we go into attack. The ground and the walls of the trenches are held up by the decomposing bodies of men I have known and liked. Men who followed me because I am their commanding officer. I am a captain in the Royal Scots Dragoon Guards. They did what I said and I carried out the orders of my superior officers. I ordered those men over the top, time after time after time, and they died, Jack. In their hundreds! They died because they did what I told them to do!"

Suddenly Oswald began to cry. Not just tears but great howling roars of deep pain. There was the sound of hurrying footsteps outside, and then the nurse came swiftly into the room and went over to Oswald.

"Captain Fairfax," she said gently, and she put her hands on Oswald's shoulders.

I sat there, looking at my brother as he rocked backwards and forwards on his chair in mental anguish, the nurse holding him, restraining him gently.

She looked at me and said, "I think it might be better if you go. We will give him something to help him sleep. That often helps, but he has a great deal of trouble sleeping."

I'm not surprised, with the brutal images in his mind, I thought. The nightmares Oswald must suffer. The memories that must come back to haunt him in his sleep as soon as his eyes close.

I nodded to her, and got up.

"Will you come and see him again?" the nurse asked me. "I'm sure your visit will have helped him."

"How?" I asked, baffled.

"Sometimes talking about the horrors the patients have experienced can be the first step on the road to recovery," she said.

"I'll do my best," I said. "But I'm off back to the Front in a day or so, and I'm not sure what the future holds."

I turned back to Oswald, but he was lost to me, just rocking on his chair, his eyes shut tight and his hands firmly over his ears as if trying to block out all sights and sounds.

"I'll see you again, Oswald," I said. "I hope you feel better soon."

As I walked back down that corridor, I kicked myself mentally for saying those last words. In view of Oswald's condition, they seemed so inadequate. But I just didn't know what else to say.

I left the hospital, and went back to the War.

JULY 1916

By the time I got to Farnborough they had my replacement De Hav2 ready for me, and I set off across the Channel. In the late afternoon I landed back at St Omer. As I came in to land I saw the airfield was full of planes. I was looking forward to meeting up with the chaps again and I wondered if Alan would mind if I told him about what had happened to Oswald. I knew that Mother and Father wouldn't like it being spread around, but I was still feeling so shocked at how Oswald had been in that hospital that part of me needed to share it with someone, just to get it off my chest.

Oofy Richards was the first person I saw as I walked into our hut. He beamed when he spotted me. "Jack! I thought you'd have had more sense than to come back to this hellhole! But the bright lights of London couldn't keep you, eh?"

"No chance!" I said with a grin. "The fine food, the luxury accommodation, the friendly Hun shooting at you every day? How could life back in England compete with that?!"

I looked around the hut, at the other chaps sitting in their chairs, ready and waiting for the command to go, and a few of them waved a hand in greeting. But Alan wasn't in the room. I guessed he was either in the mess sorting out some food, or perhaps he'd gone back to our digs at "the hotel".

"Where's Alan?" I asked.

There was an awkward pause, then Oofy said, "I'm afraid he bought it yesterday."

I looked at him in disbelief.

"Alan?" I said, stunned.

Oofy nodded.

"Anyway," he continued, his voice chirpier, "the weather's been brightening up lately, so..."

"I don't want to hear about the damned weather!" I stormed angrily. "I want to know what happened to Alan! How did he go? Was he shot down? Who did it?" My voice must have risen to a shout without my realizing it, because I heard the voice of Major Sanders snap out from behind me, "What the devil's going on here?"

I turned and faced him.

"I've just found out that Alan Dixon has been killed," I said, "and I'm trying to find out how it happened."

"He was shot down by the Hun," snapped Sanders. "That's it."

"No it isn't!" I shouted back angrily. "How did it happen? Where?"

Beside me, Oofy shuffled his feet unhappily.

Sanders glared back at me, and then he said, "You will come into my office, Lieutenant Fairfax."

I followed Sanders out into the operations hut next door. As we came in, a sergeant stood up from his desk and approached Sanders, holding a piece of paper in his hand, but Sanders waved him away.

"Not at the moment," he said. "I am not to be interrupted for the next three minutes."

With that, Sanders walked into his office. I followed him in.

"Shut the door," he said.

I could tell from his manner that I was in for a roasting. "Sir..." I began, determined to get my explanation in first.

"Silence!" snapped Sanders. "Ordinarily I would not even give you the benefit of this talk, Fairfax, but I understand that you and Dixon had been friends for a long time."

"Since we were six years old, sir," I said. "We met at prep school."

Sanders nodded, but his firm expression didn't change.

"You have just broken one of the unwritten laws of the Flying Corps – trying to get a fellow pilot to talk in detail about the death of a colleague."

I bowed my head apologetically. It was true that there was an unspoken agreement that we didn't talk openly about it when one of us "bought it". It was as if by not talking about it, it would stop it happening to us.

The view of the Top Brass was that dwelling on such things would "lower our morale" and make us less eager to fight. For that reason, there were never any empty chairs at our briefing sessions. When a man died, a chair was removed, until such time as his replacement arrived.

"I'm sorry, sir," I said. "I admit that I lost my head. As I said, Alan Dixon is ... was ... my best friend in the world. We have been together for as long as I can remember."

"That may be," said Sanders. "But the morale of this squadron is my responsibility, and I will not allow any of my pilots to do anything to undermine that. Is that clear?"

"Yes, sir," I nodded.

"Good," he said. "However, in view of these particular circumstances, I can tell you that Dixon died bravely. He was lost during an air battle with Von Klempter's outfit. I believe it was Von Klempter himself who was responsible."

So, the German I'd ridiculed as "the flying banana" had shot down Alan. The same man who'd downed me. But I had lived.

"The other pilots reported that Dixon took out four Huns before he was shot down," added Sanders. "He was an excellent pilot and a brave warrior. I have written to his parents to tell them so."

"Yes, sir," I said. But there was one more thing I had to find out. "How did he die?"

"I've just told you," replied Sanders. "He was shot down by Von Klempter."

"Yes, but ... was his plane intact?" I finally forced myself to say the words. "Did he burn?"

Sanders said nothing for a moment, but I could see the turmoil behind his eyes. Finally, he said, "That's all you need to know, Lieutenant Fairfax. You are dismissed."

Deep down I felt myself go cold, but I stood to attention, saluted smartly, and left the office.

Oofy was waiting for me outside, looking miserable.

"Is everything all right, Jack?" he asked. "I'm sorry, I didn't mean to land you in trouble like that."

I forced a smile and clapped him on the shoulder.

"You didn't do anything wrong, old boy. It was my fault entirely," I said. "I'm sorry I lost my rag the way I did. I wouldn't hurt you for the world. Forgive me?" And I held out my hand to him.

Oofy grinned as he took my hand and shook it.

"Nothing to forgive," he said. Then he added, awkwardly, "But I am most awfully sorry about Alan."

"I know," I said. "Thanks." Once again I forced myself to smile. "I'd better go and check my crate. I want to make sure it's ready for action tomorrow."

"Good egg!" Oofy replied.

I watched Oofy head back towards our hut, then I turned and walked towards where our planes were parked. I hoped that no one was around. As I walked I could feel my cheeks wet with tears. I bit my lip to try to stop them. Grown chaps don't cry. Alan would hate to see me crying like this. I'd be letting the side down. But when it came to it, there was no side, just friends.

I felt hollow inside. Worst of all was that I now knew that Alan had died in a burning plane. I remembered the fear I'd felt when I thought my plane was going to catch fire. I couldn't shake the thought of Alan – what was it the Germans called it? Gebrannt. Burnt. Well now I had a score to settle. I was going to get Von Klempter.

The next day I was ready to get up into the air again and take on the Hun, hoping that Von Klempter and his "flying circus" would be up there, but instead our whole squadron were summoned to a briefing in the mess. It was unusual for us to be taken off flying duties en masse just for a pep talk, so I guessed there was something big in the air. I was right.

Major Sanders waited until we were all sitting quietly and attentively, and then he began.

"Chaps, I don't need to tell you that the war on the ground has been at a stalemate for some time. Well, tomorrow that is going to change. The Army Top Brass have decided to go for a major push on the Somme. Those of you who've been up will have noticed our big guns have been laying an even heavier bombardment on the enemy than usual."

I assumed the increased bombardment the CO was talking about had been going on while I had been back in England, because I hadn't been aware of it when I'd been up in the air. Though when you're at 10,000 feet, as you battle with the enemy twisting and turning in the sky, it's difficult to concentrate on what's happening on the ground.

"Today, you're standing down and you're to check your machines. Tomorrow's going to be our big day. Meanwhile 21 Squadron are going on offensive duty today. They're going to add to the Hun's worries by carrying out a bombing raid."

A bombing raid usually meant a two-seater going over enemy positions, with the crewman in the rear seat throwing bombs out of the plane on to the enemy below. It was a risky business as they had to fly low enough to make sure the bombs were on target, yet not so low that they ran into flak from the German anti-aircraft guns.

"The plan for tomorrow is that the big bombardment from our heavy guns will begin at 0730 hours. They will pound the German lines in a concentrated attack until 0800. As the barrage lifts, the infantry will move forward at speed, cross the barbed wire and attack the enemy in their forward trenches. The generals believe that the Huns will still be in their deep dugouts, recovering from the heavy bombardment, and won't have time to get to their machine-guns.

"At the same time, to ensure further cover for the ground troops, bombers will fly over and attack the German positions behind the front line. Your job will be to escort and protect those bombers. If this push is successful, as I'm sure it will be, it will decimate the enemy, pushing the Germans back so far and so fast that they will be forced to surrender.

"So, gentlemen, prepare for tomorrow, and for what could be the beginning of the last days of this war."

As we headed out of the mess hall, I gave Oofy a humourless grin.

"One more push, eh, Oofy!" I said. "I wish I'd had a pound for every time we'd been promised that."

"Now don't be a cynic, Jack," said Oofy. "The Top Brass have special intelligence. They know things that we don't, about the Germans and their weaknesses, and that sort of thing. They know what they're doing. I, for one, am looking forward to doing anything that gets this war over with so I can get home." He hesitated, looked round to make sure no one else was within earshot, then added, "The thing is, I'm engaged to be married."

"My goodness, Oofy, who'd marry you?" I exclaimed. I mean, Oofy was a nice enough chap, but hardly what I'd describe as handsome. He had a head that went to a point at the top, and no real chin to speak of. His head struck me as looking like a rugby ball perched on his neck.

Oofy looked at me, put out.

"I'll have you know my fiancée, Gladys, is a woman of great taste," he said. "Everyone says so."

"Sorry, old chap," I said with a smile. "Just joking. I'm sure you'll be very happy together."

I spent the rest of the day going over my De Hav with one of the mechanics. When we ran into the Hun tomorrow, as I was certain we would, I didn't want to be put out of action on account of any mechanical failures. Nor did I want the wings collapsing on me. They'd felt a little edgy as I'd flown over the Channel the previous day, so we worked to ensure the rigging lines were firm and the wooden struts were properly lined up. Then we went through the engine and fuel lines, and lastly I checked the Lewis gun and ammunition. Whatever happened tomorrow, I was going to be ready.

The next morning at 0715 hours, the whole of our squadron was assembled on the field: fourteen single-seater fighter planes, and six two-seaters, with their bomb loads. It was early July, but the morning seemed particularly chill, and I knew it would be even colder at 10,000 feet, so I'd made sure I was dressed to withstand the cold. I had on my leather flying jacket with its big fleecy collar, a woolly scarf, thick gloves, fleece-lined flying boots, and my leather flying cap.

The bombardment of our heavy guns began on the dot at 0730 hours. Even from miles away we not only heard them, we felt them – the ground shaking under our feet as they fired and sent their huge shells raining down on the German front lines.

At the whistle we "mounted up", clambering into the cockpits of our planes. It always struck me as odd that we still used the language of the cavalry, even though we used planes instead of horses. Father would have felt at home here.

At 0740 hours we started our engines. The six two-seaters that were to carry out the bombing raid, being larger and slower, took off first and headed in a southerly direction. They were to keep behind our own lines for safety, and wait to rendezvous with us, their escort.

As the bombardment ended, exactly at 0800, we were flying across the front line, heading for the German trenches. Below me I could see our ground troops emerging from the trenches and heading into no-man's-land, hurrying forward. Even from this relatively low height they looked like ants, swarming over the grey mud. I now knew what conditions were like down there at ground level – I'd seen them up close for myself. But I could only begin to guess at the horrors that Oswald had experienced, and for such a long time, that had finally broken his spirit and driven him mad.

From below I heard the chatter of rapid machine-gunfire, and I knew it had to be the Germans firing because our men only had rifles. But I didn't have time to look closer because I saw the shapes of planes in the far distance, coming from the German lines. The enemy had been alerted about us and were on their way.

Our two-seaters had already started their bombing of the German lines, dropping down low, the observer in the rear of the plane leaning out and sending the bombs hurtling down towards the ground. As we had planned, nine of us lifted up to 12,000 feet and headed in formation towards the oncoming enemy planes. The plan was to head them off and keep them busy at a distance, while the two-seaters continued with their bombing work, protected by the remaining six members of our squadron. As soon as the two-seaters had finished, they were to turn and head back home, the six escorts staying with them to protect them against any stray German who'd managed to get past us.

As we neared the approaching German planes, I felt a thrill of excitement as I recognized their distinctive bright yellow wings and bodies, with their black crosses at the end of the wings, on the tail, and on the side. Von Klempter and his cronies had come looking for more victims. But today would be the day that Von Klempter would meet his fate. I could feel the desire for revenge burning inside me and I wanted to yell out loud, "Come on, Von Klempter! Face me!"

The planes from both sides began firing before we were in range of one another. It had now become a standard tactic, firing a burst to try and make your opponent react, throw him off his track.

I scanned their formation, searching for the huge face on the propeller mounting that was Von Klempter's trademark. At first I couldn't see it, and I felt a sense of disappointment that Von Klempter might have decided not to go up with his pals. But then I spotted it, in the middle of the pack, and I turned and flew down, aiming to fly beneath them and come up at Von Klempter from below.

One of the German pilots saw the direction I was heading in and turned and followed me down, opening up with a burst of gunfire as he did so, but I caught the movement out of the corner of my eye and managed to turn aside at the last minute, and the line of tracer missed the front of my plane by inches.

I cautioned myself to be careful, not to let my intent to get Von Klempter blind me to the fact that the rest of the German squadron were superb pilots in their own right. Any one of them could shoot me down if I didn't keep my wits about me.

The air battle was already in full swing, the yellow German planes hurtling this way and that, guns blazing. Our own planes ducked and dived and fired back, every man desperate to get an accurate, or at least a lucky, shot, before his adversary could get a sighting on him.

Two planes were already going down, both of them in flames – one German, one British – leaving a trail of black smoke behind them as they hurtled groundwards. I hoped for their sake that both pilots were already dead. No one wished being burned alive on anyone.

Another German fired a burst at me, and I felt my machine shudder as his bullets hit the woodwork behind me. I put the De Hav's nose down and took it into a short dive, then flew back up, turning as I did so, enough to bring me on to the enemy's tail. I fired off a burst and saw his tail fall to pieces, and the next second he sank like a stone, going into a spin, the wings whirling around like a spinning top.

Another German came for me, and this time I flew higher, with a quick upward glance first to make sure I wasn't on a collision course with anyone. There was one plane above me, bright yellow, and as it turned towards me I saw again that familiar face painted on the propeller mounting. Von Klempter!

Unfortunately, the jolt of realization that it was Von Klempter himself delayed my finger on the trigger for just a fraction of a second. The German ace flipped neatly away from my line of bullets, turning left, then going higher. I followed him up to 15,000 feet. It was colder up here, much colder, and I was glad I had my sheepskin gloves on or my hands would have been too cold to operate the gun.

I fired off another burst, but again the wily German avoided my gunfire, this time wheeling to the right, my bullets passing harmlessly beneath his left wing as it went up and he turned. He seemed to have some kind of sixth sense, as if he knew what I was going to do next. Suddenly he turned so sharply that I thought I was going to run into him head-on, and I pulled back on the joystick to lift my machine up. Too late. I heard the rack-ack-ack explosion of his guns, and I felt a searing pain in my right shoulder. The whole right side of my body went numb, but just for a second, and then the pain kicked in. I could feel my shirt inside my jacket starting to get wet around the shoulder and chest, and I knew I'd been shot. Von Klempter had let off a burst just above the level of my cockpit and one bullet had gone straight through my leather jacket.

It hurt like hell. Every movement of my right hand on the controls sent a jolt of pain through my upper body. I wondered how bad the wound was. How much blood had I lost already?

I was just trying to recover myself, regain control of my machine, when I saw Von Klempter coming back at me from the left-hand side, coming to finish me off. I gritted my teeth against the pain and put the De Hav into a dive. I was just in time because a burst from Von Klempter's guns tore through the sky over my head as I dropped down. If I'd delayed even by a second I'd have been riddled with bullets.

"This is no good, Jack!" I shouted at myself angrily. "He's getting you! You're supposed to be getting him!" I saw the shadow of Von Klempter's plane spiral down from above me, and guessed he was intending to come in from behind me and shoot me. Immediately I went into a further dive to take me lower. As before, Von Klempter followed me down, sure now that he had me. He must have guessed he'd hit me, and maybe thought I had lost enough blood to start losing consciousness. I began to spiral down, and then suddenly, abruptly, pulled the joystick back hard and soared up, heading straight into his flight path.

My manoeuvre caught Von Klempter by surprise and he had to turn sharply to avoid crashing into me. Although he fired off a burst, it was a reflex action because he was more concerned about getting out of my way.

I was now above him, at about 17,000 feet, and I was getting colder, which made handling my plane more difficult. The pain in my shoulder was spreading across my chest. I knew I couldn't hold out much longer. I had to do something to stop the loss of blood before I lost consciousness.

The chatter of rapid machine-gun fire coming from behind me told me that Von Klempter had recovered and followed me, and was on my tail again, trying to finish me off. Once more I put the De Hav's nose down and dived beneath his tracer of bullets, and turned, then turned quickly again to put myself on a level course with Von Klempter.

Now I was heading straight for his plane broadside on, working the trigger as I did so ... and to my shock, nothing happened. I knew I wasn't out of bullets. The firing mechanism had jammed! When he'd hit me some of his bullets must have also struck my gun.

I cursed aloud. Here I was, in an air battle with a leading German ace, and I was wounded, losing blood, and without a gun.

I saw Von Klempter soar past me, then go higher, and as he did so I was certain he turned his head towards me and smiled. He knew from the fact that my guns hadn't fired at him that there must be something wrong. He had a sitting duck for a target.

I watched him circle above me, like a hunting eagle circling its prey, and then he dived, swooping towards me. He didn't fire straightaway. He knew that he didn't have to. I was unarmed, helpless. All he had to do was draw as near as he wanted, then shoot me. Or maybe let me get away just a little and begin to head for home, then shoot me down as I fled.

But I wasn't going to head for home – though I let him think so. I turned and began to fly towards our own lines, weaving from side to side, twisting and turning as if I was trying to throw him off. I could hear the sound of his engine as he gained on me. He let off a burst from his guns, but because I was taking an erratic path as I flew, he missed. Nearer he came, determined not to miss the next time, determined to gain another kill to add to his list of victories.

Suddenly I manoeuvred, joystick hard back, full right rudder, then twisted round to face him directly, and flew straight for him. As I'd hoped, the move shocked him – a man with no guns heading straight for him, set on an instant air collision.

My life or death now depended on what he did next: whether he went up, or down and tried to go beneath me. If he went upwards, then I had lost.

He went down, putting his plane into a dive to avoid me, and I dived too, but turning to my left as I did so, pulling back on the joystick at the last moment and leaning far left, almost putting my machine sideways into the sky.

I felt a terrifying crash and heard a tearing sound, and then my plane was spinning and I had to battle to control it. Desperately I fought with the rudders, using my feet against the bars with all my might. My plane gave a last lurch, and then began to fly in a straight line again. Out of the corner of my eye I saw Von Klempter's yellow plane heading out of control down towards the ground, one of its wings flapping uselessly in the wind, before tearing away from the plane completely.

I had done it. I'd rammed Von Klempter's right wing with my undercarriage, my wheels smashing into it and tearing it half away from the fuselage of his plane. In so doing I'd torn off at least one of my wheels, if not both of them. Landing was going to be an interesting experience.

I looked around me at the sky. The survivors of Von Klempter's squadron had decided to head for home, and my own flying pals who'd lived through this encounter were also now turning and heading for our own lines.

Our battle in the skies above the Somme was over. I was still alive, and I'd had my revenge for Alan's death – as well as paying something back for all our other boys that Von Klempter had shot down.

I could feel myself growing weaker as I approached the airfield. The loss of blood from my wounds was starting to affect me. I had to fight to concentrate if I was going to land this machine successfully using just my one good arm. After all that had gone on in the air, it would be stupid to kill myself landing.

I came in lower and lower towards the field, gritting my teeth against the pain down my right side.

The green grass came rushing up towards me and I pulled back on the joystick with my left arm as the plane hit the ground with a bone-jarring crunch that sent pain coursing through my whole body. The plane leapt back up into the air, then came down again as I pushed the joystick forward. I bounced a few more times across the field, and then finally the plane came to rest at a cock-eyed angle, listing heavily to one side, the right wing tips digging into the ground.

I tried to drag myself out of the cockpit, but the effort was too great.

I heard the sound of men running across the grass towards me, then a voice saying, "Are you all right, old chap?"

I looked into the face of one of the ground crew, and gave him a grin. I was alive. Von Klempter was dead.

"Never better," I said.

EPILOGUE
NOVEMBER 1918

Von Klempter's bullets had made a nasty mess of my shoulder and I spent four months on sick leave before returning to the Front.

The Battle of the Somme didn't end the War, which went on for another two and a bit years, until finally, just a week ago, the Germans surrendered.

Incredibly, I survived. I don't know how. So many others didn't. Some died after a few months, some only lasted a few days. Oofy never made it home to marry his fiancée; he died just two days before the Germans surrendered, shot down while flying on a reconnaissance mission. Very few fighter pilots survived the War right to the end as I did.

My first act on returning to England was to call on Alan's family to offer my condolences. They, in turn, offered their condolences for my own family's losses.

In August 1918 Oswald died in the hospital. At that time I was still in France. I had a letter from Nanna telling me that he'd choked on some tablets. The official verdict was accidental death. My own feeling, though I didn't tell this to anyone in my family, was that Oswald couldn't cope with the horror he'd experienced, and that he'd taken his own life with an overdose.

The shock of Oswald's death hit Father particularly badly. Oswald had stood for everything that Father held dear: tradition, the good name and the future of the Fairfax family, the honour of the Regiment. Although there could be no doubt that Oswald had been a brave soldier at the Front, to be invalided home with shell shock had been a grave blow for Father. Despite his love for Oswald, I could tell that, for him, it sullied the family name. His hope had been that Oswald would return to his former health, and rejoin the Regiment, at least for a while. Instead, Oswald died. For Father, it was just too much for him to take. A week after Oswald's death, Father suffered a heart attack and died.

Shortly after Father's death, my plane was shot down during a battle with the Hun. I suffered only minor injuries, a broken leg and arm, but enough for me to be invalided back to England.

And so, at the age of 21, I have returned home to England and Bowness Hall as the new Lord Fairfax. It feels strange to me, being responsible for the people of the villages that make up the Fairfax estate. Men and women who knew me when I was just a small boy now call me "My Lord" and "Master". They look to me to give security to their lives. I know that I must not let them down. That was one of the things the War taught me: when you have power, and the lives and safety of other people are in your hands, you have a human duty to take care of them. I learnt that the hard way in a time of war. As the new Lord Fairfax, I hope I will not be found wanting in times of peace.

HISTORICAL NOTE

When the First World War began in 1914 aeroplanes were still a relatively recent invention. The first flight in a heavier-than-air machine was made by the brothers Orville and Wilbur Wright of the United States in 1903. The first cross-Channel flight from Calais to Dover was made six years later by Louis Blériot, in 1909, just five years before the War started.

At first there was great resistance among the senior officers in the British military to the idea of using aeroplanes as a military force. Many thought that they were a fad that wouldn't last. However, aware that other countries such as Germany and France had already taken the lead in aeroplane technology, reluctantly the British military authorities agreed to consider the matter.

In 1911 the Air Battalion of the Royal Engineers was formed, and in 1912 the Royal Flying Corps was set up, which incorporated the Air Battalion. The Navy had also decided to set up its own air service, and so the Royal Naval Air Service came into being in 1912, although it was not given an official seal of approval until 1914.

Many of the first planes were unreliable and as dangerous to the men who flew them as they were to the enemy. Flimsily constructed of wood and cloth with wire rigging, often they did not have the strength to hold together under the stresses of flying. Fabric could be stripped from the wing during a long dive; undercarriages would break off during landing. Many pilots died in training, before they ever got to meet the enemy.

As the War progressed, both sides worked to develop a fighting aeroplane that was superior to those of the enemy. In a short space of time new machines appeared with new forms of guns. The advantage swung this way and that. First the Germans had the superior position with the Fokker monoplanes, then the Allies matched them with the British De Havilland DH2 and the French Nieuport.

These, in turn, were superseded by the German Albatross, which dominated the skies, and was the favoured flying weapon of the legendary Baron Manfred Von Richthofen.

Von Richthofen was known as "the Red Baron" because his plane was painted completely red. In this book, the fictional character of Von Klempter is based in part on Von Richthofen.

By 1917 it looked as if the air war had been won by the Germans as they decimated the ranks of the RFC. (The average life expectancy of a fighter pilot in the RFC at that time was estimated at less than two weeks.)

Then, late in 1917, two new planes appeared: the British SE5A and the French Spad XIII. Both of these planes were fast and strong, with the Spad having the advantage of two Vickers guns in the fuselage. Gradually they began to turn the tide. The tide was turned completely with the appearance of the Sopwith Camel in July 1917. The Camel had a rotary engine, two Vickers guns, and excellent aerobatic qualities.

But it wasn't just the machines that won the battles in the air, it was the men who flew them. Although a pilot's life in the First World War was generally a short one, some mastered the technique of aerial fighting and survival, and their names live on in the history of aerial combat. Baron Manfred Von Richthofen may have been the most well known of the First World War fighters, but both sides had their share of aces.

For the RFC, the primary aces were Mick Mannock VC, James McCudden VC and Albert Ball. Mannock was Britain's top ace, who only started flying in 1917 but had 73 victories before he died in 1918 in aerial combat. James McCudden scored 57 victories before he was killed in July 1918. Albert Ball was 20 years old when he was shot down and killed in May 1917. By the time of his death he had 44 victories to his credit.

As well as Von Richthofen, German aces included: Oswald Boelcke, the first German ace and creator of many air-fighting techniques, who had scored 40 victories by the time he died in October 1916; Max Immelman, one of the first generation of aces, who had scored 15 victories by the time of his death in June 1916; and Werner Voss, who at one time was almost matching Von Richthofen with 22 British planes shot down in 21 days. He died in September 1917.

Manfred Von Richthofen was shot down and killed in April 1918. He had a tally of 80 victories.

By the end of the War, the casualty figures of pilots were:

British

6,166 killed

7,245 wounded

3,212 missing or taken prisoner

German

5,853 killed

7,302 wounded

2,751 missing or taken prisoner

On 1 April 1918 the RFC and RNAS were amalgamated into the Royal Air Force.

THE BATTLE OF THE SOMME – 1916

The first day of the Battle of the Somme, 1 July 1916, was a disaster for the Allies (the British and French). Despite a week of heavy bombardment of the German positions prior to 1 July, during which nearly two million shells were fired, most of the German barbed wire, dugouts, and machine-gun positions were intact. As a result, the British lost 60,000 officers and men on this first day, cut down by a hail of German gunfire, for a gain of 1,000 yards.

The Battle of the Somme continued until 18 November 1916. By the end of it, the Allies had advanced a distance of two miles along a line 15 miles long. The casualty figures for this battle were:

British: 418,000 killed or wounded
French: 194,000 killed or wounded
German: 650,000 killed or wounded.

Timeline

1903 First flight in a heavier-than-air machine by Orville and Wilbur Wright.

1907 Henri Farman creates successful biplane.

1909 First cross-Channel flight from Calais to Dover by Louis Blériot. Henri Farman makes first 100-mile flight.

1910 Louis Paulhan wins prize for powered flight from London to Manchester.

1911 First use of aircraft for offensive action by Italians in Libya.

1912 First parachute descent from an aircraft. Royal Flying Corps formed.

June 1914 Assassination of Archduke Ferdinand at Sarajevo. Austria attacks Serbia.

July 1914 Austria and Hungary at war with Russia. August 1914 Germany declares war on Russia and France, and invades Belgium. Great Britain declares war on Germany. First single-seater fighter planes made in Britain.

January 1915 First Zeppelin (giant German airship) raid on England takes place around Yarmouth. Four people were killed and 16 injured.

1916 First tank used by Heavy Machine Gun Corps (later Royal Tank Corps). First successful British airship built.

July – November 1916 The Battle of the Somme. April 1917 The United States declares war on Germany.

1917 Gotha, a German twin-engined biplane, is the first aircraft designed especially for bombing. November 1918 Allied-German armistice. Kaiser Wilhelm II of Germany abdicates.

1918 Royal Flying Corps (RFC) becomes Royal Air Force (RAF).

June 1919 Treaty of Versailles signed between Allies and Germany.

First World War Combat Planes

BRITISH

Sopwith 1½ – Strutter 2

Weight: 1,308 lbs (empty); 2,223 lbs (loaded)

Maximum speed at 10,000 ft: 87.5 mph

Time taken to climb to 10,000 ft: 29 minutes 30 seconds

Maximum altitude: 16,000 ft

Endurance: 3 hours

Engine: 110hp Clerget

Armament: 2 machine-guns (0.303 inch)

Number built: 5,990

Sopwith Pup

Weight: 856 lbs (empty); 1,225 lbs (loaded)

Maximum speed at 10,000 ft: 106 mph

Time taken to climb to 10,000 ft: 14 minutes 25 seconds

Maximum altitude: 17,500 ft

Endurance: 3 hours

Engine: 130hp Le Rhone

Armament: Vickers or Lewis 0.303 inch machine-gun

Number built: 1,770

De Havilland DH2
(also known as Airco DH2)

Weight: 943 lbs (empty); 1,441 lbs (loaded)

Maximum speed at 10,000 ft: 93 mph

Time taken to climb to 6,500 ft: 12 minutes

Maximum altitude: 14,000 ft

Endurance: 2 hours 45 minutes

Engine: 100hp Genome Monosoupape

Armament: Lewis 0.303 inch machine-gun

Number built: 400

GERMAN

Fokker EI

Weight: 787 lbs (empty); 1,238 lbs (loaded)

Maximum speed at 10,000 ft: 82 mph

Time taken to climb to 10,000 ft: over 40 minutes

Maximum altitude: 10,000 ft

Endurance: 1 hour 30 minutes

Engine: Oberusel U0 rotary 80hp

Armament: Forward-firing MG belt-fed machine-gun

Number built: 54

Fokker EIII

Weight: 878 lbs (empty); 1,342 lbs (loaded)

Maximum speed at 10,000 ft: 88 mph

Time taken to climb to 10,000 ft: over 40 minutes

Maximum altitude: 12,200 ft

Endurance: 1 hour 30 minutes

Engine: Oberusel UI 9 cylinder rotary 100hp

Armament: 0.312 inch Parabellum or MG machine-gun

Number built: 260

Albatross DII

WEIGHT: 1,367 lbs (empty); 1,954 lbs (loaded)

MAXIMUM SPEED AT 10,000 FT: 109 mph

TIME TAKEN TO CLIMB TO 10,000 FT: 14 minutes 8 seconds

MAXIMUM ALTITUDE: 17,060 ft

ENDURANCE: 1 hour 30 minutes

ENGINE: 160hp Mercedes

ARMAMENT: 2 machine-guns

NUMBER BUILT: not known

STANDING
ALONE

PART 1

THE WAR ON THE HOME FRONT
LONDON 1914 – 1915

5TH AUGUST 1914

My name's John Travers Cornwell, though everyone calls me Jack. I'm fourteen years old. Yesterday Britain declared War on Germany and my dad says he is going to volunteer and go and join the army and fight. My older brother Arthur says he's going to do the same. My dad says this isn't going to be just an ordinary war, like any we've had before, but a really big one, with the whole world caught up in it.

I was born on 8 January 1900 in Clyde Cottage, Clyde Place, in Leyton, Essex, during the last year of the reign of Queen Victoria. I was brought up in the country but in 1910 we moved to 10 Alverstone Road, Manor Park, Little Ilford, in East Ham, East London, which is where we live now.

My dad's name is Eli Cornwell. He's a tram driver. My ma's name is Lily. I've got three brothers – Ernest (who's two years older than me) and two younger brothers, George (who's a year younger), and Arthur Frederick. Ernest doesn't live at home with us. I've also got a younger sister called Lily, the same name as my ma. Lily is five years younger than me.

I have another brother and sister, but I suppose properly speaking they're my half-brother and half-sister as they're my dad's children by his first wife who died. My brother Arthur is 26 and works at a factory. My sister Alice is 24. To avoid confusion we call my younger brother, Arthur, by his second name, Fred.

When I was five years old I started school at Farmer Road School in Leyton, which wasn't very far from the house we lived in when we were in Essex. When we moved to Manor Park in London I went to Walton Road School. I stayed there until just before my fourteenth birthday, when I left to go to work for Brooke Bond & Co., a company that sells tea. My job is a van driver's boy, helping the van driver with his deliveries.

Soon after we moved to London, I joined the 11th East Ham Troop of the Boy Scouts, also known as the Little Ilford Troop, attached to St Mary's Mission, which is our local church. Our Scoutmaster is called Mr Avery. Now that war has been declared, Mr Avery says our troop are going to have to be dissolved, because all the Scout officers are going to join up and fight.

I really liked being in the Scouts because you learn so much about tying knots, and how to do so many things. I got my Tenderfoot Badge, and my Second Class and my Missions Badge. I also got a special Boy Scout Award because I saved a girl who was stuck in a drain, but my dad says that I shouldn't talk about it because I was just doing my duty and if I tell everyone about it that would be Boasting, which is not a good thing to do. My dad says that doing your duty and being respectful and honourable are the most important things in life.

My dad was a soldier before he became a tram driver. He fought in the wars in Egypt, and South Africa. Even though he is quite old, he says it is his duty to fight for the king and country, so he is going to join up in the army.

12TH SEPTEMBER 1914

Dad has enlisted as a private in the Home Service Battalion of the Essex Regiment, and he's gone to their garrison in Colchester. The home service garrison battalions are for men who've got a really bad illness or disability, which means they can't go off to the front and fight, or men who are older, like my dad who's 60. I know my dad wanted to go off to France and fight, like the old soldier he is, but I'm glad he's going to be in England. Colchester isn't that far away, and he'll be able to come home on leave now and then. Anyway, everyone seems to think the war will be over by Christmas, so he won't be away for too long.

The night before Dad left, he came out to our back yard, where I was sitting thinking about him going away. The army can be a hard life and Dad isn't a young man any more, and his health can be a bit doubtful, though he wouldn't like to hear me say so. He gets bronchitis when the winter comes, and he coughs really badly. I'd gone outside because I didn't want him to see I was worried about him, but he must have known.

"Having a quiet think, Jack?" he asked me.

"Yes and no," I answered with a smile.

He came and sat down next to me on the old wooden box I use as a seat.

"I ain't leavin' you with an easy heart, Jack," he said. "But this is duty. A man has to protect his family, and that's what I'm doin', joinin' up. Can you imagine what would happen if I didn't go, and no-one else did either?"

"The Hun would invade us, like they've done France," I replied.

"Exactly," nodded Dad. "And what would happen to you and your ma and all the rest of you if that happened?"

I fell silent, though I still felt an ache in my heart at the thought of him going, and being shot at. "I can't help worrying about you," I admitted at last. "If the Hun invade you'll be in the front line. It's going to be dangerous."

"It's dangerous wherever there's a war, son," he said, and he put his arm on my shoulder. "None of us wants to go to war." And then he hugged me to him – something he hadn't done in years, and I felt tears welling up in my eyes, but I blinked hard so they wouldn't come. Dad had often told me it wasn't manly to cry.

"I want to come with you," I blurted out. "I want to join the army too."

Dad shook his head. "Sorry, Jack. You have to be eighteen to join up. You've got a long way to go yet."

"But there are boy soldiers," I said. "You went in as a boy."

"That was in the old days," said Dad. "Things have changed, and rules are rules. Anyway, you've got a very important job to do here.

While I'm away, I want you to look after your ma and the rest of 'em. Arthur will be going out to France soon. But George and Fred will need a steadying hand. Someone to set an example."

"I'll do that, Dad," I assured him. "I promise."

"I know you will, son," he said. "You're a good boy, Jack."

He gave me another squeeze, then took his arm away. "I'll write to you, of course, when I get the chance. And I count on you to write back and let me know how things are going here at home. After all, your ma's not the greatest one at writing letters."

The truth was Ma couldn't read and write very well, because she hadn't had much schooling. Dad hadn't had much schooling either, but he'd learned to read and write when he was in the army. That's one of the reasons he said the army was good for people like us. It gave us opportunities we'd never have otherwise.

Dad and I sat there for a bit longer in the yard, until the light began to fade.

"Time for me to go in," said Dad. "Your ma's packing my things. I've got an early start tomorrow." Then he went in.

I stayed there in the yard for a little while longer, thinking about him going off to war. I'll miss him.

15TH SEPTEMBER 1914

It's just been a couple of days since Dad left and went off to Colchester. Ma has been miserable, but she's trying to pretend to be cheerful. It didn't help that Arthur left today to join the army, though Arthur won't be going to France straight away. First he has to go and be trained as a soldier.

I told Ma I wanted to go and join up myself but, just like Dad, she says I'm too young. I don't agree with them. I've been thinking about it more and more since I had that talk with Dad in our yard, and the way I see it, if I'm old enough to go out to work and earn a living, like I do, then surely I'm old enough to go and fight for my king and country? After all, I know some boys and girls who are as good as married at the age of fourteen. I think it's unfair you have to be eighteen to join up and fight.

Afterwards, it struck me that perhaps the navy might let me join. Although you have to be eighteen to join the army, I know the navy have boys in it. They start as cadets and become sailors as they get older. We learned about the navy at the Scouts and at school. Britain has the greatest navy ever, and some of our greatest heroes were navy men. People like Admiral Lord Nelson, who defeated the French at Trafalgar, and Sir Francis Drake, who was the first Englishman to sail around the world, and he was a vice admiral in the fleet that defeated the Spanish Armada.

When I read about those great men, and how they went off in ships and did exciting things, I want to be like them. Lord Nelson was only twelve when he joined the navy, which is younger than I am!

16TH SEPTEMBER 1914

I went to the navy office to volunteer, but they told me fourteen is too young. They said I had to be sixteen to join. I thought about pretending to be two years older than I was. I know of some boys who got into the army this way. One boy in our street who is only thirteen joined up in the army by pretending to be eighteen, and they let him in! I can't believe the recruiting sergeant couldn't tell how young he was! But Dad says that I mustn't ever tell a lie. He says that lying causes all manner of bad things to happen to a person and will ruin their life and the lives of others, even if they do it for what they think is a good reason. Tell the truth at all times, says Dad, otherwise you are letting yourself down as a person and no one will trust you, because you will be known as a Liar.

I felt miserable because the navy wouldn't take me. After I left the recruiting office I went down to the Thames and looked at the boats there – big ones and little ones. Some were merchant ships, which go all over the world taking goods to distant countries and bringing other stuff back here. Some were passenger liners, which take people to far places like America and Africa. My Dad was in Africa with Lord Kitchener and has told me about it. It sounds like a really strange place, and very hot!

The ships I like best are the navy ships. In the old days, which is not really so long ago, the navy ships were made of wood and their weapons were cannons. Now they're made of metal and instead of cannons they have huge guns on them which can fire shells for miles!

I watch these ships sail up and down the river and look at the sailors at work on the decks, and I wish I was with them. I want to be a gunner, firing shells at the Hun and sinking German battleships. I wish I could join the navy now and get into the action! I don't want to have to wait another two years – the war could be over before then!

4TH OCTOBER 1914

Today we got a letter from Dad! He sent two letters, one to me and one to Ma. In my letter he asked me to help Ma read his letter to her.

Dad didn't say a lot about what he's doing because he says that if you put too much information in a letter and it falls into enemy hands, they can work things out – like where your regiment is, how big it is and what morale is like. Dad's letter was quite cheerful.

Dear Jack

Well, here I am in Colchester, serving once more under Lord Kitchener. It's not really the same as before, because then he was a field general and he led us troops in battle. Now he's doing an even more important job as Secretary of State for War, running the whole thing, and there couldn't be a better man for the job. He was a great general, the best I ever served under, and he's still a good 'un! If all our generals were like Kitchener, we'd have the Hun licked in double-quick time!

Things here aren't bad. The food could be better, but then it is army food, and I've got used to the food your ma makes. There's no better cook than your ma, and her puddings could make any man happy, especially her bread pudding. I wish you could send some out, but I suppose it could get lost on the way.

I had an aunt who used to make bread pudding, but hers was as hard as a brick. We could use it right now to fire at the Germans from our big guns in France.

As you can tell, I'm in good spirits. Give your ma a hug from me, and tell George, Fred, Lily and Alice that I'm thinking of them. Tell them to keep their chins up. And that goes for you too, Jack. We have God on our side and we will win!

I remain your loving

Dad

He didn't mention Ernest. Like I say, Ernest doesn't live at home. There was a sort of falling out between Dad and Ernest last year, and Ernest went off, and we haven't seen him since. I don't know what he's doing. It's strange having a brother you never see, or even know about. I thought of asking Ma if she knows where Ernest is. I did ask her about six months ago, before Dad went off to join up, but all she said was "Don't mention Ernest. It only upsets your Dad." I never found out what the upset between them was. And Ma won't say.

6TH OCTOBER 1914

A lot of people said that when the war started it would all be over in a few weeks, or by Christmas at the latest. It's now been going on for two months and it doesn't look like it's going to be finished any time soon.

Ma worries a lot about Dad because of his health, especially his bronchitis.

I'm still not exactly clear on what this war is all about. I asked Dad just before he went off to Colchester, and he just said that it wasn't up to us ordinary people to get involved in the whys and wheres of things. It was our duty to support our king. So I asked Arthur before he went, and he told me what he knew about it.

According to Arthur, the war's happened because of treaties between countries, which means one country signs a contract with another country to say they will be friends and allies, and if anyone else attacks them then they will join together. It seems we have a contract like that with Belgium, and Germany has a contract with Austria-Hungary, and Serbia has a contract with Russia. I'm not sure who France has a contract with. I think it might be Belgium. Arthur thinks France had an agreement with Russia.

Anyway, it all started in June this year when some Duke called

Archduke Franz Ferdinand was killed by an assassin. Arthur says this assassin was either a Serbian or a Bosnian, he wasn't sure which. Whichever he was, Archduke Ferdinand was Austro-Hungarian; so the Austro-Hungarians declared war on the Serbians because of this assassination and attacked Serbia. Because the Serbians had an agreement with Russia, Russia came into the war on the Serbian side. Germany had a contract with Austria-Hungary, so they declared war on Russia. And because Russia and France had an agreement it meant Germany also declared war on France.

Then the Germans invaded France, and because France and Belgium are right next to one another, they invaded Belgium at the same time. This meant that Britain had to declare war on Germany and come in and defend Belgium, as well as France. At least, that's what Arthur said.

I must admit, it all seems a bit confusing to me, which is why I think Dad's way is best – don't ask questions, just do your duty.

15TH OCTOBER 1914

Today we had a letter from Arthur. He has finished his training and is off to France. His letter wasn't very long, but he said that he would write more once he got to France. I'm not sure if he will because Arthur doesn't like writing letters, but we'll see.

I wrote a letter to Dad today telling how things are here, and how we are thinking about him. But I didn't put in too much of that. Dad doesn't go in for being too emotional. He says that the thing that makes us British and better than anyone else is the fact we don't go to pieces when things aren't going our way. He calls it having "a stiff upper lip". I think that means that when bad things happen, you mustn't cry, you just get on with things. Mind you, although he says that, I remember him giving me that hug the night before he went off to Colchester, and I realized that underneath all the things he says, he cares a lot.

4TH NOVEMBER 1914

Yesterday the German navy attacked Great Yarmouth on the east coast. A German battlecruiser sailed right near to the coast and started shelling the town. The papers didn't say if anyone was killed, just that there was lots of damage. I'm shocked by this. I don't understand why our navy ships didn't go out and fight the Germans and attack them and sink their ships, though I didn't say it out loud to anyone because it could be *treason* if you criticize your own side.

Our neighbour, Mr Adams, who is too old to go to war, says our ships couldn't get out because the Germans had put mines in the sea. These are bombs that float just beneath the surface of the water and they blow up if anything touches them. Mr Adams says the Germans know where they have put their mines and that's why the German ships don't get blown up by them. I said that surely these mines would just float, and so any ship could hit it, but Mr Adams says the Germans weigh their mines down so they stay in the same place.

Mr Adams says that a lot of our ships are fighting the Germans in other parts of the world, and we need them back if we are to defend our coast from the German navy.

6TH NOVEMBER 1914

We have had a letter from Arthur. He says it's very wet at the front, on account of all the rain, and the trenches the soldiers live in can get filled up with water. But he tells us he's keeping fine on the whole and not to worry.

I read his letter to Ma, but I can tell she doesn't believe that everything's all right. She spends a lot of the time trying to find out from other people any news they have from their men at the front to find out what's happening. She says this war is going on a long time. I know that she is worried that the longer the fighting goes on, the more chance there is of Arthur getting wounded. There have already been quite a few families in our street whose sons or fathers have been killed or injured in the fighting. She's also worried because there are stories that the soldiers spend most of the time soaked through in the trenches. I'm glad Dad isn't in the trenches, because with his bronchitis that could kill him.

One of our neighbours, Mrs Sims, says her son Henry has caught lice out there. And not just little lice in his hair either, like everyone gets, but really big lice that crawl all over his body. She also claims that Henry has seen rats in the trenches as big as cats, but I'm not sure about that. Henry was always exaggerating things when he was at home.

1st December 1914

Judging from the stories in the newspapers, the war is spreading right over the world. What Arthur said about different countries having contracts with other countries is bigger than I realized. I know that Australia, Canada, New Zealand, India, and lots of bits of Africa, like South Africa, are all part of the British Empire and so are our allies in this war. But Germany also owns parts of Africa, and so do countries like France and Portugal, and all these other countries are coming into the war on the side of their mother country. So there is also fighting going on in Africa and around the Mediterranean.

I got out my atlas, which I won as a prize at school for doing good work, and looked up all these different places to find out where they were.

9TH DECEMBER 1914

Dad came home on leave today. It was really great to see him again. He cut a fine figure in his uniform, and lots of the neighbours came round to see him to ask about the war. Dad says they do a lot of training and practising, and they are very busy building defences around the coast. To be honest, I was surprised at how fit he looks, considering his age. I think being in the army must be good for him.

He only stayed for two days, then he had to go back to Colchester. He said he won't be able to get home for Christmas. It will be strange to have Christmas without Dad here, but, as he said, a man has to do his duty.

13TH DECEMBER 1914

I've changed my job. I left Brooke Bond and I've gone to work as a dray boy with the Whitbread brewery at their depot in Manor Park. The dray is a large, open-sided cart pulled by two horses, and it takes the barrels of beer from the brewery to the pubs. My job is to ride along with the driver and help him to unload the barrels of beer and collect the empty barrels.

I get better wages at Whitbread than I did at Brooke Bond. Working on a dray will make me stronger because it is heavier work, which will help when I join the Navy. I'm determined to join up and play my part in this war. It's what Dad would want, and if I can't get into the army until I'm eighteen, then it's the navy for me.

My driver on the dray cart is a man called Jebediah, though everyone calls him Jeb. He's a nice enough man, but a bit grumpy. He also wheezes all the time when he talks, and even when he doesn't talk. I think he has something wrong with his chest – a disease, or something. Jeb's wheezing is even worse than Dad's when he has his bronchitis. Lots of people in the East End of London have chest diseases because of the damp and smoke from all the chimneys.

Me and Jeb talked about the war as we drove around delivering our barrels of beer. He said he thought it was strange that we were at war with Germany.

"Why?" I asked.

"Because our king and their king – though they call him the Kaiser – are the same family."

"You mean their king's English?" I asked, puzzled.

"He's half English," he said. "You know the old queen's husband was German?"

"Of course I do," I nodded. "Prince Albert the German."

"Well there you are, then," said Jeb. "Their king is half English and our king is half German. First cousins and such. You can tell because even their name is German."

"Whose?"

"Our king and queen. King George and Queen Mary. Their name is Saxe-Coburg-Gotha. You can't get more German than that." He shook his head. "I always thought the next war would be against the French. It usually is."

14TH DECEMBER 1914

There was a row today between Ma and my big sister, Alice. It wasn't a big row, because Ma doesn't do big rows – she likes a quiet life. It's noticeable that since Dad went off to join up and isn't at home, Alice speaks out more, speaking her mind. Today she was talking about votes for women. Before the war started there was a campaign by a group of women called Suffragettes to give women the right to vote in elections. Most of these women were very posh and they held meetings in the West End and other places. They're led by a woman called Mrs Pankhurst. When the war started, Mrs Pankhurst said that women should stop pushing to get the vote but should put all their energy into the war effort and get behind the soldiers fighting at the front. Now it seems that one of this Mrs Pankhurst's daughters has come out and said that her mother is wrong and that this is the time for women to fight for the vote, and she is going to start up her campaign here in the East End. Alice said she thought that was a good thing. Ma said she didn't want the vote. She thinks politics and running the country are men's work. Alice blew up and said that women worked just as hard as men and had just as much right to say who ran the country as men did. Then Ma got all tearful and said it was wrong of Alice to talk like that when the menfolk were out risking their lives fighting the war.

When Alice saw that Ma was upset, she calmed down a bit because no one likes to see Ma upset, and we all know how worried she is about Dad and Arthur. But Alice still said she hoped that the politicians would do the right thing and give women the vote.

Me, I don't know what the right and wrong of this is. When there were all these meetings and protests before the war, with some of the suffragettes going to prison because of the things they did, like breaking the windows of government offices, Dad said they all ought to be locked up. He said that women didn't need the vote because the men would vote on their behalf. When he said things like that, Alice went all quiet and gave him funny looks, but she didn't go for him like she did Ma today.

15TH DECEMBER 1914

There are reports in the papers saying that our navy destroyed the German fleet in the South Atlantic, off the Falkland Islands. I have looked up the Falkland Islands in my atlas. They are small islands off the eastern coast of South America. This victory is great news! The battle was over a week ago, but news takes a long time to get back to us when things happen so far away.

18TH DECEMBER 1914

The German navy launched another attack on some English towns on the north-east coast! This time German battlecruisers came right up to the coast and fired shells on Scarborough, Hartlepool and Whitby. Eighteen people were killed, all civilians.

The newspapers are asking how these German ships were able to get past the Royal Navy ships in the North Sea to make this attack. It seems lots of people are blaming our navy for not defending the coast properly, but I am sure there is more to it than this. Our navy does its best, but many people say that the German battleships are faster than our ships, which is why we can't catch them. I think that people who say this sort of thing are *traitors*. We should be praising our navy and helping them defeat the Hun, not criticizing them. Also, most of our navy has been in the South Atlantic where they have sunk the German navy. I'm sure those ships will be able to come back and defend our shores.

25th December 1914

Christmas Day. It should have been a happy time, but as we sat around the table and ate our Christmas dinner and toasted one another's good health, all I could think of was Dad at the barracks in Colchester and Arthur in the trenches. I really do miss them both. I wish they were home with us.

I know Ma feels the same. We put out two empty chairs at the table, one for Dad and one for Arthur, and I caught her casting unhappy looks at them when she thought no one was looking.

Alice is a young woman with her own life, and although she says she worries about Dad, I don't feel she misses him like I do. I think she is more worried about Arthur. That's understandable, because Arthur is her proper brother and only two years older than her. Alice sticks by Dad's saying about keeping a stiff upper lip, and not letting her feelings show.

The ones I have to keep an eye on are young George and Fred. Since Dad went off, they can be a bit of a handful. Ma can't keep them in check as she should, so I told them that if they don't behave I'll write to Dad and tell him what they've been up to, and he'll get angry with them and have a go at them when he gets back. That usually sorts them out because Dad can have a bit of a temper, especially if he thinks anyone is being disrespectful to Ma.

8TH JANUARY 1915

My birthday. I am now fifteen years old. One year nearer to being able to join the navy. This is my first birthday without hearing Dad say to me, "Happy birthday, Jack." It feels strange and lonely without him. But I shall do what he says, which is *my duty*.

20TH JANUARY 1915

There was another attack on Great Yarmouth yesterday, but this time it was from the air! A zeppelin flew across from Germany and dropped bombs on the town and the coast. The army tried to shoot the zeppelin down but I imagine their shells couldn't reach it.

I saw a picture of a zeppelin in the paper. They're like huge, long sausage-shaped balloons filled with air, and the pilot and the crew sit in a kind of carriage underneath it.

I've heard that some of them have been shot down by pilots from the Royal Flying Corps. When the bullets hit a zeppelin they catch fire and blow up because of the kind of gas they use inside the balloon. I suppose there were none of our planes near Great Yarmouth when this zeppelin attacked.

3RD FEBRUARY 1915

I talked to Jeb today about wanting to join up and fight, and he got moody when I said this.

"It's all very well fighting for your king and country," he said. "Trouble is, no one cares about you when the fighting's finished and you come back home." He patted his chest. "I got wounded when I was in the army. I lost nearly all of one lung. No one cared. Not the army, nor the government. They just kicked me out and told me to fend for myself."

"Where were you?" I asked.

"South Africa," said Jeb. "The Boer War."

"My Dad was in Africa," I told him. "He fought with Kitchener. He's with the Essex Regiment now, but in England, defending. He joined up as soon as war was declared."

"I tried to join up," said Jeb. "When war was declared, I went down to the recruiting office, despite what had happened to me, and said I wanted to go and fight. But they wouldn't have me because of my lung." He gave a big heavy sigh, which made his wheezing even worse. "I should be fighting, not driving a horse and cart."

20 February 1915

The Hun are attacking our ships with their submarines. They sneak up on a ship and fire torpedoes at it. The people on board the ship don't have a chance! Our navy is doing its best to try and track down the German submarines and sink them. The sooner I can join the navy and play my part, the better!

24TH FEBRUARY 1915

Today something terrible happened to me and Jeb while we were on our rounds. We had stopped outside a pub and were unloading our barrels when a lady came up to Jeb. She was all dressed up in good clothes, and spoke posh. She looked at Jeb like he was something horrible and said, "A man of your age should be in uniform, fighting at the front!" Then she produced this white feather from her bag and held it out to him. Giving a white feather to someone is a sign that they are a coward.

I stood looking at the white feather and at Jeb, and I felt shocked. Jeb is no coward. Jeb glared at the woman, snatched the feather from her, scrunched it up in his fist, threw it on the ground and trod on it.

He snapped at her. "I did my bit for my country and I lost a lung because of it! Go and give a feather to your husband, if you've got one!"

With that he turned his back on her and carried on unloading the barrels. For a moment I thought the woman was going to hit him with her brolly, but then she just turned and walked off.

Jeb was really angry, and for the rest of the day he sat next to me glaring at the horse as it pulled the cart along, not saying a word, but I could tell how furious he was.

"She didn't know you've only got one lung," I said trying to make him feel better.

"She don't know and she don't care!" Jeb said angrily, and he spat down towards the cobbled road.

What I didn't say out loud was that I was worried that someone was going to give me a white feather too. What would I do if that happened? I would know I was too young, and that I'd tried to join up but had been turned down. But some people say I look older than my age. Even though it would be unfair, I don't think I could stand the shame. It's the same for Jeb. It's not his fault he's not in uniform, but I could tell that he felt angry at what had happened, and ashamed.

6TH MARCH 1915

There was another row today between Ma and Alice. Alice said that the government was going to turn the old caustic soda factory in Silvertown into a munitions factory, making gunpowder and shells and bullets. A friend of hers called Theresa said she was going for a job there because she'd be paid 25 shillings a week! Alice said she was thinking of going for a job at the factory with Theresa but Ma didn't look happy about it.

"That's not a good place to work," she said. "Making munitions is men's work really. I've heard about those places. Only rough women work there."

At this Alice got upset. "Are you saying that Theresa's rough?" she demanded angrily. "I've known Theresa ages and she's a good girl. Her husband, Bert, is away fighting in France, just like Arthur. She says she's going to do it because our troops need shells and ammunition, if we're going to win this war. She's doing it for her Bert and Arthur, and all the rest of our boys out there."

Alice's anger made Ma back off. I don't think Ma was expecting Alice to be so upset. After all, she was only saying what lots of other people were saying. I'd heard some of the men at the brewery talking about the women who were doing men's work, like a job in a munitions factory, and how the women who worked there were a bad lot, more like men in the way they acted – swearing and spitting and everything.

"I'm not saying your friend is rough," said Ma. "I'm just saying that the work is rough. Filling shell cases with gunpowder. It's dangerous. Something could blow up and you could get killed."

"Arthur could get killed fighting in France," argued Alice. "That's why they need shells and ammunition."

Ma fell silent, then said: "Well, the factory's not open yet, so I'll write to your dad and see what he says about it."

That shut Alice up, because she knew that Dad would feel the same as Ma. Dad's old-fashioned that way. So instead Alice said, "No need. I'll write to him myself." But I knew she wouldn't.

9TH MARCH 1915

I told Jeb about the row between my ma and Alice, and how the women at Silvertown were going to be paid 25 shillings a week. He told me about a niece of his who works at a munitions factory in Kent. "They may get paid well, but they work hard for it," he explained. "I went down to see my niece one Sunday a couple of weeks ago. She was all yellow."

"Yellow?" I said, completely confused.

Jeb nodded. "It's from the powder they use to make the TNT," he told me. "It gets in their skin and no matter how often they wash it stays there. Mary, that's my niece, says she washes all over when she gets in from the factory and the water turns this sort of blood-red with the chemicals, and her skin is left yellow. Even her toenails have turned yellow. Mary says she's luckier than most. Some of the women have developed skin rashes because of the chemicals."

I thought, I've got to tell Alice about how she's going to be turning yellow if she goes to work at the munitions factory. Then I thought I wouldn't, because if I did she might get mad and say I was siding with Ma against her.

25TH APRIL 1915

The war goes on. The letters we get from Arthur suggest that both sides are stuck in the same place, not able to advance. Sometimes our side makes an advance and the Germans are pushed back, then a short while later the Germans attack and push our men back. And they are back on the same piece of land they were on before, but lots of men have died.

I really want to be out there, helping Britain win this war.

There are reports in the papers that the Germans have been using gas against the troops. Arthur didn't say anything about gas in his letters. Someone said the Germans had used the gas against the French troops, which is why none of our soldiers know anything about it. I hope Arthur doesn't get gassed.

9TH MAY 1915

A German submarine has sunk a passenger liner, the *Lusitania* with torpedoes. The newspapers are calling it one of the most cowardly acts of the war, because the ship wasn't a warship of any kind, but a liner sailing from New York, in America, to Britain with nearly two thousand ordinary civilian passengers on board. The German submarine attacked the *Lusitania* when it was passing the coast of Kinsale in Ireland.

It makes me so angry when I read about things like this. It's bad enough that soldiers and sailors and airmen are dying in this war, but they are in combat and know what they are doing, and they know that being killed or wounded is a chance they take. But the people who died when the liner was torpedoed and sunk were just ordinary people.

Apparently the German submarine didn't give the ship's passengers on the ship any chance to get into the lifeboats after the first torpedo struck, because they fired a second torpedo immediately after, and the ship went straight down. Some people managed to survive, but over a thousand people died when the ship was hit and sank.

This has made me even more determined to join the navy and go to sea, and seek out these submarines, and the rest of the German navy, and sink them!

16TH MAY 1915

Yesterday Jeb and I were delivering barrels of beer to a pub next to Charing Cross railway station, and we saw all these wounded soldiers being put in buses and coaches. There were hundreds and hundreds of them. Some had legs missing. Some had arms missing. Some had bandages wrapped round their heads. Some were blind and were being led along in a line, holding on to the back of the man in front. I'd heard people talk about the soldiers coming back wounded, and I'd seen lots of them in our neighbourhood, but I'd never seen so many injured soldiers in one place before.

"They're the lucky ones," said Jeb. "The unlucky ones are lying dead back there in France."

"They're not lucky," I said. I pointed at the line of blind soldiers making their way towards one of the waiting coaches. "What are they going to do now?"

"Beg," said Jeb. "But at least they're alive."

As we drove the cart away, I looked back. More wounded soldiers were pouring out of the station, and more buses and coaches were pulling up to collect them. All I could think of was Arthur and I prayed that he wouldn't come back like that.

1ST JUNE 1915

Last night there was a zeppelin attack on London. Lots of people were killed and buildings destroyed. People are getting worried. They say that if the zeppelins can drop bombs on London, then they can drop gas on us as well.

It seems that we're under attack from all sides. The German navy is shelling our coastal towns, and the German zeppelins are dropping bombs on our towns and cities inland. I have to do something more than just driving around with Jeb delivering barrels of beer. What I do isn't going to win this war. It's been going on for nearly a year and it still looks no nearer to being won.

3RD JUNE 1915

I talked again to Jeb today about joining the navy. He said I should lie about my age. He said I'd get away with it because I look older than I am, but I told him what Dad had drilled into me about not lying. Jeb suggested I try again, and keep trying until they let me in. The trouble is, I worry that if I keep on trying and they keep sending me away, it'll count against me and the recruiting officer will just automatically turn me down when he sees me come in again. I've got to be clever about this and think about what I can say to persuade the navy to let me in when I next go there.

15TH JULY 1915

This afternoon I went to the Royal Navy office again to volunteer, and this time they said I could join! I reckon because of the war they must have relaxed the rules. The trouble was, they said that because I was only fifteen I needed my father's written permission. I told the recruiting officer that my father was away in the army, so it wasn't easy for me to get written permission from him. This was only a white lie – I could write to Dad and ask him to give his permission, but I was worried he might think I was still too young.

The officer said that if I could take him letters proving my good character from responsible adults, such as the headmaster of my old school and my employer, then that should do the trick and I could enlist and start training as a boy cadet. So I will be able to join the Navy after all without waiting!

I came home and told Ma and George and Fred and Lily. George and Fred were really jealous and said they also wanted to go and join up, too. Ma told them they were both too young. She said that she would have a husband and two sons away fighting and she needed them both at home to take care of things.

Lily got upset and hugged me, and said she was worried I'd get shot and wounded. Someone had told her that the son of a family down the road had gone to France and been killed and she was already worried that the same would happen to Arthur.

I told her not to worry, that I would be in the navy. The navy was different from the army because you were on a ship, which meant the enemy were always far away, and couldn't creep up on you and shoot you. You could see them coming across the sea. George said you wouldn't be able to see them if it was night time, and that upset Lily who started crying and saying I'd be killed. So Ma told George off, and said that I had to do what I had to do. That I was going to protect them and everyone else, and they should be proud of me.

Today I joined the navy! I am now Naval Cadet John Travers Cornwell Boy, Second Class (No J/42563).

I got the letters from my old headmaster at Walton Road School and from my boss at Whitbread's, and took them to the recruiting officer, who said they would do fine. I signed the forms and was given a rail ticket to Plymouth. I am to start my training at HMS *Vivid*, Keyham Naval Barracks in Devonport. The recruiting officer told me that the training normally takes two years, but they have speeded things up so that it will take only six months. They have an urgent need for us boys to go to sea and join the fighting ships. I'm to be paid sixpence a week, when my training's over I'll be paid a shilling a week.

I went to the brewery depot and told the manager that I was going off to war. He shook my hand and told me there'd be a job for me at the brewery when the war was over.

Then I went to where Jeb was at the dray cart and told him the news. He looked at me for a bit, then held out his hand for me to shake. I took it and he shook my hand firmly and gave me a smile.

"You're a brave boy, Jack," he said. "And good company. I'll miss having you to talk with when I'm doing my rounds. Make sure you come back safe so you can join me on the cart again."

"I will," I assured him.

Then I shook his hand again and set off home to pack my bags. After that, I sat down and wrote a letter to Dad.

Dear Dad,

Good news! I have joined the navy, so I will be fighting the Hun very soon! I start my training tomorrow at HMS Vivid. I will think of you when I am sailing the waves, sinking the German battleships and their U-boats. I will do my duty, just as you always say, and hope I make you proud of me.

I remain your ever-loving son,

Jack

PART 2

TRAINING
HMS VIVID, DEVONPORT

LONDON 1915 – 1916

29TH JULY 1915

Today I said goodbye to Ma, George, Fred, little Lily and Alice.

I got to Paddington station to catch my train. The station was packed, mainly with men and boys also going down to Plymouth. Many of them were in uniform – junior officers, able-bodied seamen and cadets – but quite a few were in their civvies, like I was. Most of those wearing ordinary clothes were boys of about my age, maybe a little older.

I found myself a seat inside a carriage with three other boys, all Londoners. It was obvious we were all going to the same place for the same reason so we shook hands and introduced ourselves.

"I'm Jack Cornwell," I said. "From East Ham."

"Jimmy Mac," said the tallest, a red-haired boy, as he shook my hand. He gestured his thumb at the smaller boy sitting next to him. "This is my cousin, Bobby. We're from Camden Town."

"I live just round the corner from him," said Bobby. "We grew up together."

"T-Terry," said the fourth one. "I-I'm…". We nodded politely and waited for him to find his words. "I'm from Pa-Paddington."

"You didn't have far to come then." Jimmy grinned.

I was pleased that Jimmy and Bobby didn't make fun of Terry because of his stammer. When I was at school we had a kid who stammered, and some of the other kids used to be really cruel to him. My dad says that picking on someone weaker than yourself is the coward's way. He says it's the duty of the strong to protect the weak. I suppose that's why we went to war with Germany, to protect the smaller and weaker countries they attacked.

The train journey to Plymouth was really long. It took hours and hours. Luckily my ma had packed me some sandwiches for the journey, and so had Terry's. Jimmy and Bobby had just a piece of bread and dripping each, which wasn't much, so me and Terry shared our food with them. Jimmy promised to pay us back when we got our first pay.

"You d-don't have to p-pay me back," said Terry. "That's what pa-pals are for."

Jimmy smiled. "Yes!" he said. "That's us! The Four Pals!"

I feel really good about having made these friends so quickly. I'm sure it will help me settle in so far away from home.

30TH JULY 1915

Yesterday we all arrived at HMS *Vivid* Keyham Barracks, in Devonport, Plymouth.

We were immediately given our uniforms and equipment and put into groups of twenty. Each group is called a mess. I was pleased that I am in the same mess as Jimmy, Bobby and Terry, so we can still be the Four Pals together!

I thought HMS *Vivid* was going to be a ship, but it turns out to be part of the barracks, which are on land, although it is next to the docks.

The name "barracks" strikes me as wrong, because it sounds like a place with lots of long huts. But Keyham Barracks is more like a small town. It even has its own church on the site, which shows how big it is. It looks as if there are thousands of people here, either training or working. I think it is going to take me a while to get used to this place and find out where everything is, and especially what I have to do in my training.

14TH AUGUST 1915

I've been here two weeks now and I'm getting the hang of things. The difficult thing at first was getting used to sleeping in a hammock instead of a bed. A hammock is like a sheet that hangs between two hooks. You have to hang it up yourself at night before going to bed, then take it down in the morning.

I don't know why we have to sleep in hammocks instead of proper beds. Jimmy says it's because there's not a lot of room below decks on ships, and beds would take up too much space. But I've noticed that sometimes Jimmy says things as if they are true, even when he doesn't really know about them. This doesn't mean he tells lies. It just means if he doesn't know why something happens, he comes up with a reason of his own, and sometimes he's right, sometimes he's wrong.

Someone else in our mess said the reason sailors sleep in hammocks is because when ships are at sea they move about all over the place, because of the winds and high seas, and a hammock is easier than a bed because it swings with the ship when it moves. That doesn't make sense to me because it could swing too hard and throw you out of bed. I'm sure I'll find out the real reason why we sleep in hammocks later.

The day's routine at the Barracks goes like this:

At half-past five in the morning the bugle is sounded to wake us up and call us to attention – I'm told the morning bugle doesn't sound until a quarter to six in winter – (a whole quarter of an hour more to sleep!) We roll up our hammocks, then we have prayers. After prayers we clean and tidy up our quarters until eight o'clock. Then we eat breakfast.

At half past eight we are inspected by the officer of the day, who checks that our boots are polished and our uniforms are clean and we have washed, including under our fingernails. I am used to this because we used to have this sort of inspection when I was in the Boy Scouts in Manor Park.

By nine o'clock we start our classes. The classes vary, depending on what we are due to learn that day. During our first week we learnt all about our kit. We learned how to roll our hammocks, how to sling them up and take them down. We also learned about the importance of washing and looking after our clothes, including sewing and mending.

This last week we have been learning semaphore, which is sending messages using flags. Luckily for me, I already did semaphore in the Boy Scouts. Next week we will have a week learning bends and hitches, which means learning to tie different sorts of knots. Once more, I shall be fine here because I did knots in the Scouts as well.

At noon we stop for dinner; then after that we start work again until three o'clock. Except on Wednesdays and Saturdays, that is. On those two days we get the afternoon off as half-holidays. On the other days we do games, or we practise rowing or sailing.

At five o'clock it's tea time, and after tea we can do what we want until half past eight, providing we don't get into trouble. Often me and the gang find somewhere to kick a football around. Terry is the best footballer of the four of us, though Jimmy likes to think he is.

At half past eight we sling our hammocks and make them ready for the night, then climb in. The bugle goes for "lights out" at nine o'clock, but by then most of us are asleep after the day's hard work. But before I go to sleep I say a prayer for Dad and Arthur, and for God to keep them safe.

16TH AUGUST 1915

Since I last wrote we had what I'm told is called "an incident". In this case it meant Terry getting badly bullied by another boy in our mess, and we didn't know how to deal with it because we didn't want to make Terry look worse.

The bully was a boy called Ted Meers. He's fifteen years old, like us, but he's big for his age. He comes from somewhere in Kent. Unfortunately, it seems wherever you go, there will always be bullies to make trouble. It was the same when I was at school, and it's the same now I'm in the navy.

What happened was that we came into our mess to put up our hammocks, and Meers shouted at Terry in a nasty way, making fun of his stammer. He started pretending to stammer, saying "D-d-d-do", and his mates started laughing. It upsets me when you see people playing up to bullies like Ted Meers, pretending they like them and laughing at their jokes, when the truth is they're just scared of them. Anyway, Terry went red, and because he was so angry, he couldn't get his words out. He started to say "Shut up", but he could only get out "Sh ..." and then he got stuck, and Meers laughed at him and repeated "S-s-sh". I was going to step in, but before I did Jimmy said to Meers, "Leave him alone!"

Meers turned on Jimmy and snapped at him, "You want to make something of it, do you?"

Instantly everyone went silent, because we all knew what Meers was like. He was a bully, but he was also strong, and he was a cheat of a fighter. In our first week he'd got into a fight with a boy from another mess and had kicked him in the leg and when he went down he kicked him in the groin. The boy's screaming brought an officer to see what the trouble was. Meers claimed that he'd only been defending himself after this other boy attacked him and Meers's mates backed him up.

The other boy went to hospital, and I heard he was sent home. Since then, everyone was wary of Meers.

For a moment I thought that Jimmy was going to back down because he'd gone all white in the face, but then he just turned and looked Meers straight in the face and said, "I'm just saying you leave him alone, unless you want to take on both of us."

"Three of us," piped up a voice, and I realized that it was Bobby who'd spoken. So, of course, because we were the Four Pals, I had to speak up as well. "That's four of us," I threw in, and walked over to join Jimmy, Bobby and Terry.

Meers looked at us, and I could see he was thinking hard. Yes, I was pretty sure he could beat any one of us on his own, but he wouldn't have as much chance against four of us. And he was clever enough to know that he couldn't depend on his so-called "mates" if it came to a real fight. People who hang around bullies do it because they want to pretend they're tough, but usually they're not. Get them on their own and they crumble.

Finally Meers sneered. He turned to Terry and said: "So, you're not m-m-man enough. You've got to have your mates to look after you. Baby!"

With that Meers turned and went out of the hut, heading for the toilet block. There was an awkward silence in the hut, and then his cronies went after him. Terry looked furious.

"You s-shouldn't have s-said anything!" He forced the words out angrily to Jimmy.

Jimmy stared at him, stunned. "Well thanks for nothing, pal!" he snapped back. "I just put my head on the line for you!"

"I d-didn't need it!" said Terry. Then he went to his hammock and started putting it up. His ears were all red and I could see how angry he was.

Jimmy was also angry. He glared at Terry, and then stormed outside the hut.

Bobby and I exchanged sympathetic looks. We both knew what was going on. In Terry's case, he didn't want to look as if he had to have someone to take care of him. He wanted to be seen to stand up for himself, even though we all knew that if it came to a fight, Meers would slaughter Terry.

From Jimmy's point of view, he'd put himself at risk to save Terry from getting beaten up by Meers. When Jimmy spoke up, he wasn't to know that me and Bobby would add our voices as well.

"What are we going to do?" asked Bobby quietly, looking towards

Terry. At the open door of our hut we could see Jimmy standing outside.

I shook my head. "I don't know," I admitted. "We've got to talk to them. We can't have the Four Pals splitting up like this."

"You're right." Bobby nodded. "If you have a word with Terry, I'll have a word with Jimmy."

While Bobby went out to talk to Jimmy, I walked over to where Terry was putting the finishing touches to his hammock. He didn't turn round to look at me, even though he must have heard the sound of my boots walking towards him on the wooden floor. And I could have been Meers coming after him.

"Terry," I said.

"I d-don't want to t-talk about it," he said. His voice was all gruff and choked, and I suddenly realized that he was crying. Though I didn't know if he was for sure, because he wouldn't turn and face me.

"You can't let someone like Meers break up the Four Pals," I said. "We've been good for each other. If we break up like this, then Meers has won, whatever happens." I waited for Terry to reply, and when he didn't I carried on. "All right, Jimmy shouldn't have spoken up like that. But he did it because he's your mate. Like I am. Like Bobby is. We're pals, and pals look after one another."

Terry still didn't speak, but he'd stopped messing with his hammock. He stood there, listening, so I carried on talking.

"Admit it, Jimmy could have got himself badly beaten up standing up to Meers the way he did. Remember what happened to that boy in that other mess, the one Meers kicked who got sent home. Trust me, Terry,

Jimmy didn't do what he did to upset you. You know what Jimmy's like, his mouth opens before his brain starts thinking."

At this, Terry nodded. "T-true," he said quietly. And he gave a sniff and he wiped his face with his sleeve.

"So, I think you ought to shake hands with him, so we can be the Four Pals again," I said.

I heard heavy clumping footsteps on the floorboards behind me, and I whirled round, thinking it might be Meers and some of his mates, but it was Jimmy and Bobby.

"I was just thinking the same," said Jimmy. He stuck out his hand towards Terry. "I'm sorry, Terry. I spoke out of turn, and I was wrong. Are we still mates?"

Terry hesitated, then he wiped his face with his sleeve again and turned to face us. His face was all tightly stretched across his cheekbones, and I could see from his eyes that he had been crying. He looked at Jimmy's outstretched hand then he took it and shook it.

"M-mates," he said, nodding firmly. Then he gulped and added, "I'm s-sorry, J...".

Jimmy shook his head. "No need to say sorry, Terry," he said. "Let's just not say any more about it." Then he grinned. "And the four of us should stick together. That way, Meers won't try it on any of us, cos he'll always be taking on four. And even for him, that's two too many."

"Good!" agreed Bobby. "Now I suggest we finish our hammocks and get some sleep. We've got a hard day in the morning."

I felt relieved as I fixed up my hammock to think that the

Four Pals hadn't broken up. But I knew that the problem of Meers wouldn't go away. And some day, I was sure, Terry would find himself standing up to Meers on his own, and getting hurt.

20TH AUGUST 1915

Today I got a letter from Dad. I was so pleased.

Dear Jack,

Thanks for your letter. So you are going to be a sailor! I'm really proud of you. You will cut a fine figure in your uniform. Always remember that whatever happens, do your duty. Avoid bad company. I know you will because you are a good and honest boy, and have been brought up to always do the Right Thing.

Things here are much the same as they have been. I would like to be in the action more, but I will be ready if and when the Hun attack us.

The men I am with are good blokes. All of us know that we are fighting for our families. Just the same as you will be doing soon.

I'm thinking of you.

Your loving,

Dad

It's been ages since I've heard from him, and I've been wondering how he was. For that reason, it's been lucky for me that we're kept so busy, and I'm so tired when we finish for the day that I go to sleep straight away. Dad didn't say anything about his health, so I hope he's all right and his bronchitis is being kept at bay.

Today our mess went out on the sea! We took a boat out under the command of a lieutenant, rowing with oars, ten to each side. It was to give us the experience of dealing with the swell of the sea, and controlling a boat according to whether it's an ebb tide (going out) or a flow (coming in).

The sea was quite rough and a few of the boys got sick. I was lucky, I didn't. I seemed to be able to handle the way the boat went up and down. Bobby was sick, so was Meers and two of the other boys. But the lieutenant wouldn't let them stop rowing. When the boat came back to shore, the four who were sick then had to clean the boat.

6TH SEPTEMBER 1915

Today I had a letter from Ma. It was short, but it meant a lot to me because I know how hard it is for her to put her thoughts down on paper. She says that George and Fred are behaving themselves. Everything is all right at home. Bill Moore, one of our neighbours who was fighting in France, has been killed, and they are worried that Evie Moore, his wife, might do something silly to herself because they were a very close couple. Ma says she and Alice are going to keep an eye on Evie Moore and make sure she is all right. Ma also says that she is thinking of having chickens in the back yard as a way of making sure they get eggs at home.

My guess is Alice gave Ma some help writing the letter. Alice writes and spells really well. She could have got herself a good career, if she had been born somewhere other than East Ham. It seems all the women from where we live have to go into factories, or else do cleaning work. To get on in this world you need education, and education costs money. Everyone says it's a waste of time to educate girls because they're going to get married and have children. I know that's what Dad says, but I think that's a pity in Alice's case.

10th September 1915

I've been given a great honour. The commander of the cadet school at HMS *Vivid* has appointed me to the post of his messenger. This means that at certain times of day I report to his office and collect and deliver messages from him to other high-ranking people at the base. The officer in charge of our mess says this shows that I'm considered to be especially honest, trustworthy and reliable. I've written to Dad to tell him about this. I know he'll be very proud. I've tried to play it down in my letter because I don't want him to think I'm boasting. But I want him to know that I'm doing my duty well enough for the commander to believe I can do this important job.

The lessons we are doing in the mornings are getting much harder. Signalling by semaphore and the different sorts of knots were things I'd already done in the Scouts, so that was easy for me. Since then it's all been new. We've learned about the compass and how to steer by it. Also how to rig and sail a small boat. There have been lessons in throwing the lead to take soundings, as well as how to cast and weigh the anchor.

Yesterday we had a lesson on lights, which are very important when you are in a ship at sea at night. This was about what different lights mean when you see a ship in the distance.

20TH SEPTEMBER 1915

Last night we had a concert in the gallery in the drill shed, which becomes a sort of theatre. The drill shed isn't a place where there's drill, which is what you'd think from its name, but is part of the canteen.

The concert was good. Some of the sailors took turns to do sketches and sing songs, and we all joined in with the singing. It seemed strange to be sitting in a concert when there was a war going on, but our officer says that there has to be room for some fun, otherwise this life would be just hard work and misery. Personally, I don't think there's anything wrong with hard work – it's how we get on. And where would we be in this war if we didn't work hard to train and learn how to fight and defeat the enemy?

I enjoyed the concert, though. The comedy sketches were funny enough, with some of the men pretending to fall off the stage, and toppling over, and throwing flour at one another. And the songs were good too, especially the rousing songs about winning the war. They made me want to get out there and do my bit even more!

24TH SEPTEMBER 1915

Trouble with Meers again this afternoon. Me, Jimmy and Bobby were out on the playing field, kicking a ball about with some of the other boys. Terry wasn't with us because he'd gone to see one of the chief petty officers about some pictures of knots he'd had to do. Terry turns out to be quite a good artist and this CPO had asked him if he'd draw some pictures of different sorts of knots so he could use them with other cadets. The next thing we knew, a boy from another mess was running towards us shouting "Fight! Fight!"

Instantly we stopped playing football and went running after him, and found Terry and Meers going hard at it behind one of the long huts. Both of them had blood on their mouths and blood coming from their noses, and Terry had a big nasty bruise over one eye.

Bobby made a move to run in and jump on Meers, but I grabbed him and stopped him. So long as Meers didn't do anything nasty and cheating, like kicking Terry like he'd kicked that other boy, it was a fair fight. Well, it was almost a fair fight. After all, Meers was much bigger than Terry.

As we watched, Meers swung a hard punch at Terry, but Terry managed to duck down and Meers's fist sailed over Terry's head. Then, so quickly that I hardly saw it, Terry jerked back up and brought his fist up hard under Meers's chin. We all heard the crack, though whether it was the sound of Meers's chin bone cracking, or Terry's fingers, I couldn't tell. Certainly, if it had been Terry's fingers, it wasn't stopping him because Terry stepped back, and then swung a punch with his other fist, straight into Meers's face.

Meers couldn't defend himself. That crack on his chin had made him groggy and his hands had dropped down by his side, so Terry's fist just thudded into his mouth, and Meers toppled backwards.

Meers lay there on the ground. We could tell he was conscious, but only just. His eyelids were flickering, like he was trying to keep them open but they wanted to stay shut. Terry stood, his fists ready, panting and waiting for Meers to get up. Then a voice boomed out behind us, demanding, "What's going on here?"

We all turned, then sprang to attention. A CPO was standing there, glaring at us. Even Terry moved to stand to attention, though I noticed he winced as he did so.

The CPO looked at us, and then at Meers lying on the ground, then at Terry, then back at us again and demanded sternly, "I asked: what's going on here?"

"Boxing, sir!" Jimmy replied quickly.

Bobby and I looked at him, stunned, then swung our eyes back to the CPO.

"Boxing?" echoed the CPO.

"Yes, sir," answered Jimmy.

I suppose it wasn't actually a lie. But it wasn't the truth, either.

The CPO stood looking at us for a moment. Then he pointed at Meers, and then at four of the boys nearest to Meers and said, "You, you, you and you. Take him to sick bay." Turning to Terry he said, "And you go to sick bay too. Get yourself seen to. Then you'll report to my office. Is that understood?"

"Y-y-yes, sir," said Terry.

Later, me, Jimmy and Bobby were hanging around close to the CPO's office while Terry and Meers were inside. We were eager to find out what the CPO said to them both. They were in there for ages. Finally the door opened and they came out. Meers said something to Terry, Terry just looked at him, and then Meers walked off. He passed us, but he didn't say anything, just gave us a glare and then trudged on.

"What happened?" asked Jimmy, gesturing at the CPO's office.

"He s-said if we d-did it again we'd be in b-big trouble," said Terry. "Then he t-told us to sh-shake hands," said Terry. "So we did."

"But what was all that just now?" asked Bobby. "What did Meers say to you?"

"He s-said I was tougher than he th-thought, and he wanted to b-be my p-pal." Terry grinned. "I told him I've already g-got three pals."

We all laughed, and Jimmy slapped Terry on the back.

"Good one!" he said. "I don't think you'll have any more trouble from Meers!"

1st October 1915

Today I spent time writing letters to Ma and all at home, to Dad in Colchester, and to Arthur in France. I didn't want to tell them how hard the work is here in case they think I'm complaining. And they're all having things a lot harder than I am. So I wrote and told them about the food and how good it is, because it is. We get a good breakfast. Usually it's sausages and sometimes – if there are any – we get an egg with it. We usually have fish for breakfast as well, a kipper or a bloater. We also get corned beef, which is very filling, and a good wedge of cheese, and in the evening we get a basin of hot cocoa, which is really good.

After I had written the letters I worried that Arthur might get upset because I guess his rations at the front won't be anything like that, and I don't want to make him feel jealous and think my life is getting soft. Life here is far from soft.

It's not so much the hard physical work that wears me out as the brain work, with all the things we have to remember. A lot of them are to do with arithmetic and angles. Like boxing the compass, for instance. This is when we have to remember all 32 points of the compass clockwise from north. Each point is at eleven and a quarter degrees, and you have to be able to work out the whole way round the compass at these intervals. They say things will get easier once every ship in the navy is using the gyrocompass, which is marked in degrees around a circle from 0 to 360, but at the moment we have to work everything out in points.

18th October 1915

Bobby got a letter today from his Ma which told him his two older brothers, Ted and Stan, were both dead, killed in action. Bobby did his best not to cry in front of us, but I could see his lips were trembling and his eyes were red. I didn't know what was in the letter at the time, but I could see he was upset by it, so I asked him if he was all right. He nodded and went out, taking the letter with him.

A short while later he came back into the mess and handed me the letter to read, then went out again. I read it, then told Jimmy and Terry what was in it. Jimmy was so shocked that he nearly fell over, and I kicked myself for not remembering that he and Bobby were cousins, so Ted and Stan had been Jimmy's cousins as well. Jimmy turned and went out, looking very upset.

Terry and I didn't know quite what to do. In the end, we went outside and found Bobby and Jimmy sitting on a tree stump.

"I'm sorry, Jimmy," I said. "I forgot they were your cousins. I didn't mean to blurt it out like that."

Jimmy shook his head. "That's all right, Jack," he said. "Anyway, me and Bobby are going to have some quiet time on our own for a bit."

"Of course," I said.

Me and Terry left them there. There's not a lot to say when something like that happens.

19TH OCTOBER 1915

Today Jimmy was a lot better. Bobby still looked pale and unhappy, but that's understandable. I'd be the same if I got that same news about Dad and Arthur. I wonder where Bobby's brothers were killed? I wonder if it is anywhere near where Arthur's fighting? I especially worry about Dad, even though he's in England. He's not as young as most of the men in the army. I know he says he's an old soldier, and he's as tough as old boots, but he needs to take care of himself.

8TH NOVEMBER 1915

We have been doing lessons in gunnery. These are the lessons I have been looking forward to the most because I want to be a gunner on a ship, and fire shells at the Germans and sink their ships. The truth is, though, I've found these lessons to be the hardest of all. It's not just about how to fire a gun, that would be easy. It's about angles of projectiles, and velocity, and all sorts of arithmetic stuff. A naval gun is not just like a rifle or a pistol, it's a big and very complicated piece of machinery with lots of parts that can go wrong. It also needs a very big crew to man, load and fire it. The whole business of loading it and firing it is pretty complicated. But I am determined to learn all there is to know.

25th December 1916

Christmas Day. Today we had a proper Christmas dinner – turkey, roast potatoes, vegetables and gravy, with a great Christmas pudding to follow. It was the best meal I've ever had. After it we all drank a toast to the King.

It seemed strange to be having Christmas away from home, but in a way it felt like home because of being part of the Four Pals. They've become like family. It sounds strange to say, but they seem more like brothers to me than George and Fred. That said, I thought of George and Fred and Lily and Alice at home with Ma, and said a prayer for them. When all this is over, we shall have our own Christmas together.

8TH JANUARY 1916.

My birthday. I am sixteen years old and in the navy. Well, at the moment I am still in training but in just a few weeks' time I shall be qualified as a Boy, First Class, and then I will be assigned a ship. It would be great if all four of us – me, Jimmy, Bobby and Terry – were assigned to the same ship, so the Four Pals would stick together. In the army they have regiments known as the Pals, where friends who've got together form a regiment of their own and go off to fight in the war together. But in those cases the Pals are usually all from the same village, or the same local area, and there are enough to form a whole regiment. With us there are just four of us. Also, it's not just numbers in ships, they need men and boys with different skills. In the army it's really just about being able to use a rifle.

The Government have introduced conscription. This means that every man over the age of eighteen has to go into the services and fight. I think this is only right. Britain is at war and needs every man she can get if we are not to lose to the Germans.

This war has been going on for a long while. I don't see that it can keep on going like this. Men are dying all the time and whole countries are being destroyed. I sometimes think that everyone's forgotten what this war is all about. All I know is that we have to beat the Germans, otherwise they will rule us.

Today the gunnery officer asked me to stay behind after the lesson. I was worried that he was going to make me stay behind and do some of the calculations again. I was surprised when he said that he was impressed with my work in the gunnery lessons, and asked me if I had thought about studying to be a sight setter or gun layer.

What a sight setter does is this: on the big gun there is a brass disc. The sight setter turns this brass disc to make the muzzle of the big gun go up, or go down, to make sure the shells that the gun fires hit on the target. If the sight setter gets it wrong, it means the shells will miss the target.

Being a sight setter is a really important job. It's not always done by boys, many men do it as well. The gunnery officer told me he has been keeping an eye on the way I apply myself to my lessons, and he thinks I could be a sight setter if I wanted to.

The trouble is, to qualify as a sight setter means extra training. As it stands, me and the rest of our mess will pass out as Boys, First Class, next month. If I volunteer to stay on and train as a sight setter, this means another two months' training.

I thanked the gunnery officer and said I would like to train. But afterwards I wondered if I'd done the right thing. If I leave the training camp next month when I pass out as a Boy, First Class, then I'll go straight on to a ship and be taking my part in the war. If I stay on for extra training to be a sight setter, it could be another eight or nine weeks before I get on board a ship.

I didn't know what to do, so I talked about it afterwards with the other three. Bobby was impressed when I told him and said he wished he'd been asked, but Jimmy and Terry felt differently.

"I want to get to grips with the Germans as soon as I can," stated Jimmy.

"M-me t-too," nodded Terry.

Bobby shook his head. "Being a sight setter means being part of a gun crew," he said. "Actually being on deck, firing shells at the Hun. Fighting them face-to-face. As ordinary sailors, we could end up being below deck and never seeing the enemy at all."

This time it was Jimmy's turn to shake his head. "That may be so," he said, "but I don't want to wait. I want to get out there! If I had my way, I'd be on a warship already, instead of being stuck in lessons day after day."

"We have to learn," put in Terry.

"I've learned all I need to know," said Jimmy. "Come February, I shall be on a ship!"

Bobby looked at me. "Well, Jack?" he asked. "What are you going to do?"

"I've already told the gunnery officer I will," I said.

"You can tell him you've changed your mind," said Jimmy. "Tell him you want to get out there and fight the Hun as soon as you can!"

I thought it over, looking at their expectant faces as I did so. All of them were waiting, wondering what I was going to do. I sighed and shook my head.

"I've got to do it," I said. "Before I started, I wanted to be a gunner on a ship. I'm being given a chance."

They fell silent, and Jimmy looked particularly unhappy. "It'll be the end of the Four Pals," he said sadly.

"No it won't," I said. "We'll always be pals. And after the war we can get together and be the Four Pals again." I grinned. "Until then you lot will just have to be the Three Musketeers."

19TH FEBRUARY 1916

Today our mess completed our basic training and have all passed out. I am now Boy, First Class!

Me and the gang shook hands to congratulate one another, then they went off to pack up their things. They are all to be assigned to their ships, and they will be shipping out early tomorrow, while I start my training to be a sight setter. I wonder if the four of us really will meet up again? I hope so.

20TH FEBRUARY 1916

It takes a great deal more than most people think to make a gun work.

When a shell arrives, it's put into a loading tray next to the breech, which is the end of the gun's firing tube – the long gun barrel. When the breech is opened, the loading tray moves in front of the breech and a man with a ramrod – which is like a hard cloth pad on the end of a long pole – pushes the shell into the breech. This ramrod is the same sort of thing they once used to push cannonballs and gunpowder into the old-fashioned cannons of Drake and Nelson!

Another man puts the cordite – the explosive that fires the shell – into the breech and the ramrodder pushes the cordite in after the shell, followed by a firing pin. The breech door is then shut. This automatically pushes the loading tray for the shells ready for the loader to put the next shell on.

The gunner pulls a trigger – a cord that hangs out of the back of the breech – which sets off the firing pin and explodes the cordite. The explosion is so powerful, it can fire a shell for miles.

If that sounds complicated, it gets worse because the gun has to move left and right, as well as up and down, to make sure that the shell hits the target when it's fired.

To move the gun there are two men, both sitting on seats fixed to the gun. One man is in charge of the elevation, which is raising or lowering the gun barrel. The other man is in charge of traverse, which means moving the barrel from side to side, to the left and right.

None of the gun crew can actually see the target they're aiming at. They act on instructions they receive from the gunnery officer. And the person who relays the instructions from the gunnery officer to the men who move the gun up or down is me, the sight setter or gun layer.

On a ship the gunnery officer is in a conning tower, which is high up in the centre of the ship. He can see the enemy and he works out what angle the gun needs to be at to hit the target. He calls his instructions to the sight setter through a telephone line, and the setter receives them through headphones.

Because we were only training, we used the gun that's set up in the grounds of the barracks. Also, because we were training and they didn't want to waste valuable ammunition, we just did it with dummy shells without cordite and firing pins.

The gunnery officer called out different angles to me through the headphones. To begin with, he wanted me to set the gun so that it would hit a target 6,000 yards away, so he called out "6,000!". I turned the brass disc on the gun until the notch that was marked 6,000 was in line with the arrow on the brass plate beneath it. Then the gunnery officer called out, "Down 300!". I turned the disc so that the arrow went down 300 to 5,700. Then the gunnery officer called out "Up 500!", and I turned the disc the other way, so that the arrow went up past 6,000 to 6,200. That meant the gun was now aimed at a target 6,200 yards away.

The gun crew is made up of ten – crew leader, shell loader, elevation, traverse, ramrodder, fuses, cordite, package disposer, reserve, and me – sight setter. If it sounds like a lot of men just to fire one gun, there are even more involved! There are the men who carry the shells up to the gun. There are the men who put the fuses in the shells and arm them ready to be fired. (Shells can't be armed before they are ready to be fired because it would be too dangerous to have them lying around armed and all set to explode.) There are also the men in the cordite room, responsible for sending up the plugs of cordite to fire the gun.

The reason so many men are needed is so that the gun can fire and be reloaded quickly. When a gun crew is working fast together, a gun can fire ten shells a minute.

17TH MARCH 1916

The war continues. I've had no news of Dad or Arthur for a while yet.
I hope they are keeping well, but the news from the front is confused.
Some reports say we are winning and the Germans have been pushed
back, yet on the same day there'll be reports that the Germans have
made ground. The only thing that everyone seems to agree on are the
casualty figures. I pray every night that Arthur is safe, and that we will
win this war.

I am now fully qualified as a gun layer or sight setter.

I was given my papers, and my travel orders and travel dockets for the journey to the ship I've been assigned to. It is the cruiser HMS *Chester*, which is based in Rosyth in Scotland. Today is one of the proudest days of my life!

I don't have to report to HMS *Chester* until next Monday, the 2nd of May, so I've been given leave to go home and spend a few days with Ma and the family. It will be good to see them and catch up with their news, and the news from Dad and Arthur. It's been almost nine months since I was home.

PART 3

BACK HOME AND ONWARD!

29TH APRIL 1916

It was so good to see Ma and the family again. George, Fred and little Lily have all grown up so much since last July.

George and Fred were really jealous of my uniform and wanted to try it on, but I said no. This uniform had to be earned. I let them wear my cap, though. Alice arrived with a young man she's been walking out with. His name is Charles and he's in a reserved occupation, which is why he isn't fighting in the war.

Just this morning Ma had letters from Dad in Colchester, and Arthur from France. My guess is that Dad's written to me in Devonport, and his letter will be forwarded on to me. At least, I hope it will be.

There have been many deaths of men in our neighbourhood, men who had been fighting overseas. Most of them had died in France and Belgium, but one of our neighbours, Mrs Clare, lost her son John in Gallipoli, which is in Turkey. According to George, who has been following the war while I've been away, Gallipoli was a terrible defeat for our side. We lost half our army in casualties, about a quarter of a million men. I told George off for spreading stories about defeats. I explained we should only be talking about our victories because spreading stories about our defeats lowers morale among our soldiers and sailors.

"So have I lowered your morale then, Jack?" asked George.

I could tell by the smile on his face that he was just being cheeky, but I thought it was time to be serious with him. "No, you haven't, George," I replied. "Because I know we're going to win this war. But there are plenty of enemies who are doing their best to stop us, and that sort of talk only helps them. You don't want to be the one who helps our enemies attack Dad and Arthur, do you?" The mention of Dad, and the reminder that Arthur was out in France fighting, made George look uncomfortable.

"I was only joking you, Jack," he said defensively.

"Well it's not something we should joke about," I told him. "This war is a serious business."

"Can we stop talking about the war for a bit?" pleaded Ma. "Jack's home after being away for nine months. We ought to be enjoying him being here, instead of going on about the war. He'll be off to it soon enough."

"Quite right," said Alice. "Let's put the kettle on for a cup of tea, and I'll make us some sandwiches."

So that's what we did. We settled down to chatter about all manner of things, and for a short while it almost seemed as if the war wasn't happening. But you only had to look at the photos of Dad and Arthur on the mantelpiece to be reminded it was.

1ST MAY 1916

My last night at home in East Ham. Tomorrow morning I will go to King's Cross station and catch the train to Rosyth in Scotland. It's a really long train journey which is going to take most of the day. The train goes right up England and into Scotland to just past Edinburgh, which is on the Firth of Forth, where HMS *Chester* is moored. I've never been north of London, so this journey will be a real adventure. But not as much of an adventure as actually going to sea and taking part in the war and doing my bit, fighting the Germans.

It's been strange, these last few days. Even though it's been good to see Ma, George, Fred, Lily and Alice, I know I'm not the same Jack Cornwell I was just nine months ago, when I left to go to HMS *Vivid* and start my training. Being away from home all that time and training, and everything else, has made me into someone else. I know people say I'm not a man yet, but I know I'm not a boy any more. My adventures at HMS *Vivid*, all the things I've done and the people I've mixed with, have put me apart from George and Ernest. Even from Ma. I feel I know what the war is about now. It's about battle – man against man, ship against ship, gun against gun. It's about facing every day as if it will be your last, and not letting it make you afraid.

2ND MAY 1916

I got off the train in Rosyth and set off to find HMS *Chester*, my kitbag over my shoulder. I'd been told that it was at anchor, so I'd have to walk along the dock until I came to the small boats that ferried sailors out to their ships. The train journey had been a long one, and it was getting dark. I was getting near to the place on the quay where the small boats left when I heard a voice call out: "Hello, shipmate!" I looked behind me, but I couldn't see anyone. Then I looked to where a stack of oil drums were piled up, and I noticed a boot sticking out from behind them. I went towards the stack of oil drums, but being very careful. I'd heard that thieves sometimes hung around the docks, waiting to attack sailors and roll them for their money. I kept well clear of the oil drums as I went round to the other side. A sailor was lying on the ground, and at first I thought he must be injured, but then he smiled and waved.

"Hello, shipmate!" he said again. "I heard you coming!"

I moved nearer to him, and as I did so the smell of drink came off him, and I realized that he was so drunk he couldn't stand up.

"You're drunk," I said.

"I am," he admitted. "Drunk as a judge."

He tried to push himself up off the ground, but instead he fell back.

I put down my kitbag and moved towards him to try and help him up, but keeping myself clear of his mouth in case he was suddenly sick and vomited over my uniform. I got my hands under his arms and managed to help him struggle to his feet. Once he was up, he reached out and held on to the nearest oil drum to help him balance. It was lucky the drums were full. If they'd been empty he'd have pulled them over on top of him.

"Where are you bound, shipmate?" he asked.

"HMS *Chester*," I replied.

He smiled broadly again. "That's my ship!" he said. "Will you give a shipmate a hand and help him get on board?"

I gave him a doubtful look. "I don't know if that's a good idea, in your condition," I said. "You'll be caught for being drunk and disorderly."

"Better than being court-martialled for desertion," he said.

"Desertion?" I said, shocked.

"Or maybe just absent without leave," he added. He blinked a few times, and then held out one hand. "My name's Wally," he said. "Wally Bones."

"Jack Cornwell," I shook his hand.

"The thing is, Jack, I was with some pals ashore on leave and I sort of got separated from them," Wally explained. "I found a girl and thought I'd have some fun. So they went off back to the ship. Me and the girl had our fun and a lot of drink, and then the next thing I knew I was out on the street, trying to get back to the good old *Chester*. But I only got this far before my legs packed up."

"For someone's who's as drunk as you are, you don't sound drunk," I said.

"That's true," agreed Wally. "That's the way it is with me. My mouth will always work when I'm drunk. It's my body, especially my legs, that doesn't. Mind, tomorrow I will have a headache."

I looked at Wally and thought about escorting him back to the ship. I was worried about arriving for my first ever duty helping to carry a man who was drunk in uniform. I'd never been drunk in my life. I'd never touched strong drink – a glass of ginger beer was enough for me. Would they think I was the same as him, his drinking companion? But I couldn't let him lie here on the ground this way. As Wally said, if he didn't get back to the ship, he'd be charged with being AWOL, or even desertion. And in a time of war that was a treasonable offence.

"All right," I said. "I'll help you. Wait 'til, I've got my kitbag on my shoulder, then lean on me."

Wally smiled an even broader smile. "You're a good pal!" he beamed. "You've just made a friend for life in Wally Bones!"

I heaved my kitbag on to my shoulder, then went to Wally and let him lean against me and put an arm round my shoulder. Then we made our way along the quayside, with him lurching along, his legs going in all directions, and every so often falling down, then hauling himself back up using me as a prop. We reached the dockside where the boats were taking sailors out to their ships. Two sailors eyed us suspiciously as we reached them.

"Where you bound?" one asked.

"The *Chester*," I said.

They looked at Wally, who was just about hanging on to me to stay upright, and the other sailor asked, "What's wrong with him?"

"He's not well," I said. Well, it wasn't a lie.

The two sailors exchanged doubtful looks. "We don't want him being sick in our boat," said one.

"He won't," I assured them, with more confidence than I really felt.

The two sailors helped me get Wally into the boat, and we set off across the choppy waters of the Firth of Forth. When we reached the *Chester*, three sailors were waiting by the steps.

"Here's Wally!" called one, and the other two let out a cheer and hurried down the steps to help Wally out.

"This here's my pal, Jack Cornwell," said Wally. "He got me here."

One of the sailors patted me on the shoulder. "Good man!" he said, and I realized from his accent he was Welsh. "We was wondering what had happened to Wally. We owe you one!" And with that he carried Wally up the steps. I picked up my kitbag and went up after them. And that's how I arrived for my posting at HMS *Chester*.

9TH MAY 1916

The *Chester* is a very busy ship. It's got a crew of 402, which means there are lots of men on it, crammed into small spaces. You notice it most below deck. There's not much room to hang hammocks, just eighteen inches between each hook, so many hammocks are hung up wherever the men can find a place. At dinner times we cram sixteen to a table, sometimes more, which doesn't give a lot of elbow room when you're eating.

It's also very hot below decks. Ships like this are built for battle, so there are very few portholes. Also the hull is made of metal, which doesn't let in ventilation like the old wooden hulls used to. There are fans which bring in air from the ventilators on deck, but it's so hot that you don't seem to feel the effect of it much.

Wally Bones and his pals have been as good as their word about looking after me. They sought me out the day after I came aboard and helped show me where everything was on the ship. They also spread the word amongst their pals not to play tricks on me. Sometimes when a new boy comes on board the old hands play practical jokes on him for fun. Wally and his friends said if anybody played serious tricks on me (like locking me in a cupboard, or something where I might get seriously hurt) they would take revenge. So it seems it was lucky for me that I found Wally when I did!

12TH MAY 1916

Today we were lined up on deck ready for inspection by Captain Lawson. He's a tall man with a grey beard, very imposing, but – the men say – very fair. He keeps his pet dog on board with him. It's a large sheepdog called Skipper, and when he came to inspect us his dog came with him, following him and stopping when he did. It almost seemed to be sitting to attention at one point. The men say that the dog is really one of the crew, and the man next to me, Dobby, said afterwards that he thinks the dog actually gets a rum ration.

15TH MAY 1916

Today we had gun practice. The men with me on my gun are a good bunch and have worked together before. I'm the only new one in the crew, but they helped me settle in. The man I work with, who sits in the seat controlling the elevation of the gun, is called Patch, and he winked at me as we were preparing. "Don't worry about getting hurt, son," he told me cheerfully. "Just remember, we're sitting on thousands of tons of explosives. If we get hit, we'll all be blown to kingdom come and we won't know a thing about it!"

Our gun has thick armour in front of it, which is fixed to the gun and turns with the gun as it moves, so we're protected. One of the gun crew, the shell loader, Batty, doesn't seem convinced by this, though. "It may look safe enough," he said "but look at that space below the armour. There's a gap between it and the deck. If shrapnel or something comes under there, it'll take our feet off!"

"Then there'll be no more football for you, Batty!" laughed Patch, and the other men laughed too. But Batty didn't laugh.

"I've said all along they ought to put something there as better protection," he insisted.

"Stop complaining," our gun leader, Fred, told him. "It's just as bad for the Germans on their ships."

"That don't make it any better for us!" protested Batty. "I ain't worried about the Germans. I'm worried about getting home alive, and with my feet! I'm supposed to be getting married when this war's over!"

"And she needs your feet to keep her warm, does she?" chuckled Ned. He was on the traverse controls for the gun.

"I think we ought to stop all this talk about getting killed," said Mick, the ramrodder, sternly. "We don't want to upset the boy on his first day with us."

"I'm not upset," I said. "God's on our side. He'll look after us."

"I'd rather have proper armour right down to the deck floor," Batty persisted, still looking sulky. But then he stopped talking about it, as Mick had told him.

17TH MAY 1916

HMS *Chester* is just one of about fifty ships in the Battlecruiser Fleet. The Battle Squadron, which is even bigger and has the really big battleships, is further north, at Scarpa Flow off the Orkney Islands. This is because some of the battleships are so huge, they are too big to be anchored at Rosyth, especially at low tide, so they have to stay in deep water.

The two fleets, our Battlecruiser Fleet and the Battle Squadron, are called the British Grand Fleet when they are together. It's such a great name, the Grand Fleet. And it really is grand.

19TH MAY 1916

There are rumours on board that we will be going into battle soon. There have been reports of some of the German fleet planning to come out into the North Sea and head towards Britain for an attack, supported by a whole fleet of U-boats. Everyone is glad about the news because we have been stuck here for ages with no sign of going into action, and that makes everyone edgy and tense. We are here because we want to fight!

26TH MAY 1916

In spite of the rumours about us going into action, a week has gone by
and nothing has happened. We don't know if the reports of the German
fleet coming to attack was a true story, or one that someone made up.
It's been a month since I left Devonport and I've still seen no action. All
I've done is drill and practise and train. Our gun crew can now work
together to load and fire the gun like clockwork, but I want us to do it
for real, in a battle against the Germans, not just practising and firing
unfused shells into the sea as target practice.

Letters today from both Dad and Ma! Dad wrote:

Dear Jack

Thank you for your letter. I hope you have got your sea legs by now.

I know you can't write and tell me what you're doing, and what ship you're on, so I have to imagine it.

Do they photograph you at all? A pal of mine here says that sometimes the new members of a ship line up with the rest of the crew to have their photos taken. If they do it on your ship, I'd like it if you can let me have a copy.

Sorry this is only a short letter, but things are very busy here, as I am sure you can understand.

I'm sending you some stamps with this so you can write back.

I look forward to seeing you again soon.

Your loving dad

And the one from Ma:

Dear Jack

How are you? We are all well at home. You know Mrs Lester from four doors away, the one we called A.L.? Well she died. The doctor said it was her heart. She was always a good neighbour to us.

Alice says to tell you not to worry about us. Also, to tell you that George and Fred are behaving.

Do write. I like getting your letters.

Love from your

Ma

I shall write back to them both tomorrow. I shall also write letters to Alice, and George.

31ST MAY 1916

This is it! At last! We have been given the order to set sail! And not just the *Chester* and the Battlecruiser Fleet, but the whole British Grand Fleet! We are going into battle! The word is that we are heading for Jutland. I've never heard of Jutland, nor do I know where it is, so I asked Patch.

"Jutland is the northern part of Denmark," he explained. "Although Denmark is neutral, it's right next to Germany, and they say the German fleet is gathering there, ready to make an attack. So we're going out to meet them and stop them."

This morning the order was given to prepare the *Chester* for action, and at half past eleven we weighed anchor and cast off, in convoy with the other light cruisers and the destroyers in our Battlecruiser Fleet.

As we passed beneath the Forth Bridge, with our crew standing in lines on deck, I had never felt so proud. Looking at all the other ships, with their crews also standing in lines on deck and the fleet stretching in each direction port to starboard and fore and aft, as far as the eye could see, was an incredible sight. There is nothing like a naval fleet leaving harbour and sailing out in the open sea to war. And this is just part of the British Grand Fleet! Once we are out in the North Sea we will be joining up with the Battle Squadron, which is steaming south-east from Scapa Flow. We will meet up and head together towards the coast of Denmark, where reports say the German High Seas Fleet has assembled.

Our fleet is hundreds of ships strong! We are an armada! We are powerful! We are invincible! The British Navy rules the waves!

As we cleared the Firth of Forth, the bugles sounded general quarters, and we all went below to prepare for action.

Shortly after, the bugles sounded again, this time signalling "action stations". We are going into battle! May God be with us.

PART 4

THE BATTLE OF JUTLAND
31ST MAY – 2ND JUNE 1916

31st May 1916

It was three o'clock in the afternoon when we met up with the Battle Squadron. We'd been sailing eastwards towards the Danish coast for about three hours since we left the Firth of Forth. The whole of that time our crew had been ready by our gun. I had been standing with my headphones on, waiting for instructions, but so far there had been silence from the gunnery officer. As I stood there I could feel excitement churning inside me. The Germans were out there! Were they heading towards us, or were they hiding, waiting for us in the coves and harbours of Germany?

So far the sea had been calm and the weather good. There was a haze over the sea. It could have been from the effect of sunlight on the water, but it also could have been from the chimneys of the hundreds of ships. Every ship's funnel was pouring out thick smoke, and in this weather it hung lower. The problem was that so many of the ships were burning coal, and coal smoke is much thicker than the smoke from ships like ours, which had oil boilers. This thick smoke can make it difficult for the observers who are watching out for enemy ships, and also for the signallers who have to send messages by flags to the other ships in the fleet.

"The Germans won't come out yet," muttered Ned. "They'll wait 'till our battleships are with us."

"Why?" I asked.

"Because if they attack us now, they could get cut off by our battleships arriving, and they won't want to be trapped by them. The Germans like a clear run between their ships and the coast so they can run for their rivers."

Just then Batty shouted out, "There they are!"

For a moment I thought he meant he'd seen the Germans, but when I looked I saw our Battle Squadron in the distance, heading towards us. Even from this distance, it was a sight to take your breath away. The really big battleships, the dreadnoughts, were enormous. They made some of the other ships look like toys next to them. To give you an idea of how massive these dreadnoughts were, the displacement of our ship, the *Chester*, was 5,185 tons. Dreadnoughts such as Benbow and Iron Duke had a displacement of 25,000 tons – nearly five times as big as our ship. And I thought our ship was big!

Sailing behind and on either side of the dreadnoughts were more cruisers and destroyers. Hundreds of ships, all ready for battle! It was a sight that filled me with pride. The British Grand Fleet on its way to defeat the Hun, and I was part of it! I wished my Dad could see me!

The *Chester* began to turn, and I noticed that the approaching dreadnoughts and the rest of the Battle Squadron were doing the same, and now we were all heading east towards Jutland.

I glanced around at the other men on the gun. Like me, all of them were straining their ears and eyes, staring out towards the horizon, watching for any sign of the German ships. There was a silence on deck. No one hummed a tune, or cracked any jokes, or started telling stories. We were all just watching and waiting. My whole body felt alive, like every nerve ending was alert and waiting, ready to spring into action as soon as the order was given. But all the time there was nothing. Just our own ships, sailing together, yet at a safe distance apart, and the haze of smoke settling over the sea.

We sailed on for about another hour. The whole time I was alert and tense, standing, waiting, ready. I looked towards the other ships, especially the dreadnoughts, with their hulls painted such a dark grey that they almost looked black. The German ships were painted with light grey paint, so each side could recognize its own ships and the enemy from a distance.

More time passed. The swell of the sea rose and fell, the waters getting choppier now, but I remained standing, holding on to the gun mounting, ready for action.

Then suddenly we heard it! The sound of heavy gunfire just a few miles distant, towards the south-east!

"We've found 'em!" shouted Patch. "Get ready, boys!"

"Signals," said Fred, pointing at one of the nearest ships, and I saw the flags go up with signals to us and the other ships around us, ordering us to change direction. We could all feel the ship begin to turn, heading south-east and gaining speed as it did, pushing towards the German fleet. All the time we could hear the sound of heavy gunfire continuing.

I wondered who the gunfire was coming from. Was it from our own ships or was it from the Germans?

As the ships increased their speed the funnels pushed out more smoke, increasing the haze. I started to pray. Please God, let me be brave!

I knew that all I had to do was follow orders and carry out my duties as I had done hundreds of times during training and practice, but it's a different situation when the enemy are firing live shells at you. I thought of Arthur, who would be going through this hour after hour, day after day, in France. Every day, shells falling on their positions and machine-gun bullets flying at him. Now it was my turn.

All the ships had now turned south-east and we were racing onward, the sea rising, the *Chester* catching the wash from the other ships ahead of us.

I could feel a knot in my stomach as I heard the sounds of battle, of big guns firing, and wondered if the rest of the men felt the same. I knew that, whatever happened, I mustn't let them down. I mustn't let Arthur and Dad down.

I tried to imagine the scene on the rest of the ship. We had trained and practised so many times for action stations and combat, I knew that below deck all of the steel doors were being shut. The medical parties would be getting ready in the sick bays, setting out surgical instruments, medicines and dressings for wounds. The men that would be carrying out emergency fire repairs would be preparing their equipment –

mallets, wedges and boxes of sand.

In the turret and the foretop the range-finders would be hard at work, getting ready to pin down the position of the enemy ships and calculate how fast they were travelling and in which direction, then pass that information on to the gunnery officer, who would then pass it on to the gun crews.

Below deck the steel doors would be locked tight with all eight catches instead of the usual two. This would make sure they didn't blow open if there was an explosion.

That was another thing they'd be worrying about below decks – a German shell hitting the store of explosives and fuses. If that happened, it would blow the ship sky-high. That's why the hull of each ship was so heavily armoured.

All this time the thud-thud-thud of the heavy guns in the distance was getting louder, now accompanied by crashes and explosions, the sound of metal being torn apart, and black smoke billowing up in a thick cloud. The battle was raging and the haze of smoke on the water was getting thicker, turning into a fog. We could hardly see those of our ships that were nearest to us, at least not with the naked eye. We all knew we were far enough away from them for a German ship to slip past.

Now, as we got nearer and nearer to the German ships, I had to fight to keep calm. I glanced at the rest of the men in the gun crew. All of them seemed concentrated on manning the gun, getting ready for battle. I wondered if they'd felt the same nervousness as I did when they went into battle for the first time. They'd been joking before, but now all jokiness had gone. I gritted my teeth. I had a job to do. This was no time to start thinking about being afraid.

I continued looking out to sea. My eyes were almost burning now from the strain of peering into the distance, at the ship-filled sea, at the smoke, watching for a ship to appear with a German flag fluttering aloft.

With ships criss-crossing and turning back on their own course, the sea was now getting higher, waves lifting and crashing against the side of the *Chester*. I didn't know what the time was, or how long we had been sailing since the bugles had first blown with the order for "action stations". All I knew was that the enemy was out there, that we were closing in on them, and they were closing in on us, and already the ships at the head of our fleet were engaged in a full-scale battle.

Suddenly I heard the voice of the gunnery officer through my headphones, giving me the elevation for the gun, and I pushed the brass disc to the right marker. Immediately Patch started winding his wheel, bringing the gun down, which meant the Germans were right near us! As Patch stopped winding, Fred pulled the lead connecting to the firing pin. There was an almighty *BOOM!!* from the gun and it recoiled as the shell hurtled out from the end of the barrel. At the same time the shell casing ejected backwards, where Batty dealt with it, hurling it safely to one side.

Fred opened the breech and the next shell slid into place, and Mick pushed it in with his ramrodder. The gunnery officer's voice through my headphones ordered me to lower the elevation just twenty points, so I changed the setting on the brass disc, and just then I saw the German ships appear from out of the black smoke. There were four of them, light cruisers, the same as us. I heard a thud from one of them – and saw smoke coming from it, then realized they had fired a shell at us. I heard a whining sound and saw the shell getting larger and larger, then instantly the deck near me blew up.

There was a flash of white that almost blinded me, then intense heat as flames leaped up, followed by thick, black smoke, so thick that I couldn't see. I put my hand over my nose and mouth to stop myself from choking on the smoke.

I looked round and saw Ned lying on the deck. He had a massive hole in his chest where a piece of shrapnel had torn into him, almost cutting him in half.

All at once there was another explosion, even louder than the first, right by me, and I heard screaming. The smoke shifted and I could see two men rolling in agony on the deck, and I saw that their legs had been cut off just below the knees.

I stayed standing at my post, waiting for instructions over my headphones to set the gun, and I heard a voice say "six…", then the rest of his words were lost as another explosion hit us. The whole gun seemed to lift up off the deck with the force of the explosion, as if it was being torn off, and I immediately knew I'd been hit. I looked down at my front and saw that parts of my uniform had been torn open, shredded across the chest, and I saw the glint of metal among the tattered blue cloth.

At first my body went numb, but then the pain hit me. I'd never felt pain like it. It felt as if my whole body was on fire, as if my skin had been torn off and I was being burned.

I gritted my teeth against the pain. I wouldn't cry out! The Germans wouldn't beat me! Arthur and his mates were suffering this kind of thing every day, and for months and months. If they could take it, so could I.

I was just turning to look at the rest of my gun crew when there was a *BOOOOM!!* from an explosion, the force of the blast throwing me back against the metal of the gun. I nearly slipped down, but I managed to grab hold of one of the handles and held on, determined to stay on my feet. I was afraid that if I went down, I'd never get up again, and I had to stay standing. I had to stay by my gun. I was the sight setter. Without me the gun couldn't fire at the enemy.

Even though I couldn't see because of the smoke, I knew that the rest of my crew were either dead, or badly injured like me. But I was certain they'd be sending other men to replace them. And when they did, they'd need me as their sight setter. I would not desert my post.

The pain was really bad now, like red-hot blades cutting into my chest and my shoulders, but it was in my chest where the pain was worse. I looked down at my wounds. The front of my uniform was now soaked in blood and it was sticking to my skin. It sounds stupid but my first thought was: "I'm going to have a devil of a job trying to get this uniform clean!"

I can't die, I told myself. *I have to stay alive and stay here for when the others come to take over the gun. I have to stay at my post. I'm the sight setter. I'm needed here.*

I started to feel sick, and I felt dizzy, though whether that was from the smoke or the bits of metal that had pierced into my chest, I didn't know. Possibly a bit of both. I could feel myself sagging back against the metal of the gun and starting to slide down, but I clenched my teeth and forced myself to stand up. I mustn't sit down. I must keep my eyes open.

All the time I listened, waiting for instructions through my headphones, but I knew the instructions wouldn't come until another gun crew arrived. I waited, but no one appeared.

I could hear other explosions on-board, but further away from my position. The Germans were targeting the rest of our ship.

The pain in my chest was getting more severe now. It was a dull ache, but if I tried to move, or even coughed, a sharp pain shot through me like a burning knife, so I did my best to stay still.

Suddenly I heard footsteps on the deck rushing towards my position. Another gun crew, I thought! We're going after the Germans! I gritted my teeth against the pain in my chest. I hard to hold firm and set the gun sights! But it wasn't a replacement gun crew. It was the ship's medical orderlies, four of them. Three of them began checking on the bodies of the men lying by the gun on the deck, and one of them came over to me.

"Where you hit, son?" he asked.

"Chest," I managed to say.

He knelt down and quickly examined my chest, and reached out a hand to touch it, but I stopped him with my own hand.

"Hurts," I said, my voice shaking.

He nodded. "I bet it does," he said.

He stood up and called to the others. "Boy here badly hurt! Looks like shrapnel in his chest!"

One of the other orderlies came over and joined him, shaking his head. "The others are dead," he announced. "We're heading back to port," he said to me. "We'll get you properly looked at there."

"We can't go back to port!" I protested. "The Germans are here! We have to attack them!"

"We could if we had any guns and gunners to fire them," said the man, "but our guns have been shot to bits. The battle's over for us. We're heading to Immingham."

They gave me an injection of something that knocked me out.

When I came to I was lying on the floor of a cabin inside the ship. I still felt pain in my chest, but not as much as I had before. I suppose the injection they gave me had dulled the pain.

I looked down at my body. My uniform had been torn open at the front and a bandage had been wrapped around my chest and back. It was heavily bloodstained, I saw the bandage was almost flat, so I knew they must have taken some of the pieces of metal out of me. But it felt as if some of them were still there, stuck in my chest. I coughed, and the pain that went through me was awful, like someone had taken a saw to my lungs.

One of the medical orderlies was attending to another man, but when he heard me cough he got up and came over.

"How are you doing?" he asked.

I opened my mouth to speak, but my mouth was very dry and my throat seemed to have swollen up, and I found I couldn't talk. Instead I gave a slight nod and tried to smile to show him I was all right, even though I knew I wasn't.

"Not long before we get to Immingham," he said. "Then we'll have you sorted out."

"Did…?" I stammered, battling to force the words out, "did … we … win?"

The medic's expression clouded.

"The battle's still going on," he said. He must have seen the bitter disappointment on my face, because he forced a smile and said, "Don't worry, I'm sure it's going to be fine. Our fleet's bigger than theirs. I've no doubt we've got the Germans on the run. Old Admiral Jellicoe knows what he's doing!"

I tried to smile with him, but a sudden spasm of pain tore through my chest and I coughed, and I saw blood spurt out of my mouth in a spray. The orderly suddenly looked worried. "Just hold on there, son," he urged. "They'll be able to sort you out at the hospital."

When we arrived at the docks there were ambulances waiting to collect the wounded. I was put on a stretcher and carried to one of the ambulances, and loaded in.

"Won't be long now before we get you to hospital," said a medical orderly cheerfully. "You'll see, once we get you there you'll be as right as rain. We'll soon have you fixed up and back fighting the Hun!"

My head felt like it was swimming and all I could feel was pain. Not just in my chest, but all over my legs, my arms, my head, every part of me felt like it was broken and burning with pain.

I was aware of a face appearing at the door of the ambulance, and I recognized it as being one of the officers, Lieutenant Macfarlane. "See you keep this boy alive!" he told the MO firmly. "He's a hero! Stayed at his post when the rest of his gun crew were killed. If we had an army and a navy of men with the same sort of guts as him, we'd have won this war before now!"

"I was just doing my duty, sir," I said. At least, I hope I said it. My voice had gone all sort of croaky and I wasn't sure if all my words came out properly.

Then the door of the ambulance slammed shut and I could feel the vehicle shudder, then start to move. And, then I passed out.

PART 5

MA

1ST JUNE 1916

I'm in hospital. The nurses tell me this is Grimsby General Hospital. One also told me that we won the battle! The matron and the officers have told the hospital staff that they're not supposed to talk about the battle, or mention anything about the war, but this one nurse, Nurse Edwards, who's Welsh, says that I deserve to know.

She says she doesn't know the whole story, but from what she's heard from doctors and men who've come in, and from some of the telephone calls and other things, she says the Germans retreated to their own ports. She doesn't know how many ships the Germans lost, but she says it looks like the German navy has been defeated. Britannia rules the waves! I smiled when she told me this, then the pain in my chest came back again and I started coughing, and there was a lot of blood. Nurse Edwards ran off to get someone, but I passed out before she got back.

Later

I've been given more medicine, which made my head swim. Nurse Edwards was tidying up my bed and she told me the doctors were going to try and operate on me to get the other bits of metal out of my chest.

But just as she said this, another nurse, Nurse Mariner, who was passing, told her to shush. Nurse Edwards looked surprised at this, and Nurse Mariner jerked her head and took Nurse Edwards away so I couldn't hear what they were saying. But I could guess it wasn't good news from the way that Nurse Edwards put her hand to her mouth sharply, and then to her eyes, like she was wiping away tears. Then she hurried out of the ward, and Nurse Mariner came over to me and carried on tidying my bed in place of Nurse Edwards.

"What was all that about?" I asked.

Nurse Mariner gave me a smile. "Nothing."

"Whatever it was upset Nurse Edwards," I pointed out.

Nurse Mariner smiled again. "Nurse Edwards gets upset at the slightest thing," she said. "Don't let it worry you."

Then she went on to tidy the next patient's bed.

I lay there for a while, thinking about what had happened. It was true Nurse Edwards did get emotional. I'd only been in the hospital for a short while, and I'd already seen her cry quite a few times. I don't think she was cut out for dealing with men with the sort of injuries suffered in times of war – legs and arms missing, blinded, and lots of them dying right there in the ward.

I was lying there when the matron appeared by my bed. She had a different uniform from the other nurses. They wore white and she wore dark blue. I had heard the nurses talk and they all seemed to be scared of matron. It was like she was their senior officer and they were terrified of doing something wrong and upsetting her. But she didn't look terrifying when she came and stood by my bed. In fact she smiled, and it was a real genuine smile.

"Hello, John," she said.

"Jack," I replied, correcting her. Then I thought how rude that sounded, correcting her like that. And what was worse, correcting someone who was a senior officer, even if it was in a hospital! I forced a smile, and hoped she'd let me off. "John's my given name but everyone calls me Jack," I explained.

Matron smiled again, which surprised me. From the way the nurses talked about her I'd expected her to tell me off for answering her back.

"Jack," she nodded. "That's a good name. Do you have brothers and sisters?"

I said I did, and told her about my brothers Ernest, George and Fred, and my sister, Lily, and also Arthur and Alice. "Arthur's fighting with the infantry in France," I added.

"I'm sure they will be very proud of you," said matron. "I understand you fought bravely in the battle."

"Oh, we carried on all right," I said, remembering what Dad had always told me about not boasting, because no one likes a braggart.

Matron smiled again. "I'm sure you did."

The way she went off, and I thought, she's not as scary as the nurses say at all.

Later the doctor, Dr Stephenson, came to see me. "I know you are a brave boy, Jack," he said. "No one could have stayed at his post as you did, as badly wounded as you were, unless they are brave. And, because you are brave and have courage, I know that you will be able to cope with the truth. The fact is, Jack, we can do nothing for you except make you as comfortable as we can. Your injuries are too bad for repair."

I looked at him. He looked so unhappy at having to tell me this.

"So I am going to die?" I asked.

Dr Stephenson nodded. "I'm afraid you are, Jack."

"How long do I have?" I asked.

"I'm guessing you have just a day. Maybe two," he replied. "You are very badly wounded."

I let this sink in. I suppose I had been lucky. I could have been killed along with the rest of the gun crew on the *Chester*. At least I hoped I would have time to say goodbye.

"My Ma—" I began.

"A telegram has been sent to her," said Dr Stephenson. "She's on her way to see you."

"Then I shall stay alive until she gets here," I told him.

Dr Stephenson nodded and patted my hand, and then withdrew to go and attend to other patients.

Later

I don't know how long I have been here in the hospital. The nurses give me medicine to ease the pain of my wounds, and it makes me sleep. There is no clock in the ward so I don't know what the time is when I wake up.

The nurses are very caring towards me. They come to me when I'm awake and ask me how I feel, and do their best to make me comfortable. I think it's still the same day because every time I wake up I can still see daylight coming in through the windows. Unless I've the whole night without waking and it is now the next day.

I asked if Ma has arrived yet, but she hasn't. It's a long journey from East Ham to here.

Later

When I woke again it was night. The ward was dark except for low lights. I have survived the whole day. The nurses say Ma hasn't arrived yet. I am sure she will come tomorrow. All I have to do is stay alive for the night and get through to the morning. I want to say goodbye to her before I go, and let her know how much I love her and Dad. I want her to tell Dad that I was thinking of both of them as I lay here, that my last thoughts were of them.

Later

Daylight. I have made it through to the new day. Unfortunately, there's a kind of dullness to my eyes and I can't see as clearly as I should. I can see things and people when they're up close, but it's all a bit dim when they are away from me. It feels like there's a weight on my chest the whole time now, and I'm having difficulty breathing. The nurses have given me more medicine for the pain in my legs and chest, but they say they can't do much to help my breathing.

It also seems that everything is muffled, as if my ears are blocked. When I was young I once had wax build up in my ears. Ma cleared it out with warm water. It came out in a lump and then I could hear properly again. I wonder if I've got wax in my ears again? I can't think why I would get wax all of a sudden like this, so maybe it's something else. I wonder if this is dying? I keep hoping to see my ma, but so far she hasn't come.

Still daylight coming in through the windows. Lots of action in the hospital. Nurses hurrying around, patients coughing and choking, and metal basins being put down and picked up, and trolleys being wheeled. At least, I think that's what it is. It's all a bit of a muddle of noise. I try to pick out particular sounds, but they all seem to blur into one whooshing sound that keeps coming and going. I can hear voices and I can sort out men's and women's, but I can't recognize who is talking. I keep thinking I hear my Ma's voice, but the nurses say she hasn't come yet. It's hard to tell who is who around me. My eyes are dimmer now. I can see it's daylight, but I can't see people's faces clearly. I hope my ma comes while I can still see. I would dearly like to see her face before I die.

Later

Sleep again. Wake again. Sleep again. All the noise seems further away now. A nurse came to me and bent over me. I knew it was a nurse because I could smell the starch of her uniform. I hope the same will happen when my ma arrives. I will know her by her smell, and I'll be able to see the outline of her face.

The weight on my chest is really heavy now. It's like it's pushing me down on to the bed. I know I can never sit up. My ma will have to lean right over me for me to see her, but I will know she is here. All I have to do is hang on. She will be here soon, I know.

Later

Someone touched me and I woke up. "Ma?" I said. "Is that you?"

"Not yet," said a woman's voice, and I realized it was a nurse.

I tried to sit up, but the weight on me was too heavy.

"Give Ma my love," I said. "I know she's coming."

Those were Jack Cornwell's last words. He died on June 2 1916. Unfortunately, the telegram informing his mother, Lily Cornwell, of Jack's injuries didn't arrive until too late. By the time she reached Grimsby, Jack was dead.

EPILOGUE

BY GEORGE CORNWELL

CANADA, 8TH JANUARY 1921

Today would have been Jack's 21st birthday, if he'd lived. But he didn't. He died, killed in the Battle of Jutland. Dad also died. Ma died. Arthur died. Me, I'm now living in Canada, and glad to be here.

The war ended just over two years ago in November 1918, when Germany surrendered. The armistice was signed on 11 November. The eleventh hour of the eleventh day of the eleventh month, so that everyone would always remember it as the day the worst war the world had ever known ended.

How do I feel? Relieved that the war ended, and also angry. Not as angry as I was at first, after Jack died. They say time makes things feel better, but it doesn't. All it does is soften things a bit.

Jack died – aged sixteen – on the 2 June 1916. He was part of a gun crew on HMS *Chester*. His ship was hit by four German battlecruisers just minutes after they'd gone into battle. They'd only managed to fire off one salvo when the Germans hit the place where Jack's gun was. All the rest of that gun crew were killed, Jack was the only one who survived. Not that he survived long. He had pieces of metal deep inside his chest and the rest of his body was torn up with shrapnel. But he stayed at his post, by the gun, with the rest of his crew dead all around him. And he didn't just stay at his post, he *stood* at his post. That's what we heard later from the medical orderlies on board who found him. When they reached him, Jack was standing there, with his headphones on, bleeding, but still waiting for orders. That's the sort of person Jack was. Brave. Someone who always did his duty. I wish the people in charge had done their duty by Jack, and the rest of us.

We were told later by the nurses at Grimsby General that Jack kept asking for his ma. He'd been told she was on her way. The truth is that the telegram that was sent to Ma telling her Jack was dying didn't arrive until after he was dead. Whether someone made a mistake, or was lazy and didn't send the telegram as soon as they should have, or just got things wrong, we never found out. As soon as Ma got the telegram telling her Jack was in hospital and not expected to live, she hurried off and caught the train north to Grimsby, determined to see Jack before he died. But when she got there he was already dead.

The navy sent Jack's body home to us for burial. We'd have loved to have given him a proper burial in a churchyard with a headstone and everything. But we were just a poor family from the East End of London. We didn't have any money to bury Jack properly, so he was laid to rest in a communal grave in Manor Park Cemetery, East Ham. A communal grave means that lots of coffins are buried in the same grave. They dig a pit 25 feet [about eight metres] deep and the coffins are placed in one on top of the other. Then the grave's marked with a wooden numbered post rather than any headstone or ceremonial marking. Jack was buried in Communal Grave Number 323.

It was only after Jack had been buried that word began to come out about what had really happened during the Battle of Jutland. I think the government wanted to keep quiet the fact that large numbers of British sailors had died, about 6,000 – and a big number of British ships that had been sunk. But Jutland had been a British victory. The German fleet had been forced back into their own rivers in Germany, and they never came out again. Well, not in the same great numbers.

And word spread about the bravery of the men who'd been involved in the battle. Not just the admirals and the captains, but about the ordinary sailors. And word began to be heard about Jack.

One of the big papers, *The Daily Sketch*, sent a reporter to our house to ask about Jack, and asked where he was buried because they wanted a photograph of his grave for their paper. We showed them the wooden marker post on the communal grave.

Next thing we know, there's a whole article about Jack in the paper, calling him a hero, and saying what a disgrace that he was buried in a "pauper's grave" without even a headstone with his name on it.

Ma was upset about this. She preferred things to be private and didn't like all the world knowing our business, especially the bit about the "pauper's grave". I knew she was worried what Dad would say when he read about that because he didn't like other people knowing our business either.

Me, I told her I was glad the paper was saying it, because I felt it was wrong that Jack hadn't had a decent burial. It wasn't our fault we couldn't afford to bury him in the way he should have been buried. Jack deserved a grave and a headstone fit for a hero.

The paper began its campaign, demanding that the authorities do the decent thing by Jack. Letters from ordinary people came in to the paper, and to the government and the navy, protesting about the fact that Jack was in an unmarked grave. Finally the authorities announced that Jack's coffin was to be exhumed, which meant it was going to be taken out of the communal grave, and reburied in a proper grave with full military honours.

Luckily, Jack's coffin was at the top of the pile of coffins. If his coffin had been at the bottom, it would have been a terrible mess, lifting out all the other coffins on top of him. Bearing in mind what happened much later, my guess is that they wouldn't have bothered. They would have just taken out the top coffin and said that was Jack's anyway. But we'll come to that later.

They opened the grave and took out Jack's coffin, and made a new and better looking coffin around it. Then, on 29 July 1916, Jack was reburied, again in Manor Park Cemetery, but this time with full military honours.

In all my life I have never seen anything like it. It seemed to me like the whole world was there. For a start, the entire route of the funeral procession, from East Ham Town Hall to Manor Park Cemetery, was lined by members of the armed forces, especially sailors, all standing to attention and saluting as Jack's coffin came past them.

The funeral procession left East Ham Town Hall at 3 o'clock in the afternoon. Mounted police officers were right at the front. Behind them came a band from the Royal Navy playing stirring marches, followed by a firing party with their rifles at "slope arms" on their shoulders. Behind the firing party came Jack's new coffin, mounted on a gun carriage and draped over with a Union Jack. Sitting on top of the coffin was Jack's naval cap.

Immediately behind the coffin walked a massive procession of dignitaries, all moving in a slow and sombre way, including the Mayor of East Ham, the Member of Parliament for the local area, the Bishop of Barking and a lot of other churchmen. Behind them came the St Nicholas Boys' School Band, also playing. Behind them was a procession of boys from our old school, Walton Road. Behind all that lot were a load of boy sailors from HMS *Chester*, plus the 2nd Battalion of the Essex Regiment, and also Boy Scout troops, as a mark of Jack's time as a Boy Scout.

I was at the back of all these people, and as the funeral march came past the Alverstone Road area of Manor Park, the rest of our family joined me. Dad had been given compassionate leave to come home for the funeral, and he joined the procession along with Ma, Fred, Lily, Alice, and Ernest. I was glad to see Ernest was there

We all walked along behind this procession to Manor Park Cemetery. There may have been bigger funerals for kings and queens and prime ministers and such, but I never was part of anything so big in my whole life.

When we got to Manor Park the bishop made a speech about sacrifice and Jack being a hero, then they reburied Jack in a newly dug grave, and as his coffin was lowered the firing party let out a volley of shots and the last post was sounded. Then the men who'd been on HMS *Chester*, placed a big floral tribute in the shape of an anchor by Jack's grave.

After that, there were more speeches, most of them on the same theme – sacrifice, doing your duty as Jack had done, all words and sentiments that would have made Jack proud to hear. Then the funeral was over, and we went home, back to our little house in Alverstone Road. And the next day Dad went back to the barracks at Colchester.

That wasn't the end of it, though. The outpouring of grief and pride in Jack from the general public, and not just in London but right across the country – indeed right across the whole British Empire – made the government decide to use Jack to raise morale for the war effort. Jack was going to be an example to all other young men to do their duty and fight for their country. There were demands made in the press and in Parliament for there to be a proper award to honour his bravery, not just the big funeral that had been held in July. So, in the middle of September, Ma got a letter from the government that said:

"The King has been graciously pleased to approve the grant of the Victoria Cross to Boy, First Class, John Travers Cornwell O.N. J. 42563 (died 2 June 1916), for the conspicuous act of bravery specified below:

"Mortally wounded early in the action, Boy, First Class, John Travers Cornwell remained standing alone at a most exposed post, quietly awaiting orders, until the end of the action, with the gun's crew dead and wounded all around him. His age was under sixteen-and-a-half years."

The Victoria Cross! The highest award for bravery! It was the biggest honour the country could have given Jack. Ma was told she would have to go to Buckingham Palace to receive the medal on Jack's behalf from King George V himself. I must admit, I felt a great deal of pride as I helped Ma write the letter to Dad in which she told him about Jack being awarded the VC. I knew it would buck him up. And we both felt Dad would need bucking up, because his last letter to us had been written from a hospital. He'd been taken ill, he said. Nothing serious, just a bit of a cough, and he was being well looked after. He hoped to get back to see us soon, because he was overdue for some leave, and he wanted to visit Jack's grave.

I wrote to Dad, sending him a copy of the letter from the government telling us about Jack being awarded the VC. I got Alice to copy it out because her writing is much neater than mine, and a letter as important as that needed to look proper when Dad read it.

After the story of Jack being awarded the Victoria Cross appeared in the newspapers, the government decided to use this latest news, and Jack's bravery, to raise money from the public. In the same month that Jack's VC was announced, September 1916, the Boy Cornwell Memorial Fund was set up. The aim of this fund was to provide a ward for disabled servicemen at the Star and Garter Home in Richmond. Every schoolchild in the British Empire was encouraged to give a penny towards the fund.

In addition, a local memorial fund in East Ham was set up for Jack's grave. Money was raised from all the schools in the area, and all the local schoolchildren were urged to make donations to the cost of a memorial, as well as other charitable causes.

To help raise money, the government decided to use a photo of Jack. Their plan was to print this photo of Jack on things like postcards, cigarette cards, beer mats, badges, and all sorts of items, and then sell them. The only problem was, there weren't any photos of Jack. Growing up, there was hardly enough money for important things like paying the rent and buying food and coal, let alone luxuries like paying to have photos of us taken. So they decided to cheat.

A man from one of the government departments – I don't know which one – turned up at our house and asked if I'd like to help our country. I was fifteen at the time, so I wasn't sure how I could help. I was too young to join the army or the navy and – with Jack dead and Dad and Arthur away – it was only my wages that were keeping us.

"They say you look a lot like your brother, Jack," the man said.

"So they say," I replied.

Personally, I didn't think I did look very much like Jack. He was a bit podgier than me about the face, but we were certainly similar.

"Would you let us photograph you?" he asked.

"Why?" I replied, puzzled.

"Because we need a photo of your brother, Jack, but we haven't got one. So what we'd like to do is photograph you, dressed up in a sailor's uniform, and put it out as being Jack."

I stared at him. "But that's a cheat and a lie!" I said.

"No it isn't," he replied. "There aren't any photos of Jack so no-one knows what he looks like, and people want to know. We need a photo to honour him. We need it to make people remember him, and help this country win this war."

Well, when he put it like that, I couldn't really refuse. I knew it was what Jack would have wanted. And, like he said, outside the family, no one would know the photo wasn't really of Jack. So I went along to this photographer's studio, and they gave me a sailor's outfit to put on, complete with a navy hat. I was a bit annoyed that they didn't have a cap with the name of Jack's ship HMS *Chester* on it. Instead, it had HMS *Lancaster* on the tallyband. I pointed this out to the photographer, but he just said "No one will notice". Then I stood with my arms folded and a serious look on my face while he took my photo. Afterwards I changed into my everyday clothes and went home.

Pretty soon that photograph of me was everywhere – in the papers, in magazines, on badges and postcards – with the caption "The hero Jack Cornwell" under it. Everyone in our family and our area knew the truth, but, like the man said, no one else did. So that's the true story of the famous photo of my brother Jack that went all round the world – it isn't Jack, it's me.

After the photo was printed, other people wanted pictures of Jack. Some artist got in touch because the government were paying him to paint Jack standing alone by the gun of the *Chester*, and the government had told him it was actually me in that photo, so he asked if I would pose for him at his studio, wearing the sailor uniform again. I told him I couldn't because I was working and we needed the money. He offered to pay me, but I said that if I took time off, I could get the sack, and I couldn't afford for that to happen. So instead he asked my younger brother, Fred, if he'd pose for him instead.

Fred was as pleased as punch to think that someone wanted to paint a picture of him, even though it was supposed to be of Jack. So Fred posed for the picture and it became famous and was hung in some important gallery, and copies of it were made and sold all over the world.

It was while all this was going on that we got the bad news. Dad died on 25 October 1916. The "cough that's nothing to worry about," as he'd written in his letter, had turned into pneumonia. He died just four months after Jack. In my opinion, Jack being killed took the life out of him.

When his body was returned home, he was buried in the same grave as Jack, and his name added to the headstone.

Ma was shattered when she got the news about Dad dying. What was worse, with Dad gone, the government stopped his pay, so she had even less money to live on. Me and Alice did our best, but we were struggling to look after ourselves, let alone look after Fred and young Lily. Despite that, on 16 November 1916, Ma went to Buckingham Palace and received the Victoria Cross from King George V on Jack's behalf. She wore her best dress and her best coat for the occasion.

After that, it was back to life as normal in Alverstone Road. Well, not really life as normal. Dad was gone, Jack was gone. Then, in 1918, Arthur was killed in action.

During all this time I supposed that money had been rolling in to the different funds set up in Jack's name. One thing was for sure, we never saw any of it. Ma was the one who suffered most. She got a small pension because of Dad dying, but it wasn't enough to live on. Me and Alice helped her when we could, but it was a struggle for us. By the time the war was over, young Fred was working as well, and he moved away with his work.

Ma took a job at a hostel for sailors to try and make ends meet, but she only got a very small wage, so it wasn't a great deal of help. Finally, desperate, she went to the memorial fund set up in Jack's name and asked for some money. After all, the fund had been set up to help charitable causes, and what was more charitable than to help a woman whose son the fund had been named after and who had lost her husband and another son to the war?

The people who ran the fund said no. They told her she wasn't a worthy cause.

I felt so angry when they said that. These people, none of whom fought in the war, or did anything to help the country except sit behind desks and push pieces of paper around, had the nerve to say no. All the money they had hold of had been raised in the name of Ma's dead son, Jack. He had been her sacrifice. And yet they gave her nothing. They said that the money was to be used to erect a memorial at Jack's grave. Surely, our Ma was Jack's greatest memorial. She'd brought him into this world, she'd hurried to his bedside as soon as she'd been told he was dying.

Finally, Ma couldn't afford to pay the rent on the house at Alverstone Road. Me and Alice had already told her she ought to give it up and move somewhere smaller, because with me also leaving home, the house would be too big for her to manage on her own. In the end she moved into a couple of tiny rooms in Commercial Road in Stepney. There, things went from bad to worse. She cut down on eating to try and save money, and starved. Because I wasn't living at home, I didn't see it happening. Poor Ma was found dead in her rooms on 31 October 1919. She was just 48 years old.

She was buried in the same grave as Jack and Dad at Manor Park Cemetery, but even in death they did her a further injustice. Someone put the wrong name on the headstone. Instead of "Lily, wife of Eli Cornwell and mother of Jack Cornwell, VC" they put "Alice...".

Alice was the name of Dad's first wife. Someone in some office somewhere must have just looked up the records of marriage for Eli Cornwell, seen the name "Alice" and given that name to the stonemason. I went to see the stonemason and told him to remove "Alice" and carve "Lily" instead, but he said he couldn't. He'd been paid to carve that name, and that's what he'd done. He demanded to know who'd pay him to take it off and carve another name on there instead.

That was it for me. I decided that there was nothing left for me in England, and I made up my mind to start a new life in Canada. I've been in Canada for nearly two years now, and I'm glad I made the move. I've been in touch with the others to tell them how I'm doing, and what a great country this is, and Lily says she's planning to come out here too, as soon as she's 18 and can legally move.

I still see that famous photo of me dressed up as Jack, in shops and different places, and every now and then someone comes up and tells me how much I look like Jack Cornwell, the famous boy VC, and I have to smile. I'm tempted to tell them the truth, and a few of my friends know the real story, but mostly I just smile and say, "Yes, I do. But then, I'm his brother." Then I tell them about Jack and what he was like as a boy, and what a hero he was. Because he was. He was brave and he died doing his duty. My brother was a true hero.

One final thing: I read in the papers that last month they finally erected the marble memorial to Jack in East Ham. The story says:

"On 31 December 1920, at a ceremony presided over by Dr Macnamara, MP, representing the Admiralty, the Mayor of East Ham, along with members of the Cornwell family, local Boy Scouts and Sea Scouts as a guard of honour, the memorial to Jack Cornwell was unveiled in his home borough of East Ham, London…

The inscription on the memorial reads: 'In memoriam. First Class Boy JOHN TRAVERS CORNWELL, VC. Born 8 January 1900. Died of wounds received at the Battle of Jutland 2 June 1916. This stone was erected by scholars and ex-scholars of schools in East Ham. 'It is not wealth or ancestry but honourable conduct and a noble disposition that makes man great.' DM"

HISTORICAL NOTE

The Battle of Jutland – which took place in the North Sea off the coast of Denmark, between the British Grand Fleet and the German High Seas Fleet – is considered by many naval historians to be the biggest sea battle since Henry VIII's time. Bigger even than Trafalgar, or the defeat of the Spanish Armada, it was the last great naval battle. All subsequent sea battles were dominated by the addition of aircraft.

Up until 1916 the German fleet, wary of the supposed superiority of the British fleet at the start of the First World War, kept mainly to German waters. The German naval war was mainly conducted by U-boats (German submarines), determined to stop supplies to and from Britain. During the U-boat offensive many civilian liners were attacked and sunk, including the *Lusitania*.

In January 1915 the German fleet launched an attack on the British fleet, but were repulsed at the Battle of Dogger Bank in the North Sea. After this, the German fleet returned to German waters until 24 April 1916, when they launched a surprise attack on the east coast of England, bombarding the towns of Lowestoft and Yarmouth.

The German fleet then withdrew, but were planning a major naval offensive against Britain in late May 1916.

However, a German code book had been captured by British Intelligence, and experts used this code book to decipher messages intercepted over German wireless, and it was realized that Germany was planning a major naval assault on the North Sea coast at the end of May. The British Grand Fleet was ordered into the North Sea to confront the German fleet.

The two opposing fleets were huge. The British Grand Fleet (commanded by Admiral Sir John Jellicoe, with Admiral Sir David Beatty as his second in command) consisted of 28 battleships, 9 battlecruisers, 8 armoured cruisers, 26 light cruisers, 78 destroyers, 1 minelayer and 1 seaplane carrier. The German High Seas Fleet (commanded by Admiral Reinhard Scheer, with Admiral Franz Hipper as his second-in-command) consisted of 16 battleships, 5 battlecruisers, 6 pre-dreadnoughts, 11 light cruisers and 61 torpedo boats.

But the scale of the fleets wasn't just about the number of ships; it was their size and construction. The battleships, especially the dreadnoughts, were unlike anything ever seen before. Huge iron ships, replacing the wooden ships that had sailed the seas for centuries.

On 31 May 1916 Admiral Scheer sent a fleet of battleships along the Danish coast, hoping to tempt the British fleet out from its harbours. He planned to use U-boats to attack the British ships.

The British commander-in-chief, Admiral Jellicoe, had received information about Scheer's plans from the code-breaking unit of British naval intelligence the day before, 30 May, and decided to engage the German fleet head-on.

Both fleets set sail in the early hours of the morning of 31 May, but they didn't meet up until mid-afternoon, when cruisers from both sides, scouting for sightings of the enemy, spotted the other. After a brief exchange of gunfire, the cruisers alerted their commanders.

At this stage, the Battle of Jutland was noticeable for another "first" – the use of a ship as an aircraft carrier in action. HMS *Engadine* launched a Short 184 seaplane, piloted by Flight Lieutenant Rutland, Assistant Paymaster Trewin as observer. The seaplane flew over the German fleet to assess the size of the enemy and their positions. Because of heavy cloud, the seaplane was forced to fly low at a height of 900 metres, and the German light cruisers fired on the plane with (in the words of Admiral Beatty) "every gun they could bear". The seaplane survived this barrage and was able to return. It reported that the German fleet was indeed a massive force.

On both sides, the giant battlecruisers and the rest of the fleet were signalled to be brought up into their respective formations, ready for battle.

At 15.48 hours, with both sides about 18,500 metres apart, both fleets opened fire. Firing continued, with the ships doing their best to steer a zig-zag course at the same time to avoid being hit by enemy ordinance. The result of all this gunfire was a haze, which prevented any clear sightings of the enemy, or indeed of the ships in their own fleet.

The British fleet suffered the first major blows: at 16.03 the *Indefatigable* suffered five hits in rapid succession and blew up. At 16.25 the *Queen Mary* received a broadside from the German battlecruiser

Derfflinger, and the *Queen Mary* blew up and sank within 90 seconds.

At 17.27 the ship on which Jack Cornwell served, HMS *Chester*, was attacked by four German Kaiserliche marine cruisers, each the same size as the *Chester* at close range of 6,000 yards, and it was hit seventeen times by 150mm shells. The *Chester's* armour meant that the interior of the ship suffered little serious damage. On deck, however, the situation was appalling: the casualties amounted to 29 men killed and 49 wounded. The *Chester's* gun mounting were open-backed shields and did not reach the deck. Because of this, splinters passed beneath the shields or hit the open back when shells exploded nearby, or behind, and many of the wounded lost their legs. The gun mounting where Jack Cornwell was serving as a sight-setter took at least four hits. It is believed this gun only just managed to get off one salvo before it was hit.

After the action, Jack was found to be the only survivor at his gun. Shards of steel had penetrated his chest; but he had stayed standing at his gun sight and told the sailors who found him he was still awaiting orders.

Before the German cruisers could finish the *Chester* off, the 3rd Battlecruiser Squadron (HMS *Invincible*, HMS Inflexible, and HMS *Indomitable*) came to the aid of the *Chester* and the other British light cruisers that were engaged in the action.

The *Chester* was now effectively out of action, and was forced to return to the port of Immingham.

As the *Chester* journeyed south, the crew members who had died, including those from the crew of Jack's gun, were buried at sea. Usually the ship's chaplain carried out the service, but in this case the *Chester's* chaplain was among the dead, so the funeral oration was read by Captain Lawson. Lawson had himself been wounded in the attack and those who were there said he made an impressive sight, standing at the head of a ladder that led up from the starboard wait of the ship, his head bandaged and his grey beard stained with blood. (As a footnote, Lawson's pet sheepdog, which was on board with him, was also wounded in the attack, but the wound wasn't serious.)

When the *Chester* reached the port of Immingham, Jack Cornwell was transferred to Grimsby General Hospital. He was clearly dying. He died on 2 June 1916.

Off the Danish coast, the battle at sea raged for some hours more, with both sides hampered by the thick haze from gunsmoke, combined with the blinding light from the setting sun. The British fleet were also troubled with problems caused by poor signalling.

At 18.30 hours the German fleet headed back towards the German coast. Initially, Jellicoe was reluctant to send the British fleet in pursuit, fearing there could be traps ahead of minefields, and especially ambushes by German submarines. However, the German fleet then separated and doubled back, apparently attempting to get around to the rear of the British line. The sea battle then resumed, with as full force as before.

As night fell the battle continued, with more ships being sunk. Action continued throughout the night into the early hours of the following morning (1 June). The final casualty of the battle was the

German dreadnought *Ostfriesland*, which was severely damaged by a British mine as it approached the Jade River at 05.30 hours on 1 June.

The final casualties, both in shipping and men, were as massive as the two respective fleets. The British fleet suffered 6,094 men killed, 510 wounded, and 177 captured; the German fleet lost 2,551 killed with 507 wounded. The British fleet lost 3 battlecruisers, 3 armoured cruisers and 8 destroyers. The German fleet lost 1 pre-dreadnought, 1 battlecruiser, 4 light cruisers and 5 torpedo boats. The total tonnage sunk for the British Fleet was 113,300 tons and the German Fleet, 62,300 tons.

Afterwards the British government did their best to hush up the British losses in the Battle of Jutland. Officers and men who had taken part in the battle were ordered not to mention it, but the Admiralty were forced to issue a press statement in which they grudgingly admitted that there had been a "naval engagement" off the Jutland coast. Why the secrecy? Because the British losses, both in ships and men, had been so high that the government were worried that it would be seen as a failure. The losses of the huge battlecruisers *Queen Mary*, *Invincible* and *Indefatigable*, all destroyed with all hands. 3,000 men dead in those three sinkings, with another 3,000 British dead among the rest of the British fleet.

But the Battle of Jutland marked the demise of the German fleet. Defeated at Jutland, the German fleet retreated to German waters, and remained there until the end of the First World War.

The father of Queen Elizabeth II, then known as Sub-Lieutenant Prince Albert, later King George VI, fought in the battle as a sub-lieutenant on board the *Collingwood*.

Grand Fleet of the British Royal Navy:
2nd Battle Squadron:
1st Division: *King George V* (Capt. Field Vice Admiral Jerram); *Ajax* (Capt. Baird); *Centurion* (Capt. Culme-Seymour); *Erin* (Capt. Stanley).
2nd Division: *Orion* (Capt. Backhouse; Rear Admiral Leveson); *Monarch* (Capt. Borrett); *Conqueror* (Capt. Tothill); *Thunderer* (Capt. Fergusson).
4th Battle Squadron:
3rd Division: *Iron Duke* (Capt. Dreyer; Admiral Jellicoe); *Royal Oak* (Capt. MacLachlan); *Superb* (Capt. Hyde-Parker; Rear Admiral Duff); *Canada* (Capt. Nicholson).
4th Division: *Benbow* (Capt. Parker; Vice Admiral Sturdee); *Bellerophon*; *Temeraire* (Capt. Underhill); *Vanguard* (Capt. Dick).
1st Battle Squadron:
5th Division: *Colossus* (Capt. Pound; Rear Admiral Gaunt); *Collingwood* (Capt. Ley); *Neptune* (Capt. Bernard); *St Vincent* (Capt. Fisher).
6th Division: *Marlborough* (Capt. Ross; Vice-Admiral Burney); *Revenge* (Capt. Kiddle); *Hercules* (Capt. Bernard); *Agincourt* (Capt. Doughty).
3rd Battlecruiser Squadron: *Invincible* (Capt. Cay; Rear-Admiral Hood); *Inflexible* (Capt. Heaton-Ellis); *Indomitable* (Capt. Kennedy).
Armoured Cruisers:
1st Cruiser Squadron: Defence (Capt. Ellis; Rear-Admiral Arbuthnot); *Warrior* (Capt. Molteno); *Duke of Edinburgh* (Capt. Blackett); *Black*

Prince (Capt. Bonham).

2nd Cruiser Squadron: *Minotaur* (Capt. d'Aeth; Rear-Admiral Heath); *Hampshire* (Capt. Savill); *Cochrane* (Capt. Leatham); *Shannon* (Capt. Dumaresq).

4th Light Cruiser Squadron: *Calliope* (Commodore Le Mesurier); *Constance* (Capt. Townsend); *Caroline* (Capt. Crooke); *Royalist* (Capt. Meade); *Comus* (Capt. Hotham).

Attached Light Cruisers

Active (Capt. Withers); *Bellona* (Capt. Dutton); *Blanche* (Capt. Casement); *Boadicea* (Capt. Casement); *Canterbury* (Capt. Royds); *Chester* (Capt. Lawson).

Destroyers:

4th Flotilla: *Tipperary* (Capt. Wintour); *Acasta*; *Achates*; *Ambuscade*; *Ardent*; *Broke*; *Christopher*; *Contest*; *Fortune*; *Garland*; *Hardy*; *Midge*; *Ophelia*; *Owl*; *Porpoise*; *Shark*; *Sparrowhawk*; *Spitfire*; *Unity*.

11th Flotilla: *Castor* (Commodore Hawksley); *Kempenfelt*; *Magic*; *Mandate*; *Manners*; *Marne*; *Martial*; *Michael*; *Millbrook*; *Minion*; *Mons*; *Moon*; *Morning Star*; *Mounsey*; *Mystic*; *Ossory*.

12th Flotilla: *Faulknor* (Capt. Stirling); *Maenad*; *Marksman*; *Marvel*; *Mary Rose*; *Menace*; *Mindful*; *Mischief*; *Munster*; *Narwhal*; *Nessus*; *Noble*; *Nonsuch*; *Obedient*; *Onslaught*; *Opal*.

Minelayer: *Abdiel*.

Oak: tender to HMS Iron Duke

Seaplane carrier: *Engadine*.

The Battlecruiser Fleet:

1st Battlecruiser squadron: *Lion* (Capt. Chatfield; Vice-Admiral Beatty); *Princess Royal* (Capt. Cowan; Rear-Admiral de Brock); *Queen Mary* (Capt. Prowse); *Tiger* (Capt. Pelly).

2nd Battlecruiser Squadron: *New Zealand* (Capt. Green; Rear-Admiral Pakenham); *Indefatigable* (Capt. Sowerby).

5th Battle Squadron: *Barham* (Capt. Craig; Rear-Admiral Evan-Thomas); *Valiant* (Capt. Woollcombe); *Warspite* (Capt. Philpotts); *Malaya* (Capt. Boyle).

1st Light Cruiser: Squadron: *Galatea* (Commodore Alexander-Sinclair); *Phaeton* (Capt. Cameron); *Inconstant* (Capt. Thesiger); *Cordelia* (Capt. Beamish).

2nd Light Cruiser Squadron: *Southampton* (Commodore Goodenough); *Birmingham* (Capt. Duff); *Nottingham* (Capt. Miller); *Dublin* (Capt. Scott).

3rd Light Cruiser Squadron: *Falmouth* (Capt. Edwards; Rear-Admiral Napier); *Yarmouth* (Capt. Pratt); *Birkenhead* (Capt. Reeves); *Gloucester* (Capt. Blunt).

1st Destroyer Flotilla: *Fearless* (Capt. Roper); *Acheron*; *Ariel*; *Attack*; *Badger*; *Defender*; *Goshawk*; *Hydra*; *Lapwing*; *Lizard*.

9th and 10th Destroyer Flotillas (combined): *Lydiard* (Commander Goldsmith); *Landrail*; *Laurel*; *Liberty*; *Moorsom*; *Morris*; *Termagant*; *Turbulent*.

13th Destroyer Flotilla: *Champion* (Capt. Farie); *Moresby*; *Narborough*; *Nerisaa*; *Nestor*; *Nicator*; *Nomad*; *Obdurate*; *Onslow*; *Pelican*; *Petard*.

High Seas Fleet of the Imperial German Navy:

III Battle Squadron:

5th Division: *Konig* (Capt. Bruninghaus; Rear-Admiral Behncke); *Grosser Kurfurst* (Capt. Goette); *Kronprinz* (Capt. Feldt); *Markgraf* (Capt. Seiferling).

6th Division: *Kaiser* (Capt. von Keyserlingk; Rear-Admiral Nordmann); *Kaiserin* (Capt. Sievers); *Prinzregent Luitpold* (Capt. Heuser); *Friedrich der Grosse* (Capt. Fuchs; Vice-Admiral Scheer).

1st Battle Squadron:

1st Division: *Ostfriesland* (Capt. von Natzmer; Vice-Admiral Schmidt); *Thuringen* (Capt. Kusel); *Helgoland* (Capt. von Kameke); *Oldenburg* (Capt. Redlich).

2nd Division: *Posen* (Capt. Lange; Rear-Admiral Engelhardt); *Rheinland* (Capt. Rohardt); *Nassau* (Capt. Klappenbach); *Westfalen* (Capt. Redlich).

III Battle Squadron:

3rd Division: *Deutschland* (Capt. Meurer; Rear-Admiral Mauve); *Hessen* (Capt. Bartels); *Pommern* (Capt. Bolken).

4th Division: *Hannover* (Capt. Heine; Rear-Admiral von Dalwigk zu Lichtenfels); *Schlesien* (Capt. Behncke); *Schleswig-Holstein* (Capt. Barrentrapp).

Light Cruisers:

IV Scouting Group: *Stettin* (Capt. Rebensburg; Commodore von Reuter); *Munchen* (Capt. Bocker); *Hamburg* (Capt. von Gaudecker); *Frauenlob* (Capt. Hoffmann); *Stuttgart* (Capt. Hagedorn).

Torpedo-Boat Flotillas

Light Cruiser Torpedo Boat: Rostock (Capt. Feldmann; Commodore Michelson).

Torpedo-Boat Flotilla: *G39* (Commander Albrecht); *G40*; *G38*; *S32*.

III Torpedo-Boat Flotilla: *S53* (Commander Hollmann); *V71*; *V73*; *G88*; *S54*; *V48*; *G42*.

V Torpedo-Boat Flotilla:*G11* (Commander Heinecke); *V1*; *V2*; *V3*; *V4*; *V5*; *V6*; *V7*; *G7*; *G8*; *G9*; *G10*.

VII Torpedo-Boat Flotilla: *S24* (Commander von Koch); *S15*; *S16*; *S17*; *S18*; *S19*; *S20*; *S23*; *V186*; *V189*.

The Battlecruiser Force:

I Scouting Group (Battlecruisers): Lutzow (Capt. Harder; Vice-Admiral Hipper); *Derfflinger* (Capt. Hartog); *Seydlitz* (Capt. von Egidy); *Moltke* (Capt. von Karpf); *Von der Tann* (Capt. Zenker).

II Scouting Group (Light Cruisers): *Frankfurt* (Capt. von Trotha; Rear-Admiral Bodicker); *Wiesbaden* (Capt. Reiss); *Pillau* (Capt. Mommsen); *Elbing* (Capt. Madlung).

Light Cruiser Boats:

Regensburg (Capt. Heuberer; Commodore Henrich)

II Torpedo-Boat Flotilla: B98 (Capt. Schuur); G1010; G102; G103; G104; B97; B109; B110; B111; B112.

VI Torpedo-Boat Flotilla: G41 (Commander Schultz); V44; V45; V46; V69; G37; G86; G87; S50.

IX Torpedo-Boat Flotilla: V28 (Commander Goehle); V26; V27; V29; V30; S33; S34; S35; S36; S51; S52.

HMS *Chester*

HMS *Chester* was built at the Cammell Laird shipyard in Birkenhead, and was a town-class light cruiser. It was launched in December 1915. It had a displacement of 5,185 tons. It was 456 and a half feet long and 50 feet wide, with a draught of fifteen and a half feet. The engines that drove it were Parsons reaction steam turbines, with twelve Yarrow oil boilers.

It had four propellers, giving it 31,000 horsepower, which meant it could travel at 26 knots, which meant 26 nautical miles an hour. It carried 1,172 tons of fuel oil to power the boilers.

The armour plating of the hull was two inches thick, and on the actual deck the armour was one-and-a-half inches thick. On the conning tower the steel armour was four inches thick.

The *Chester* had ten five-and-a-half-inch Mark 1 guns made by the Coventry Ordnance Works. They fired an 85-pound shell. This meant the ship had a higher firing rate than a ship with six-inch guns, which fired a 100-pound shell and were slower to reload. The five-and a-half-inch guns were rare in ships of the Royal Navy. In fact the Chester was only one of two ships in the navy with this size of gun. The reason for this is that the *Chester* and the other ship were originally being built for the Greek navy, and the Greek navy wanted ships with smaller guns because they would be lighter and meant the ships would be faster in the water. But when war was declared the British government commandeered both of those ships for the Royal Navy.

Jack Cornwell and the Boy Scouts.

Jack's membership of the Boy Scouts was very important to him, and his strong association with them can be seen in the fact that the Scouts provided the guard of honour at both Jack's funeral, and at the commemoration of the memorial to him.

After Jack's death the Cornwell Award was created, which was also known as the Scout VC. This is a badge of courage awarded for acts of special bravery to Scouts. The bronze badge is in the shape of the letter "C" encircling the fleur-de-lys, the symbol of the Scouting Movement. The "C" stands for both Cornwell and Courage.

The Canadian Connection.

Jack's brother, George, emigrated to Canada shortly after the end of the First World War. Their sister, Lily, joined George in Canada in 1923 when she was eighteen. A further Canadian connection was made when one of the highest mountains on the border between Alberta and British Columbia was named Mount Cornwell in Jack's honour by the Geographic Board of Canada.

Silvertown Munitions Works

The munitions factory at Silvertown, West Ham, blew up on Friday 19 January 1917, killing 73 people and laying waste to a huge area surrounding the explosion.

The munitions factory was set up in September 1915 at an existing empty factory to produce the explosive TNT for the war effort. Concerns were expressed because TNT was produced and stored in the same building, which many thought was dangerous. Dr F. A. Freeth, who was chief chemist for Brunner Mond, the parent firm that owned the factory, wrote reports to the Ministry of Defence expressing his concerns about the safety of the plant. He later stated that "At the end of every month we used to write to Silvertown to say that their plant would go up sooner or later, and we were told that it was worth the risk to get the TNT".

At 6.52pm on Friday 19th January 1917 a fire in the melting-pot room led to 50 tons of TNT exploding. The blast was heard as far away as Guildford and Cambridge. Around 70,000 in the surrounding area were damaged by the blast. Sixty-nine people were killed in the immediate explosion and another four died later. Four hundred people were injured.

Appendices:

The last letter Jack wrote to his father, Eli Cornwell, just before the Battle of Jutland:

Dear Dad

Just a few lines in answer to your most welcome letter, which we received on Monday – first post for a week. That is why you have not had a letter for a long while. Thanks for the stamps you sent me. We are up in the (CENSORED) somewhere, and they have just put me up as a sight setter at a gun.

Dear Dad, I have just had to start in pencil, as I have run out of ink, but still, I suppose you don't mind as long as you get a letter, and I am sorry to tell you that poor old A.L. is dead, and I dare say by the time you get this letter she will be buried. I have got a lot of letters to send home and about, so I can't afford much more, and we are just about to close up at the gun, so this is all for now: have more next time.

I remain, your ever-loving son,

Jack.

PS – "Cheer up, Buller me lad, we're not dead yet!"

Part of a letter that was written by the captain of HMS *Chester*, Captain

Lawson, to Jack's mother after the Battle of Jutland:

Dear Mrs Cornwell

I know you would wish to hear of the splendid fortitude shown by your boy during the action of May 31. His devotion to duty was an example for all of us. The wounds which resulted in his death within a short time were received in the first few minutes of the action. He remained steady at his most exposed post at the gun, waiting for orders.

His gun would not bear on the enemy, all but two of the ten of the crew were killed or wounded, and he was the only one who was in such an exposed position. But he felt he might be needed – as indeed he might have – so he stayed there, standing and waiting, under heavy fire, with just his own brave heart and God's help to support him. I cannot express to you my admiration of the son you have lost from this world. No other comfort would I attempt to give to the mother of so brave a lad, but to assure her of what he was and what he did, and what an example he gave. I hope to place in the boys' mess a plate with his name on and the date, and the words "Faithful unto death". I hope some day you may be able to come and see it there.

THE TRENCHES

CARLISLE, 1919

It all began just five years ago, but in those five years everything has changed. In that time I've lost good friends, and made new ones. I've changed from Billy Stevens, the innocent boy from Carlisle, to Billy Stevens, a man whose mind is still filled with memories of terrible sights that I hope no one else has to see or live through. This is my story, told while those memories are still vivid in my mind. But I don't think they'll ever go away...

1914

My family – that is, me, my parents, my two brothers and two sisters – lived in a part of Carlisle called Denton Holme. It was all red-brick terraced houses and cramped cobbled streets. Other parts of Carlisle were richer, with bigger houses, but I liked where we lived. It was friendly. In Denton everyone knew everyone else, and you'd always find someone to help you out if you were in trouble, or short of money for milk, or coal or anything.

Rob Matthews and I had been best mates since we started at school together. I suppose we became best pals because we were sat together when we were first in Miss Pursley's class and we used to walk home together because our houses were round the corner from each other. But there's more to it than that. You don't stay best pals with someone just because you live near them.

Rob was always the dare-devil of the two of us, the one leading the way. He was the one who climbed the highest up the trees to get the pick of the crop when we scrumped apples from Mrs Gardner's orchard. Me, I was content to pick up windfalls from the ground. And Rob wasn't afraid to tell our bullying teacher, Mr Dickens, what he thought of him when Dickens picked on some poor innocent kid in our class. It got Rob a beating from Dickens with the cane, but Rob just took it and didn't let him see that it hurt him.

Like I say, that was Rob Matthews. He was a hero to the boys – and the girls – at school and around Denton, and he was my best pal. What he saw in me, I don't know. Although he said once, "You're clever with your head. I like that."

Rob and I were both thirteen years old when the War broke out. There'd been talk about it coming for some time, though I hadn't paid much interest before because it was all just politics as far as I was concerned, and politicians talking was just boring. But I had picked up things from listening to my dad when he'd sit and read the paper and talk about what was going on about the Kaiser – who was the Emperor of Germany – with my Uncle Stanley when he came round.

I remember sitting in our tiny kitchen cooking potatoes in their skins in the range, while my dad and Uncle Stanley shared the newspaper, and Dad read out from his bit, the sports pages, and Uncle Stanley read bits out from the pages that had the news.

"There's a horse racing at Epsom today called Stevens Luck," said Dad, rustling his paper. "I wonder if it's worth a shilling each way?"

That was the way it was with my dad: he'd check the horses and spend all day thinking about whether to put a bet on or not. I had no doubt that if he'd had spare money he would have, but in our house money was so tight that he never did. This was lucky, because most of the horses he mentioned as likely winners never came anywhere.

The front page of the section that Uncle Stanley held said "WAR

DECLARED" in big letters. "It had to come," sighed Uncle Stanley. "I could tell it was coming when they killed Franz Ferdinand."

"Who's Franz Ferdinand?" I asked.

"He was the Archduke Franz Ferdinand of Austria," Uncle Stanley told me. "Him and his wife were on a visit to Serbia and they got killed by a bunch of lunatics. Anarchists."

"Why?" I asked.

"Politics," said my dad. "Believe me, son, politics is to blame for most of the troubles in this world."

"As soon as that happened, I knew we were in for trouble," Uncle Stanley continued. That was the way with Uncle Stanley. Once something major had happened he could tell you how he always knew that it was going to happen. However, just like with Dad's racing forecasts, Uncle Stanley never seemed to be able to tell us what was going to happen *before* it did.

"Once Franz Ferdinand was killed there was only one thing that was bound to happen: Austria and Hungary declared war on Serbia. It was obvious."

"Why?" I asked.

Uncle Stanley ignored my question, and carried on: "Of course, straight away Russia declared its support for Serbia."

"There's another horse here called Archduke," muttered Dad, still studying the racing form. "It's 100-1. Now that's what I call good odds."

Uncle Stanley glared at my dad, slightly annoyed because he wasn't paying attention to all this knowledge unfolding, but my dad just ignored him. He was used to Uncle Stanley.

"Why did Russia get involved?" I asked. "And why are we at war?"

"Alliances," said my dad, still concentrating on his racing page. "Countries sign agreements to back each other up in case they're attacked."

"Exactly," nodded Uncle Stanley. "In this case, Germany, who are on Austria and Hungary's side, told Russia to stay out of it. Russia refused, so Germany declared war on Russia. Then straight away Germany set out to invade France."

"Which had been the Germans' plan all along, if you ask me," said Dad.

"Exactly," nodded Uncle Stanley again. "That's what I've always said. It's obvious. But to do that the Germans have got to go through Belgium. And Britain has got a treaty with Belgium, so that if Belgium were ever attacked we would come to its defence. So, when Germany invaded Belgium, we had no choice but to declare war on Germany." Uncle Stanley prodded the headline on the paper with his finger. "And that, Billy, is how this war started." He gave a smile, pleased at having imparted his knowledge of world politics to me. "Mind," he added, "it'll all be over by Christmas. The Germans can't fight a war against proper soldiers like ours. I know what I'm talking about…"

As you can imagine, as soon as we knew that war had been declared, me and Rob and all the boys in our street all went down to the army recruiting office to join up and fight the Hun. But the Sergeant there just laughed and told us all to go away.

"Don't you worry," he said. "It'll all be over in a few weeks. We'll soon kick the Kaiser back to Germany."

I was really disappointed. All the way down to the Recruiting Office I'd had visions of myself in my khaki uniform and my tin helmet rushing forward in battle, firing my rifle, and taking loads of Germans prisoners and getting medals. I could even see myself at Buckingham Palace getting my medal for bravery from the King. Instead of fighting bravely we were being sent home and we'd all still have to go to school tomorrow.

Rob was even angrier than I was. "It's not fair," he said. "When there's a war on they ought to take everyone who wants to go. It makes sense that the more soldiers we've got on our side the bigger our army will be and the quicker we'll win."

"Maybe the Germans'll be harder to beat than the Sergeant thinks," I suggested. "Maybe it'll go on for longer and then they'll want us soon enough."

"Maybe," said Rob. "We can but hope."

Well, the Kaiser didn't get kicked back to Germany in a few weeks. In fact the weeks turned into months, and then the months turned into years, and all those people who'd been so confident it would all be over in a short space of time were now moaning and groaning about the country going to ruin because of the War.

My Grandfather Pickles, my dad's father, told me, "It wouldn't be going on this long if the old Queen, Victoria, were still alive. She'd have put a stop to it. She'd just have a word with her nephew, Kaiser Billy, and tell him to pack up his soldiers and go back home."

I must admit, I was surprised to find out that our king and the German kaiser were cousins. But when I told Rob this he just laughed and said didn't I know how families were always fighting among themselves. Like his mother and her sister, who were always arguing hammer and tongs.

As the War dragged on, Rob and I often talked about joining up and going out and fighting. We saw ourselves as the heroes who would go over to Belgium and France and sort those Germans out. Both of us were really eager to get out there, but there was one problem: our mums.

When my mum found out that I'd been down to the Recruiting Office soon after the War started, she was furious. "Don't you even think about joining up!" she said. "If you go over to France I'll never see you again!"

"Course you will," I said. "I'll be allowed home on leave."

"That's not what I mean and you know it!" she said angrily. "You're not going and that's that! So don't you even think about it!"

After a few months, I brought the matter up again, but Mum hadn't changed her mind about it one bit.

"You're not going!" she said when I mentioned I was thinking of joining up.

"He's only thinking of defending his country!" my dad put in, defending me.

"Oh yes," snapped back my mum. "And he'll come home with bits missing, like Brian Cotterill over in Botchergate. Twenty years old, and no legs now. What chance has Brian Cotterill got of ever earning a decent living?"

"They don't all come home injured," said my dad.

"No, some come home dead," snapped my mum. "And some don't come home at all."

With that she gathered up the bundle of washing she'd been packing in a sheet and went next door to use Mrs Higsons's copper washer.

Dad looked at me and sighed. "Your mum's got very strong opinions," he said. "That's because she lost an uncle in the Boer War. She doesn't really mean it."

But I knew she did, and it made me feel miserable. I wanted to be out there, fighting for my king and country. Instead I was stuck at home while other boys from Carlisle went off and became heroes.

At the start of 1917, the year I turned sixteen, the War had been going on for over two years. I'd been working as a trainee telegraph operator at the Citadel Railway Station in Carlisle for two years, ever since I left school. Being a telegraph operator meant sitting at a desk and operating a telegraph key. This key sent messages along cables to the other railway stations along the lines. It also received them, printing the messages out in Morse code, a series of short buzzes and long buzzes, each one representing a letter, so the telegraph operator had to be able to understand the code to be able to read and send messages.

Rob had also got a job on the railway. He didn't work on the telegraph, though, he worked as a track layer, laying railway lines. He was a big tough lad, was Rob, and he could wield a hammer and drive a spike as good as men twice his age.

By January 1917, stories were coming back from Belgium about how our troops only needed one last push and they'd break the Germans, but the Germans had dug in tight. If only more troops could be got out there to the Front, which was where the fighting was going on, the Germans would crack and the war would be over. More men were all that was needed. I was getting more and more eager to get out there, and so was Rob.

"We have to go!" he said to me one day as we walked home from work. "I can't stand just hanging around reading about the War in the papers. I want to be out there, winning it!"

But Rob's mum felt as strongly about him not going as mine did. And so we stayed in Carlisle, getting more and more frustrated.

Around February time, posters started being put up on walls around Carlisle and leaflets put through letter boxes, all saying the same thing: "Are You A Man or A Mouse?" They were put out by Lord Lonsdale, the local lord, who had set up his own regiment for local men soon after the War started.

I read one of the posters. It said:

Are You A Man or A Mouse? Are you a man who will forever be handed down to posterity as a Gallant Patriot? Or are you to be handed down to posterity as a ROTTER and a COWARD? If you are a Man, NOW is your opportunity of proving it. Enlist at once and go to the nearest Recruiting Officer."

Rob had also seen the poster. "They're calling us cowards now," he said angrily.

I knew how he felt. Sometimes I felt ashamed, walking to work, and knowing that other boys of my age were already out in Belgium fighting to defend us. Some women had been seen giving out white feathers to young men who they felt should have been out fighting on the Front. I dreaded the moment when a woman might come up and give me a white feather in the street in front of everyone.

After seeing the poster, I brooded all day at work on the whole business of going off to war. Rob must have been doing the same, because as we met up after work, Rob said suddenly: "Do you still want to join up?"

"Of course I do," I said.

"Then let's go and do it."

I frowned.

"What's the problem?" Rob asked. "We both want to go out there and do our bit, stop the Hun. Lord Lonsdale wants people like us."

"My mum won't like it," I said doubtfully. "Nor will yours."

Rob laughed. "Then we won't tell them till we've done it," he said. "Once we're in, they won't be able to say anything about it. And I bet you that secretly your mum will be pleased to have a soldier in the family."

I thought about it and hoped Rob was right. Maybe once I'd joined, Mum would accept it. She wouldn't have a choice.

"Right," I agreed determinedly. "Let's do it."

So that very afternoon, instead of going straight home, we went to the Recruiting Office the Lonsdale Battalion had set up in the town centre. A Recruiting Sergeant was standing guard at the door, looking very smart and straight, his boots shining, his uniform smelling of starch.

"Yes, young men," he boomed. "What can I do for you?"

"We've come to join up," said Rob.

"Good!" beamed the Recruiting Sergeant. "How old are you?"

"Sixteen," said Rob.

The Sergeant looked at Rob and said, "Sorry, son, you're too young. Come back when you're nineteen." Then he gave Rob a wink and said, "Tomorrow, eh?"

Next he turned to me and said, "And what about you?"

"I'm nineteen," I said, thinking quickly.

"Good," smiled the Sergeant. "Come on in. Your country needs you."

Rob looked at me, his mouth open. For the first time in our lives I had beaten him to something. Then his face broke into a grin and he said: "I'll see you tomorrow, Billy. When I'm nineteen."

With that, he gave me a wink, and then hurried home.

"Don't tell your mum!" I called after him. "She might tell mine and I want to tell her myself!"

"Don't worry," he called back. "I won't."

When I got home, Mum was looking worried.

"Where have you been?" she demanded. "Your supper's been in the oven this whole hour, waiting for you."

"I joined up in the army," I said. "I'm going to fight in the War."

Mum looked at me, shocked, and her mouth dropped open. Then she almost fell backwards on to one of the kitchen chairs so hard I thought she'd break it. Then she began to cry.

At that moment my dad came home from work. "What's up?" he asked.

"I've joined up," I said. "I've joined the Lonsdale Battalion. I start my training the day after tomorrow."

Dad gave me a big smile. I could tell he was proud of me. "Well done, son!" he said.

"No! You can't go!" sobbed my mum. "Harry, tell him he can't go! He's too young! He can't join up! He's under age!"

"I wasn't the only one who was under age," I protested. "About half of the recruits who were in the Recruiting Office were under nineteen. In fact they let William Chambers join up, and he's only thirteen."

"That's criminal!" said my mum angrily, and she burst into tears again.

"There, there," said my dad, and he went to her and put his arm around her to cuddle her. He then gave me a wink and a nod of his head to say, "Leave this to me, son. I'll take it from here."

I went out and round the corner to Rob's house and told him what had happened.

"Your mum'll get over it," he assured me. "When do you start your training?"

"Day after tomorrow," I said. "I've got tomorrow to tell them at the Citadel Station what I'm going to do, and get packed."

"Well don't go off to France without me," said Rob. "You may have joined up first, but I'm going to be there with you, and I bet when we're there I get more Huns than you do."

I don't know what Dad said to Mum, but although it didn't make her change her mind, it quietened her down. Or maybe it was just that she accepted my going. She still sniffled a lot and wiped her eyes whenever she saw me the next day, but on the whole it wasn't as bad as I thought it would be.

My brothers and sisters thought my going off to war was very exciting, and John asked me if I'd bring him back a Hun helmet as a souvenir. I promised him I'd do my best.

Rob enlisted the next day, claiming to be nineteen, and persuaded the Recruiting Sergeant that he and I needed to start our training together because we were best friends. Because the army was keen to get friends to join up together, they agreed. I had to smile at this. It was typical of Rob, being able to talk the army into letting him start training a day earlier. Anything, rather than miss out and let me be ahead of the game.

On 15 March, Rob and I began our training at Blackhall Camp, which had been set up on the racecourse just outside Carlisle. We were given uniforms of a rough, grey material with the Lonsdale's very own badge and shoulder flashes sewn on the sleeves. We were billeted in long wooden huts, with bunk-beds running along the two long walls. Rob grabbed the bottom bunk of our pair and I took the one on top.

The huts were pretty basic, just light, timber buildings, but considering they'd been put up quickly, they weren't too bad. The only thing really wrong with them was that they were cold. The walls seemed strong, but when the wind blew at night when we were asleep, it came in through the timber sheets and caused a terrible draught.

During the day we did our marching drill using wooden poles instead of rifles because we were told the soldiers at the Front needed all the rifles.

At the end of the first day, Rob looked at his pole and sniffed scornfully and said, "I hope I get a chance to practise with a real rifle before I go into battle. I don't think a wooden pole will be much use against the Hun."

We dug trenches and then filled them in again for three days on the trot. By the end of those three days my back and arms were killing me! It seemed so stupid to me, digging a trench just to fill it in again. One of the boys in our hut, Jed Lowe, said we had to learn how to dig trenches because that's what we'd be living in when we got to the Front. He reckoned he knew because his older brother was already out there in Flanders. He said we needed to fill the trenches in again so that the next lot of recruits would have somewhere to dig up, otherwise they wouldn't be able to practise digging. I supposed Jed knew what he was talking about, having a brother at the Front, but it still seemed a big waste of effort to me. To my mind, we should have been spending our energy fighting the Hun.

The weeks passed. We dug trenches. We filled them in again. We drilled. We marched. We drilled some more. I became an expert in handling a wooden pole and pretending it was a rifle.

It was in the middle of the third week that I was sent for by our Commanding Officer. I was puzzled, as was Rob. What had I done wrong that I was being summoned in this way?

An awful thought struck me. Had my mum gone to the authorities and complained about them taking me when I was under age? Was that what it was?

I put this to Rob, and he frowned and said it was possible. "The only way to find out is to go and see what he wants," he said. That was the way with Rob. Straightforward.

Knowing he was right, but with a sinking feeling in my chest, I went to the Commanding Officer's Quarters.

Our Commanding Officer, Brigadier Reynolds, motioned me to stand at ease after I had saluted.

"Private Stevens," he said. "I understand that you worked as a trainee telegraph operator at the Citadel Railway Station in Carlisle. Is that correct?"

I was surprised by the question. I couldn't see what it had to do with my being in the army and going to fight the Huns.

"Yes, sir!" I replied.

"In that case, it looks like we'll be losing you," he said.

I was shocked. Did that mean I was going to be thrown out of the army? I knew that some people had what they called "reserve occupation" jobs, which meant the authorities felt it was more important that that person stayed in England to do that job rather than go and fight, but I couldn't see that a trainee telegraph operator came under that heading. How could they be losing me?

"But I want to go to France, sir!" I blurted out.

"Oh, you'll be going to France all right," said the Brigadier. "Only not with the Lonsdale Battalion. The Engineers are desperate for men with technical experience, especially in telegraphs and communications. So, you're being assigned to the Royal Engineers, Signals."

For the first time since we were tiny nippers, Rob and I were split up. It was strange to be saying goodbye to him. We'd been together as best mates all our lives, living in the same area, in the same classes at school, and even working at the same place, the railway station.

"Don't worry," grinned Rob as I packed my stuff up that evening, ready to go. "We'll meet up again on the Front. While I'm shooting Huns and winning medals and you're mending bits of broken wire."

I forced a grin back at this, but I had to admit that what he said rankled with me. I'd joined up to fight, not to work a telegraph key, or repair signalling equipment. I could have stayed behind in Carlisle and done that.

"Huh! Don't *you* worry," I responded. "Once I get over there I won't just be stuck working on the telegraph. As soon as the officers see how brave I am under fire I expect they'll put me up at the Front as well. I'll be shooting as many Huns as you, you can count on it."

"I'll have a head start on you," said Rob. "We're off the week after next."

I thought of what lay before me then. More training. More things to learn. Meanwhile, Rob would be out there at the Front, getting all the glory.

My face must have showed how miserable I felt about it, because Rob laughed and slapped me on the back.

"Don't put on such a long face, Billy," he grinned. "I didn't really mean it about getting more Hun than you. Come on, cheer up. We're all in the War together."

"Yes, but you'll be actually *in* the War," I said gloomily. "Me, I'll be on the edges, sending messages, just like you said."

Next morning I went off to a camp in Yorkshire for further training to be an Engineer, while Rob carried on at Blackhall Camp.

If I thought Engineer training would be easier, I was wrong. It still meant lots of digging trenches and filling them in again, just the same as before. The difference was I had extra stuff to learn.

I already knew quite a bit about Morse code and telegraph keys from my work at the Citadel Station, plus a bit about wireless. Now I had to go to lessons to learn even more. Most of it was practical stuff, how to repair a cable, fitting connections, that sort of thing.

Most of the other blokes were like me, they'd joined up to fight and found themselves put into the Engineers because of the work they did in civilian life.

One of my new pals was a fellow called Charlie Morgan. He was from Newcastle. He worked at the railway as a telegraph operator, but, being 21, he wasn't a trainee any more but a fully trained-up operator.

I liked Charlie because he was so confident about everything. He was sure we were going to win the War. He was sure he was going to be rich one day. He was going to have one of the biggest houses in Newcastle. All it took was time. It was good to have someone like Charlie as a mate, it sort of took the edge off Rob not being around any more to keep things cheerful.

I spent four weeks at the Engineers Training Camp, by the end of which I could mend a telegraph cable, and dig a ditch (and fill it in again) in my sleep. During the training, six of us Engineers had palled up. As well as me and Charlie there was Ginger Smith, Wally Clarke, Danny MacDonald and Alf Tupper. Danny was just a year older than me at eighteen, Ginger was nineteen, Charlie, Wally and Alf were in their early twenties. We'd all been working on the telegraph, which gave us something in common. Plus, we'd all volunteered to go out and fight the Hun, but had all ended up in the Engineers learning how to repair telegraph and telephone cables instead, which had annoyed all of us. But, as we'd all learned during our training, orders are orders and you didn't argue. As one of our sergeants had told us during training, "When I say 'Jump!' you don't even ask how high – you just jump! You're not in the army to ask questions!"

I knew that by now Rob and the rest of the Lonsdale Battalion would have been in France for some time, and I wondered how he was. Had he managed to bag his first Hun?

At the end of the four weeks, we were told that our training was over and at long last we were headed for the Front. I almost cheered when we got our sailing orders. At last, I was going to War!

For someone like me who'd never travelled much farther from Carlisle than the coast at Silloth, a distance of about 30 miles (unless you counted the journey from Carlisle to the Signals Unit in Yorkshire), the journey to Belgium was a really big adventure.

Charlie put on the air that this journey was nothing to him. "I've been all over the place," he told me. "Wales. Scotland. Cornwall. I've been everywhere."

"London?" asked Ginger.

"Loads of times," shrugged Charlie. "London's nothing but another Newcastle, only maybe a bit bigger."

We took a train south to London, and then another train from London to Folkestone. There we were loaded on to a troopship, which took us across the Channel from Folkestone to Boulogne. I didn't think the sea was too bad, although it was rough enough for Charlie and Alf to get seasick. At first Charlie tried to pretend that he was a seasoned traveller and it wasn't seasickness, it must have been something he ate, but when other men got seasick as well he stopped pretending.

During this long journey there was a sense of excitement among all of us. Not only were we going abroad, we were going to fight the Hun!

The train from Boulogne took us to a town called St Omer. All the way along on the train I kept expecting to see signs of the War, but the only real signs were the large amount of soldiers everywhere all dressed in khaki. That, and big guns on wheels being hauled along.

I saw a few tanks as well. I'd never seen tanks before. They were huge metal monsters with caterpillar tracks, and big guns poking out. It was said they could crawl over any sort of mud and just keep firing, the shots from the enemy would just bounce off the metal casing.

"Not much sign of any fighting," said Wally, looking disappointed.

"Don't worry, you'll find it soon enough all right," said another soldier who was pushing his way through the crowded train. "And if you don't, it'll find you."

When we reached St Omer we were transferred to buses taking us to a smaller town called Poperinghe.

"How d'you spell that?" Danny asked an older soldier.

"Why d'you want to know how to spell it?" asked the soldier. "This war's about fighting, not about reading."

"I need to know so when I write home to my mum I can tell her where I am," said Danny.

The older soldier laughed out loud.

"What's so funny?" asked Danny, puzzled.

"It's a waste of time putting place names in any letters back home," said the soldier. "They cross 'em out."

"Who do?" asked Alf.

"The army censors," replied the soldier. "It's in case our letters fall into enemy hands. They don't want the Hun knowing where our units are, or what we're doing, do they?"

I was a bit annoyed at the thought of someone else reading my letters home. Letters are supposed to be private. Mind, I could see that what the soldier said made sense.

The village we were headed for, this Poperinghe, was in an area called Passchendaele. It was near a town they said was called Wipers (which I found out later was spelled Ypres and was actually pronounced Eepre).

I kept my eyes on the landscape as our bus rolled along. It was flat country, really flat, made up of green fields with a small wood every now and then. I could see a few houses scattered about here and there in between the fields. It reminded me a bit of the flat part of Cumberland back home, up by the Solway Plain, but even that had more hills than this place.

It was nightfall when we finally got to Poperinghe. There was no time to take a look at the town and get an idea of what it was like: as soon as we got off our bus we were lined up and marched off towards some fields just outside the town where the army had set up camp. Rows and rows of tents stretched for what looked like miles. The Union Jack flew on a flag-pole. In other fields further away I could see other flags flying.

"Australians," nodded Wally, pointing at one of the other flags, which seemed to be stars and a small Union Jack on a blue flag. "I recognize the flag 'cos I've got an uncle who lives out there."

"Maybe he'll be over here with the Australian troops?" suggested Danny.

"Unlikely," said Wally. "He's 70 years old."

We were assigned six men to a tent, and our group snaffled a tent quick so that we could all be together. We'd each grabbed a bunk and were starting to sort our gear out, when a soldier from another unit poked his head into our tent.

"New arrivals?" he asked.

"Aye," said Charlie. "Just got here."

"Well, in a minute the bugle's going to blow for food, so if you want to make sure you get there among the first, take my tip and head over to the mess tent right now."

With that he gave us a wink, then hurried off.

"Food!" sighed Alf. "About time! Come on, lads, let's get over there!"

The six of us hurried towards the mess tent. Signs had been put up pointing out where it was. Also, the smell of food cooking was wafting over the camp, so we just followed our noses.

Until I sat down at a long wooden trestle table with a plate of stew and mashed potato, I hadn't realized how hungry I was. I hadn't sat down to a proper meal since just before getting on the boat at Folkestone. We'd grabbed some food at Boulogne, and then again at St Omer while we were waiting for our bus, but this was our first proper meal since leaving England. I wolfed down my food in a state of excitement. I was in Belgium with my mates, ready to start winning the War!

After mess, it was back to the tent and lights out, and sleep. Not that I could really get to sleep. After the long journey I'd had, all the way from

Yorkshire, I thought I'd be worn out and ready to sleep, but my mind was in a whirl. All I could think of was that I was finally here, ready for battle. What would it be like at the Front? What would we be doing as Engineers?

Next morning the six of us loaded up our packs and joined the column of men heading for the Front. Our column was about 100 men strong, and made up of men from different regiments, some going to fighting units in the trenches, others – like us – being sent to support units. The routine, our Sergeant told us, was seven days in the front-line trenches, followed by seven days back at our billets, then seven days in the trenches again, and so on. We were being thrown in at the deep end straight away, off for our first week at the very heart of the battle.

We marched towards the Front along roads made of cobbles. The nearer we got to the Front, the worse the roads became, the cobbles sinking into mud and disappearing beneath the surface, until in the end we were marching as best we could on a potholed muddy track.

We were lucky that our training back home had made us fit, because the weight we had to carry on our backs in our haversacks made the marching even more difficult. As Engineers, we didn't have rifles and ammunition to weigh us down, but in their places we had bigger and heavier picks and shovels, as well as our mess tin and our water bottle. We also had our gas mask, which we'd been told might one day save our lives, so I made sure mine was within easy grabbing distance.

We Engineers were near the back of the column, and I couldn't help a feeling of envy when I looked at the fighting men marching in front of us. That was where I wanted to be. Armed and ready to fight. Not for the first time, I wondered how Rob was doing out here. Had he killed his first Hun yet?

After miles of marching our legs and shoulders ached, but as we neared the Front we could hear the booming sounds of heavy guns in the distance, and even at this range we could feel the ground shuddering beneath our feet from the heavy shells.

"Looks like we've found the War at last," grinned Charlie, and me and Wally started to chuckle nervously, but we were soon cut short by a yell of, "No talking in the ranks!" from one of the Sergeants just behind us.

We marched on in silence. So this was the Front. I had never seen anything so desolate before. Just a sea of mud as far as the eye could see. Mud and barbed wire, and deep craters. And miles and miles of trenches filled with soldiers. I wondered where our trenches stopped and the German trenches began. Where was the enemy? I felt a knot of excitement in my belly as I craned my head, scanning the horizon for any sign of them.

"Right turn!" came the order from the Sergeant at the front of our column, and we turned off the road and descended into a trench. I'd dug ditches back home but these trenches were deeper than any of them. This one was about 7 feet deep and about 3 feet wide, its stinking clay walls held back by anything that was available: bits of timber, strands of wire, pieces of corrugated iron, sandbags.

Wooden duckboards formed a kind of walkway along the trench, but they were slippery with mud, and in many places they'd broken and sunk under the water. As we made our way along the trench, doing our best to keep our footing, we passed soldiers covered with mud. The holes were filled with freezing cold and stinking water.

"More lambs for the slaughter!" commented one mud-covered soldier as we passed him.

The other soldiers laughed, but their laughter was cut short with a shout from their Sergeant Major, who hollered, "Shut up in the ranks, you lot, or I'll have you all shot for treasonous talk!"

The Royal Engineers were among the first to be dispersed. There were a dozen of us, including Charlie and me, and as we stumbled down the rickety wooden steps into what appeared to be a hole in the ground lit by smoky kerosene lamps, a cheer went up from the grimy soldiers inside the hole.

"Look, lads! Relief is here!" chuckled one.

Charlie looked round at the wet clay walls held up by shafts of timber.

"You'd need to be a rabbit to be able to live here," he said.

"Think yourself lucky we've got somewhere like this," said one of the grimy soldiers. "It's only because we're Engineers. The fighting units don't even have this luxury!"

"Their officers do, Paddy," commented another soldier. "Caves with proper chairs and tables in them. I've seen them."

"Don't mind him, he's just jealous," grinned the soldier called Paddy. "He can't get used to sleeping in muddy water. Anyway, let's get you lot sorted out. Believe me, you're going to be busy!"

Paddy was right. During those first weeks I was busier than I'd ever been in my life.

At the Front there was a complicated system of trenches. Each Infantry trench had two others behind it: a support trench, and then a reserve trench behind that. They were all connected by a communications trench, along which supplies and relief operations were carried out. The telegraph cables were laid along the reserve trench, so the Infantry wouldn't get caught up in them when they went over the top. The whole thing was a bit like a maze, except made out of mud.

Most of our work consisted of repairing lengths of telegraph cables that had been broken during German artillery attacks. The cables were supposed to have been buried at least 6 feet below ground level so they didn't get broken when bombs came down, but the shells the Hun had been using of late were so big they were churning up holes in the mud 10 feet deep. There was only one way to repair a smashed cable when that happened and that was to run new lengths and join them on to the last good bit.

We went out on repair missions and worked in teams of two. My team was Charlie and me. Ginger and Wally were a team, and Danny and Alf were the third. The work was tough. You had to cut through the damaged cable, which was hard because it was covered in steel, lead or brass for added protection, and then make the connections. And all the time you were knee-deep in mud, sometimes waist-deep, and waiting for the Hun to launch another artillery attack, or send over a wave of troops armed with guns with bayonets.

The cables were vital for HQ to keep in contact with the troops at the Front. They'd tried using wireless, but it only really worked between aeroplanes and a ground station. Here in the trenches it was almost impossible. Our side had tried it. There was a thing called the British Field Trench Set, which you were supposed to be able to carry about and pick up and transmit messages. The trouble was it needed at least three men to carry it, and another six to carry the batteries needed to work it.

The Engineers had also recently tried a newer wireless set, the Loop Set. This was a bit more efficient. For one thing its aerial could be attached to a bayonet stuck in the ground, and it didn't need as many men to lug it around. The problem was it only had a range of about 2,000 yards, and lots of the time it just packed up and didn't work. Which meant we Engineers were always busy laying miles and miles of cables to keep communications going.

During my first few days in the trenches I discovered that what Paddy had said about us "living in luxury" in our hole in the ground was right. In our trench a cave had been dug out of the walls to store our equipment and we could use it as a shelter. For the soldiers of the fighting units, only officers had dugouts, ordinary soldiers had to make do with a waterproof sheet for shelter. Some of them had scraped small holes in the walls of the trench themselves, just large enough to fit in one man sitting down, but it didn't give much protection either from the elements or from shrapnel. These were known as "funk holes" and the only advantage they offered was that a soldier had a clay seat to sit on and a bit of muddy cover when waiting for action, rather than squatting in a deep puddle of icy muddy water in the open.

I was told by soldiers who'd been in the trenches for some time that this was a quiet patch. It didn't seem quiet to me. Every time Charlie and me and the other Engineers went out the Germans seemed to be shelling our positions. The first few days I spent most of my time throwing myself into the walls of the trenches, waiting to be hit by a bomb, or by flying shrapnel. Now I knew why soldiers were covered in mud from head to foot.

The first time I heard a high explosive going off it was terrifying. It makes an ear-splitting roar and the world around you shakes violently. Every time I expected the walls of the trench to fall in. Mostly the clay stuck together and held, but sometimes a crack would appear and a thick slice of clay, several feet thick, would topple over and fill in the trench, covering everything beneath it.

Shrapnel was the really terrifying thing. Bits of metal of different sizes, some large, some small, exploding out of a shell and hurtling through the air at incredible speed, slicing through anything in their way.

The mules and horses that hauled the gun carriages and the supply wagons were often caught in the bombing. On my first day I saw two of these poor animals with their legs destroyed by shrapnel, screaming with pain in the mud until they were put out of their misery by a bullet in their head.

On my second day out repairing cables, I saw my first dead man. His head was out of sight, covered in mud. All I could see was the remains of an arm and some ribs, with rotting flesh and bits of uniform sticking to it. Maggots were coming out from the hole in his ribs. I took one look at him and was sick.

"Get it out," said Charlie, patting me on the back as I vomited. "You'll see worse than this before this is over."

The sight of that dead soldier made me think of Rob and Jed and the rest of my old mates from the Lonsdales. I wondered how they were. Had any of them been wounded, or killed? I felt a sinking feeling in my stomach at the thought that, all the time I'd been feeling jealous of Rob because he was with a fighting unit, he might have actually been wounded in the fighting. Or, even worse, been killed. The thought made me shiver.

When we were out working we had to be alert for gas, especially mustard gas. We were told that the Germans also used chlorine and phosgene gas, which got into your lungs and filled them up with water so you drowned. But mustard gas was the worst of all.

Mustard gas didn't have a smell to warn you, it just crept up on you and next thing you knew you were retching and coughing and blinded, your eyes burning. It killed you by filling your lungs and burning you from the inside. The only defence against gas was the respirator, a weird-looking mask that you pulled on over your face. It had big goggles over your eyes and a hose like an elephant's trunk coming down to the canister on your front. But those funny-looking respirators saved many men's lives.

Then there were the rats. I'd seen rats back home in Cumberland, but these trench rats were as big as cats. I was told they fed off the bodies of the men who were left to rot in the muddy waters of the trenches. They had become so used to sharing the trenches with us soldiers that they didn't run away and hide like rats back home, they walked about quite openly. So you had to make sure that your rations were well and truly hidden away inside your mess tin, otherwise you'd find a rat had got in and eaten them.

With all of this, at the end of my first seven days in the trenches, I was more than ready when the order came for us to return to our billets at Poperinghe.

"It's a long walk back!" complained Charlie as we trudged our way along the muddy track.

"True, but at least we'll be in a bed tonight," I said. "And for the next six nights after that."

"Quiet back there!" shouted our Sergeant Major. "No talking in the ranks!"

We shut up and marched. Or, rather, trudged. After seven days and nights in the trenches we were all weary, battle-shocked and sore. I noticed that the numbers of the men coming back from the fighting units were fewer than had come out, and for the first time it struck me that I might be lucky that I was with the Engineers rather than the Infantry.

When we arrived back at our billets and were given the order to "Dismiss!", Charlie took the opportunity to head for the latrines before they got too full. I headed straight for the bathhouse, aiming to get some of the muck off, and get rid of the lice.

Charlie and I realized we'd caught lice after we'd been in the trenches for just two days. That first night I realized I'd got them I'd stripped off all my clothes as soon as I got back to our dugout and started searching for them by the light of a kerosene lamp and began picking them off my skin. It was a waste of time. What I didn't know was that lice laid their eggs in the seams of your clothes, so you could pick off as many as you liked, but more would come as soon as you put your clothes back on. You just had to get used to the fact that lice lived off you, eating at your skin under your clothes, and all you could do was try not to scratch or you'd just make the sores on your skin worse.

Because the problems of lice were so bad, a Delousing Station had been set up for the troops at Poperinghe. It was an old converted brewery.

The Delousing Station was full of men like me who'd just come back from their week in the trenches, all covered with mud. I followed their example. I stripped off and tied my uniform and my underwear into a bundle, and then tied my hat and boots to it.

My clothes were put into a fumigator along with everyone else's. Then I followed the others, all naked and with their skin covered in blotches and bites from the lice, into the delousing area.

The three large vats that they once used to brew beer in were full of water. The water in the first one was hot and soapy, but very, very dirty. It looked more like soup. Along with a bunch of other men I stepped in and jumped up and down a bit, letting the hot water get into my skin.

"Come on, no hanging about," complained a voice behind me.

"There's others waiting."

I took the hint. I grabbed hold of the rope that was hung across the vats and pulled myself along to the other side. Then I climbed out and got into the next vat. The water was hot and not quite so dirty. After that it was into the third vat – and the shock of freezing cold water.

I got out quickly and towelled myself as dry as I could, and collected my clothes, which now stank of smoke and disinfectant.

Once I was cleaned up, I went off to our billet and collected Charlie and the others, and we set off for Poperinghe, and the place where I'd been told all the soldiers went for relaxation, Marguerite's café.

The place looked tiny from the outside, but inside it seemed to go on for ever. And it was packed with blokes in khaki. The air was thick with smoke from cigarettes. And the noise! Soldiers singing and laughing. Looking at this lot it was hard to think there was a war on. It was very different to the pubs back home in Carlisle. They were places for serious drinking of beer. This place was more like a cafeteria or a club.

Ginger, Wally, Danny and Alf hurried straight in, heading for the bar, while Charlie and I stood just inside the entrance looking for a table, when I heard a familiar voice call out, "Billy! Over here!" I turned, and there was Rob! He was sitting at a table in one corner of the café where Jed Lowe and a couple of other blokes from the Lonsdales were sitting.

I waved at him, and Charlie and me began to battle our way through the crowd to the table. Rob had managed to grab a couple of empty chairs.

I made the introductions, and Charlie and Rob and the others shook hands.

"This is amazing, Rob!" I said. "I was thinking about you, wondering how you were!"

"As you can see, still alive," grinned Rob.

"How long have you been out here?" I asked.

"About four weeks," replied Rob. "We're going back to the Front tomorrow." He looked around at the smoky, noisy café and said, "You'll like this place, Billy. They do really great chips. Not as good as back home in Carlisle, but still very good. That is, if you can catch the waiter's eye."

He poured Charlie and me a glass of white wine.

"Here you are, try some of this," said Rob.

"No beer?" asked Charlie.

"Yeah, but this stuff's cheaper," said Rob. "*Vin rouge* or *vin blanc*. Red or white. Take your choice." He grinned. "Listen to me. Only been here four weeks and I'm talking French like a native."

For the rest of the evening, against the noise of soldiers at other tables around us playing cards, or dominoes, and a local man playing popular songs on his old accordion, Rob and I caught up.

I wanted to know what it was like in the Infantry, but Rob said he'd prefer to leave the trenches back at the Front where they belonged and concentrate on what I'd been up to.

Of course, my experiences had been much the same as his, but without a rifle and going into attack. We'd both spent most of the time up to our knees in muddy water.

I did learn that there didn't seem to be much of an advance going on, either by our side or by the Germans.

"A stalemate, that's what it is," said Rob, sipping at his wine. "Our lot lob bombs at them. Their lot lob bombs at us. Then sometimes we go over the top and charge at them, and then we come back again. And sometimes they charge at us, and then they go back again. Or, at least, the lucky ones do." And his face darkened as the memories of the battlefield came back to him. "Lots never make it back. Their bodies just lie there, in the middle of No Man's Land. Too many of them to go out and bring back. And if you tried you'd only end up there yourself." Then he smiled again and the shadow on his brow vanished. "Still, forget that. Let's get back to you. What's it like being in the Royal Engineers?"

And so I told him of my training, and the classes I'd had to go to back in England. Yet here I was, still digging trenches.

"Think yourself lucky you are," grinned Rob. "You wouldn't like it in the Infantry. Apart from the fact the Hun keep shooting at us every time we pop our heads over the top of the trench, our Sergeant Major is worse than old Mr Dickens back at school. Shouts and hollers like he's angrier with us than he is with the Germans!"

And so the night went on, until finally the man playing the accordion stopped and a woman shouted out, "*Allez! Allez!*", which I was told meant "Time to go home".

And so we went back to barracks. "I'll see you, old pal," said Rob when we got back to camp, and Charlie and I were heading off for our billets.

I shook his hand. "Take care of yourself, Rob," I said. "And we'll keep in touch whenever we can."

"With lots more nights like tonight at Marguerite's," grinned Rob.

June 1917

All too soon our leave was over, and we were back in the trenches. Just after midnight on 6 June we were all summoned to assemble for a briefing.

"A briefing at midnight!" snorted Charlie. "Why couldn't they tell us what they've got to tell us at a reasonable hour, instead of us having to scramble about in the mud in the dark?"

"Got to be some sort of top secret," suggested Wally. "They don't want the Germans to see us all standing in line in the trenches and giving the game away that something's up."

We filed out of our cave and lined up with the rest of the men in our reserve trench, where our Commanding Officer, Lieutenant Jackson, addressed us. I felt we were lucky because Lieutenant Jackson was all right. He wasn't friendly with us and he kept his distance, which suited us fine, but he wasn't like some of the officers I'd seen. They treated the soldiers under them like they were schoolkids, or like they were prisoners who were under constant punishment.

"Men," he said, "a major offensive is about to be launched on the Messines Ridge at just after 0300 hours. Although the ridge is some distance away from us, we will all be affected, because just before the offensive a series of explosions will be set off beneath the German lines. You will all feel the shock waves and they will be larger than you are used to. They will be nothing to worry about. However, we have been instructed that it will be considered safest if, when the explosives are detonated, all men are in full view in the trench and not in a dugout. Dismissed, and carry on about your duties."

Me, Charlie, Wally, Danny, Ginger and Alf scrambled back inside our cave where we were fixing cable lengths together.

"The Messines Ridge is miles away to the south," commented Danny. "I can't see why we have to stand out in the trench just because they're letting off a few explosions. It won't affect us."

As most of the others nodded, I noticed that Alf was looking thoughtful.

"What's the matter, Alf?" I asked. "You look worried."

"No, I was just thinking," said Alf. "I don't think this is going to be just any old explosion. It's going to be a big one."

The tone of his voice made us all look at him, surprised. Alf wasn't one for making up stories. As a rule he didn't say a lot.

"What makes you say that?" asked Danny.

Alf hesitated, and I threw in, "Come on, Alf, you've said enough to whet our appetites. We're your mates. If something big's going to be happening in less than three hours and it affects us, and you know about it, you ought to tell us."

Ginger, Wally, Charlie and Danny all nodded in agreement.

"OK," said Alf. "But first, go out and check that there's no one outside listening. I don't want to get arrested for betraying official secrets."

"It's not an official secret any more," I pointed out. "Lieutenant Jackson's just told us all it's all going to happen at 0300 hours. So what's the secrecy for?"

Alf wasn't convinced. He had to go to the entrance of our cave and look up and down the trench to make sure there was no one outside listening, before he came back and started to tell us what he knew.

"Just before I left home to go training I met up with my Uncle Harry. He was a coalminer back home and one night he was telling us about a job he and loads of his miner mates had been sent on, but because it was all Top Secret he wasn't supposed to tell anyone."

"So why did he tell you?" I asked, puzzled.

Alf gave a rueful sigh. "Because Uncle Harry can't keep a secret," he said. "He talks all the time. Drives my Aunt Ethel mad."

"Forget about your Aunt Ethel, get back to what he told you," said Charlie impatiently.

"Right," said Alf. "Well, according to Uncle Harry the army were digging tunnels under this place in Belgium called Messines Ridge. They needed coalminers instead of just ordinary soldiers. From Wales, Yorkshire, Nottinghamshire. And not just coalminers. They also brought over all these cockneys from London, the ones who'd built the London underground, because they were also used to digging tunnels in clay."

I looked around at the dripping wet walls of our cave and shivered at the thought of digging deep underground in this muck.

"I wouldn't fancy doing that job," I said.

"You might when you hear what Uncle Harry told us they were being paid. Six shillings a day."

"Six shillings!" said Charlie, outraged, so loudly that we had to tell him to shut up. I must admit I felt a bit annoyed when I heard that as well. After all, we were only paid one shilling a day.

"And how many of these tunnels are there?" I asked.

"Twenty, so Uncle Harry said. And each one packed with high explosives."

"That's a lot of explosives," I commented.

"A million tons, Uncle Harry reckoned."

We exchanged horrified looks. One million tons of explosives packed into twenty tunnels under the German lines.

"No," said Charlie, shaking his head. "I don't believe it. They couldn't do that much tunnelling without the Germans finding out. They'd hear the work going on. The drilling machines, for one thing."

"No," Alf shook his head. "Uncle Harry said they couldn't use drilling machines in case the Germans heard the sound of the machinery, so they tunnelled using just picks and shovels. The only machines they had were pumps to pump the water out, otherwise they would have drowned."

"If what your Uncle Harry says is true, I'm not sure I want to be in a trench when it all goes up," said Danny. "I think I'd rather be on the top. At least the walls won't be able to fall in on me."

At 0300 hours me, Charlie, Ginger, Wally, Danny and Alf lined up in the trench with the rest of our unit and waited, all looking south towards

Messines Ridge. Not that we could see anything because the top of the trench was another foot above our heads, and none of us fancied poking our heads over the top to see what was happening. Knowing what I knew made me feel a knot tighten in my stomach.

The minutes ticked by. 0301. 0302. 0303. And nothing happened. 0304. 0305. Still nothing.

"I bet they've forgotten to connect the detonators," muttered Charlie, and we all laughed.

0309, and still nothing.

And then, at exactly 0310, the whole world heaved upwards, lifting us with it. In a split second it settled down again, but continued to shake. I felt as if I was on a boat that had just hit a big wave. Danny had actually fallen over from the shock of the blast and was picking himself up out of the mud. The shock was so huge I bet they even felt it as far away as London.

Even though it was the middle of the night we could see as clearly as if it was broad daylight. The whole sky just lit up, a huge mass of flames reaching upwards. For a minute we all just stood there, looking at one another. My body was still shaking.

"Good old Uncle Harry," muttered Charlie.

And then, seconds later, our big guns opened up. The barrage was deafening even from this many miles away. About five minutes after the big guns had stopped, there came the sounds of distant whistles. In the trenches at the Front, our Infantry were going over the top.

The attack that followed carried on for three days, driving for about a mile through the lines of shattered Germans, until our boys came up against stronger Hun defences, which stopped them, making them dig in.

We found out afterwards that in the attack over 5,000 Germans were taken prisoner. Most of them had been so stunned by the explosion they didn't know what day it was, or where they were. It was like killing fish by dropping dynamite into a pool.

But the Huns started to fight back. Bombardment after bombardment came over at us from the German lines. Shells rained down on our trenches. Our workload increased as they scored hits on our communication cables.

After one raid, Charlie and I were sent out to repair yet another broken telegraph cable in yet another water-filled trench, this one even closer to the German lines. One look at the cable told us it was smashed beyond repair. It would have to be replaced.

We rolled the huge reel of replacement cable along the trench as best we could in the mud, then we set about hauling out a length. The only way to stop it from sinking in the mud and disappearing before we'd made the connections was to push the blades of our spades into the clay walls of the trench sides, and then drape the cable over them.

I was pulling at the cable when, suddenly, out of nowhere, something hit the wall of the trench just above us, landing with a sort of plop.

There was another plop, and this time I saw something falling into the mud just near us. For a second I thought it was a grenade and I threw myself backwards, expecting it to go off. Then Charlie started coughing and retching, and I saw him scramble to pull his respirator over his face. In that second I realized what it was and I felt sick to my stomach.

Mustard gas!

A feeling of panic hit me and I scrambled to get my respirator over my face before the killer gas got into my mouth and nose and burnt my lungs. It burned everything it touched. Eyes. Skin. And it always found a way in. Like now, I could feel where it had crept up inside the sleeves of my uniform and the skin on my arms felt like it was on fire. I threw myself into a muddy hole, pushing my arms under water, but I knew it was already too late.

My neck was burning too. My collar must have come undone while I was hauling the cables. It only needed one little opening for the gas to get in, and now I could feel it spreading down the skin on to my chest. Frantically, I pushed myself right up to my goggles in the muddy water, anything to stop the burning, but the water blocked the ventilator outlet for my respirator. My goggles started to mist up and I could feel myself choking.

I stumbled to my feet, saturated, with the weight of wet mud clinging to me. I couldn't move. I couldn't see. I couldn't feel anything except my skin burning. I screamed for help but was stunned by a searing pain in my head. It was as if someone had taken an axe to it and cut it in two.

I woke up to the sound of screaming. There was a smell of blood and rotting flesh mixed with the strong smell of disinfectant.

As the screaming died down I became aware of the sounds of tin plates being clattered together, and the whispering of voices.

I struggled to open my eyes. My eyelids felt heavy. At first everything looked a bit hazy, but after I blinked a few times my vision started to clear.

I was in a Casualty Station. All around me were men laid out on beds.

I tried to sit up, but the pain in my head made me lay down again. I let out a groan as I fell back on my pillow, which brought a medical orderly over to the side of my bed.

"Awake, are you?" he said cheerfully. "You were lucky."

"What happened?" I asked. My voice felt hoarse, my throat dry.

"A piece of shrapnel caught you," said the orderly. "If you hadn't had your helmet on it might've taken the top of your head clean off. I've seen it happen. Sliced open like a melon."

I looked down at my body and was surprised to see that both my arms were bandaged from fingertip to just above the elbow.

"My arms?" I asked, my voice still a rasp.

"Hang on, I'll give you some water," said the orderly.

He helped me to sit up in the bed and put a tin mug to my lips.

"Here you are," he said. "Get a sip of this."

I sipped at the water. It felt strange. My tongue and lips and the inside of my mouth seemed to have swollen to twice their normal size.

"There," he said, taking the mug away.

"My arms," I said again. "What happened to my arms?"

"Burns from the mustard gas," replied the orderly. "Like I say, you were very lucky on so many counts. Lucky you were wearing your helmet. Lucky you were wearing your respirator. Lucky you didn't go right under in the mud. Lucky the stretcher party found you. All in all, you are a very lucky young man."

I looked around the Casualty Station at the patients in the beds near me. Many of the men were heavily wrapped up like Egyptian mummies, their bandages soaked in blood.

"Johnson!" barked a man standing by one of the other beds, bandaging a soldier. "I need you here!"

"Coming, sir!" said the orderly, and he trotted off.

It was in my third day in bed in the Casualty Station when a familiar figure walked in, a smile on his face.

"Hello, Billy! Having a nice rest?" It was Charlie.

"Thank heavens you're OK," I said. "I asked the orderly what had happened to you, but no one seemed to know."

"I fell in a hole," said Charlie. "Lucky for me it seemed to keep most of the gas off me. Looks like you caught most of it. And the shrapnel. How's the head?"

"Hurts now and then," I said. "But lucky for me I've still got a head. Where have you been? Another Casualty Station?"

"No. Still in the trenches at the Front," said Charlie. "I thought, after you copped it, they might let me take a bit of time off, but no. 'The cables won't lay themselves,' they told me. That's why I haven't been able to get in to see you before."

Charlie settled himself down on the rickety chair beside my bed and proceeded to fill me in on what had happened to our unit during the German attack. Apparently I'd come off the worst. Of the other blokes from our unit who'd been working near us, Ginger had been half-drowned in a mud-slide, but nothing too bad. Wally and Danny had got away with just a few scratches and burns from hot shrapnel. They'd all managed to escape from serious gassing.

"Though the Infantry further along the trench weren't so lucky," said Charlie. "That's where most of the gas bombs fell and a lot of them hadn't got their gas mask packed so they could get at it easily. Seems they preferred to keep their rifles and grenades nearer to hand. Some of them got tangled up in all the stuff they were carrying as the gas came down and they couldn't see to find their gas masks. Hundreds of them got caught in it."

"Many dead?" I asked.

Charlie nodded. "Most of 'em. Those that aren't are blind. We were lucky."

"Any news of my mate Rob?" I asked.

Charlie shook his head. "No," he said. "Just that he wasn't one of the casualties. I checked the list they posted just before I came to see you. I thought you'd be worried about him."

"Thanks," I said.

Charlie stayed a bit longer, chatting and telling stories about the other men in our unit, until an orderly came over and told him it was time to go.

"Your talking is disturbing the other patients," the orderly snapped. "This is a Casualty Station, not a café."

Charlie shrugged, gave me a wink, and said: "OK, Billy, looks like I've got my marching orders. I'll see you in a couple of days back in the mud, when they kick you out of here."

I gave him a smile, and after he'd gone I thought about what Charlie had said. A couple more days here in the hospital and I'd be going back to the Front. Back to the mud and the bullets and the barbed wire and the gas, and I knew I didn't want to go back. I wanted to be back at home, back in Carlisle. Back to safety and my job at the railway station and my mum's cooking. But I knew I couldn't. None of us could. We were going to be here until this war was over. Or until we were killed.

As it turned out, Charlie was wrong about me going straight back to the Front. The doctor who examined me the next day told me: "Right, Stevens, we're discharging you. We need your bed. There are injured men waiting to be treated."

"Right, sir," I said.

I indicated the bandages that covered my arms. "Can I have your permission to get something from the stores that will keep these bandages covered in the trenches, though, sir? Otherwise they'll just fall off on the first day, with all the wet and the mud and everything."

"You're not going straight back to the trenches, not with those burns," said the doctor.

I looked at him, puzzled. If I wasn't being sent back to the trenches, then where was I going? Not back home, surely? Men with worse injuries than mine were still fighting out here.

The doctor saw the look on my face, so he explained: "I've arranged for you to go to Base HQ. You can carry on your work as a telegraph operator there. You'll be out of the mud for a while, at least until your skin heals. But don't worry. A week or two and you'll be all right to go back and join your pals."

JULY 1917

Base HQ was in an old town hall in St Omer. It reminded me of some of the town halls back in England, or the big old libraries. It was an enormous building, made of blocks of stone, and inside it was absolutely spick-and-span clean. You could have eaten your dinner off the floor of the entrance lobby. It was such an amazing contrast after the dirt and mess of life in the trenches, or even back at camp in Poperinghe.

The big entrance lobby had a marble floor that made an echoing sound when I walked in and the soles of my boots hit the marble. It made me feel like I ought to tiptoe and whisper, just like I used to when I was in the Town Hall back home in Carlisle.

I went to the desk and gave my name and the piece of paper they'd given me at the Casualty Station, and was sent immediately to see the man who'd be my officer while I was here, Sergeant MacWilliams. The Sergeant told me that I was to replace the regular telegraph operator who had been sent back home on leave. Then he told me how I was to act while I was here.

"Here, Stevens, you are like the three wise monkeys. You see nothing, you hear nothing, and you say nothing. Is that clear?"

"Yes, Sarge," I said.

"Good. Because if word gets back to me – and it will, believe me – that you've said one word of what goes on in this place, or repeated what's been said to anybody, I'll make sure you're shot for treason. Is that clear?"

He then called for another private to show me where I would be based.

I couldn't believe the luxury of it! All right, it was in a wooden hut that had been set up in the grounds at the back of the building, but I had a real bunk, with real sheets and pillows.

After weeks of sleeping on a rickety cot, or trying to sleep in a mud-hole in the trenches, this was like being in heaven. That night I had the best night's sleep I'd had in ages.

And then there was the food at Base HQ. Hot dinners. Real meat and potatoes with gravy. Back at the Front we never saw a hot meal from one day till the next, not unless we could cook it ourselves over the flame of a kerosene lamp. And finding something edible to cook in the trenches was hard. Because of the rats everything had to be kept in tins. So we had tins of meat, usually bully beef, which was just stewed beef pressed into tins. Then there were tins of vegetable stew that tasted like nothing I'd ever had at home. And hard biscuits that were more like dog biscuits.

So I was shocked when I heard some of the officers at Base HQ complaining because they couldn't get the food they liked. "No grouse. No venison," complained one. "How can a man live?"

I just kept my head down and my mouth shut and wondered what they'd say if they had to live on bully beef and dog biscuits like most of us in the trenches.

Next day I started work, operating the telegraph keys, receiving and transmitting messages using Morse code. My key for sending messages was like a small metal knob balanced on a spring on a piece of flat board. This was connected to an electric cable. When I pressed this key down, it completed the electric circuit. I could send messages to another telegraph operator by tapping this key, quickly for a "dot", a bit longer for a "dash". Different combinations of dots and dashes represented different words.

I received messages using a sounder key, which was a small brass arm on a pivot. When it was pressed down, it also completed an electric circuit, and I could receive messages, printed out on long strips of paper.

Because it took so long for a message to come through this way, they tended to be short, using as few words as possible. It also took a good memory to know what each of the symbols stood for, without having to keep looking them up. Being the one who could translate the coded messages meant that I saw all the information that came in and went out, and I quickly realized what the Sergeant had meant about seeing nothing and hearing nothing, and keeping my mouth shut.

And it wasn't just the messages. All the Top Brass came through this building, and once they were inside the building they all talked about the War and how it was going, and what the plans were. It was as if we lower ranks were deaf and couldn't hear them, or couldn't understand what they were talking about. Or maybe they just didn't notice us. I'd noticed that about some rich people, they talk about all sorts of private things when the servants are around, things they'd never talk about in front of other people of their same class. I suppose servants are sort of invisible to them; they're people who don't count so they don't notice them.

With all these field marshals and brigadiers and generals around, and messages going backwards and forwards on the telegraph, I learnt more about the War than I'd have ever found out if I'd asked one of the officers from my own unit. I expect that if I had asked questions about what the plans were, and how the War was really going, I'd have been court-martialled as a spy. But officers talked about these things in the same room as me, or gave me messages to send, or receive, with all this important information.

One thing that really seemed to have the Top Brass worried was what was happening in Russia. Earlier in the year there'd been a revolution there and a new People's Government had taken over the country. The ordinary people of Russia were fed up with the way they were treated by the rich people.

The Top Brass were worried that Russia might pull out of the War. If this happened, the Germans would be able to release their troops from the Russian Front and send them to back up their troops here in Flanders.

But they were more worried that the ordinary people in Britain, especially us troops, might hear about the revolution and decide to start one of our own. In our trenches and at camp we'd heard rumours that there had already been mutinies among the French soldiers over bad food, terrible living conditions and no leave. I reckoned that the Top Brass were right to be worried.

I thought about what life was like for me and Charlie and the others in the trenches. And about Rob and Jed Lowe and all the other fighting units going over the top and being cut down, and I couldn't help but feel that Base HQ and the way the generals lived was a long way from what the War was really like. The dirt and the bullets and the blood and the mud. But I didn't say it out loud.

I also found out that not all the Top Brass agreed with the way the War was being fought. A lot of the generals wanted a quick end to the War and I heard one say to another that the Commander-in-chief ought to go for one all-out attack and finish the Germans off and get it over and done with. Messages came through from London, from the Secretary to the Prime Minister, saying much the same thing. But then I overheard General Plumer, who was the Commander's right-hand man, say to one of his major generals that the Commander's view was "to wear down the Hun bit by bit, like a dripping tap". He added: "It's not worth throwing our weight against the Hun while he's still strong. We've got to weaken him first before we strike with everything we've got."

When I heard this I thought, "That's all very well, but back in the trenches we're throwing everything we've got at the Germans already and they seem to be as strong as ever." But I didn't say it out loud, I kept my mouth shut.

I'd been at Base HQ for about four days when the Commander-in-chief himself, Field Marshal Sir Douglas Haig, arrived. He'd been on a tour of his commanders at their different positions at the Front to see how the War was going. He came into the Communications Room with General Plumer and immediately Sergeant MacWilliams leapt out of his chair and snapped stiffly to attention, banging the heels of his boots smartly together, saluting as he did so. I followed his lead and leapt to my feet, snatching off my earphones.

I was amazed to find that Haig was much smaller than I'd thought he'd be. I don't know why I expected him to be tall, but I did. His hair was white, and he had a big moustache. He carried himself absolutely stiff and straight.

"Stand easy, Sergeant," said Plumer.

Sergeant MacWilliams and I stood easy, and the Sergeant gave me a hard look which meant "Get back to work", so I sat down, put my earphones back on and turned back to my telegraph key.

"Any messages, Sergeant?" asked Plumer.

"All today's messages have gone to Brigadier General Davidson, sir!" bellowed the Sergeant.

That was one of the odd things about sergeants, they seemed to shout all the time, even when they were talking to someone just a few feet away.

Haig and Plumer nodded, then turned and walked out of the room. In the whole time Haig hadn't said one word.

Sergeant MacWilliams turned to me and said: "You are a very privileged man, Stevens. You have just seen one of the greatest men in the world. If we had more men like Field Marshal Haig this war would be over by Christmas."

The day after Field Marshal Haig arrived a new phrase started to crop up in messages that I sent and received. "Big Push". At first I hadn't got the faintest idea what this meant, and I'd learnt that it didn't do to ask questions. Over the next couple of days, though, I kept my eyes and ears open trying to find out more about it. I soon learnt from the mutterings that went on between generals and brigadiers and other officers, that this Big Push was going to be a major offensive. No one said when it was going to be, or where it was going to be, but a decision had definitely been taken to launch a massive all-out assault.

I was surprised, especially after what I'd heard General Plumer say about "the dripping tap" and that Haig didn't believe in launching a major offensive until the Germans were already weakened. From the telegraph messages that I was taking the Germans seemed as strong as ever. It occurred to me that maybe the Commander wasn't the one taking the big decisions. But then, if Field Marshal Haig wasn't, who *was* taking the decisions? Was it the politicians back in London? I'd heard rumours that there had been a lot of arguments between Haig and the Prime Minister, David Lloyd George, about how this war was being run. A couple of days later I heard solid proof.

I was in the Communications Room, taking down messages that were coming in from stations at the Front, when I heard Field Marshal Haig and General Plumer talking together in the corridor just outside my door. They were talking about the Americans coming into the

War. So far, although the Canadians and the New Zealanders and the Australians had come into the War on our side, the Americans had kept out of it and stayed neutral. Charlie and some of the others said this was because there were so many Germans living in America that the Yanks wouldn't know which side to fight on if they came in.

"The first contingent of Americans have arrived in France," I heard Plumer's voice say.

"How many?" came Haig's question.

"Just a few hundred," said Plumer.

"A few hundred!" exploded Haig. "What does President Wilson think this is? A tea party that's got out of control?"

"The Americans say it's just a token force," said Plumer. "They say most of their men are in training and they'll be over here by Christmas."

"Before Christmas!" snapped Haig. "We need them now, not by Christmas! It's bad enough that Lloyd George has taken our planes just to make sure he gets votes! Now he won't ask Wilson to bring his men in earlier! Sometimes I don't think that fool Lloyd George wants us to win this war!"

Then I heard the heels of their boots ringing as they both marched off along the corridor.

The business of the planes I'd only found out about since I'd been at Base HQ. It seems that the Germans had sent over planes and carried out air raids on Britain. The month before, in June, a bomber had scored a direct hit on an infants' school and killed all the little kids. The public back home had been up in arms, demanding to know what the

Government was doing to protect it from more German air raids. As a result, the War Cabinet had ordered two squadrons of the Royal Flying Corps to be sent back to England to defend it against German bombers. This meant that the numbers of British planes here in Flanders had been cut and all the generals had been livid.

"We're losing thousands of men a day over here!" I'd heard one general rage to another. "They lose a few kids and we have to send our flying boys back to protect them. Next thing they'll demand our army goes back to protect them as well!"

Personally, I was glad I was just an ordinary soldier and didn't have to make decisions about where to send the planes or the troops. It seemed to me that whatever the Top Brass did was wrong. If they refused to send planes back to defend England and bombing raids killed more kids, then they'd be in the wrong. But if they sent the planes back to England and our troops were killed because they didn't have protection, they'd be wrong again.

AUGUST 1917

At the end of three weeks, the bloke I had been filling in for at Base HQ returned from leave. By this time, by keeping my skin dry, my burns had healed enough for me to be classed as fit to return to active service. I still had scars on my arms where the skin had been burnt, but many men had worse souvenirs of this war.

I had mixed feelings about going back to the Front. On the down side, after the safety and luxury of life at Base HQ, including a real bed and proper hot food, I was going back to an uncomfortable cot in a tent on a muddy field. Then back into the real mud of the trenches. But I was really looking forward to getting back together with Charlie and the others. Always having to be on my guard about what I might say while I was at HQ, which mainly meant saying nothing at all, had been wearing me down. I never felt relaxed the whole time I was there. It sounds ridiculous that I could feel more relaxed back at the Front, with bombs falling and the Hun firing at us, and the mud and the mess, but I did. And that was because I didn't feel relaxed surrounded by generals and brigadiers, but I did when I was with my own mates.

I managed to squeeze on to one of the transit buses taking the new influx of troops to Poperinghe, and got back to camp by late afternoon.

Charlie was in our tent playing cards with Ginger and Wally as I came in. They all let out a cheer as I walked in.

"Here comes the General!" chuckled Charlie. "Fresh from HQ. Give us a word, General. What are your orders for us ordinary soldiers!"

"You can poke your head in a mud-hole!" I responded with a grin.

The others laughed, and then all started asking questions at once, eager to find out what life was like at Base HQ. Did the generals really eat their food off silver plates? Did they have servants? Was it true they could actually telephone their families back home whenever they wanted? And could they go off on leave every few weeks?

"Later, later!" I protested. "Don't forget, I'm a man who's suffered. I've been forced to eat hot food and lay in a bed with a comfortable pillow and clean cotton sheets. And I've had to have hot baths and wear clean clothes."

Ginger laughed and picked up his pillow, a wet mass of straw, and threw it at me.

I looked round the tent. "Where are Danny and Alf?" I asked. "On leave?"

A silence fell, and then Ginger said awkwardly, "They were both killed."

"How?" I asked weakly.

"Blown to smithereens," said Ginger soberly. "Shrapnel killed Alf. No one knew where Danny was at first, there was so little left of him. He must've taken the whole force of the blast. The people who were first on the scene thought he might have been buried under the mud. Then they found bits all over the place. One of them was Danny's hand. They only knew it was his because of his ring."

I sat there stunned. Alf and Danny killed. One minute alive, the next second … dead.

We'd all seen men killed and all felt bad for them, but when it happened to someone I'd spent time with, worked with, had fun with, it hit me hard.

As well as Danny and Alf, I discovered that another six of the original dozen Engineers had been killed in the last few weeks. Me, Charlie, Ginger and Wally were the only ones left.

"They're bringing out new boys to replace them," said Wally. "They should be here the day after tomorrow. Till then, it's up to us to keep the communications of this war up and running."

I'd been so looking forward to getting back together with my old mates, and now I found two of my closest pals had been killed. I couldn't help but think about Rob. Was he still alive?

The next day me, Charlie, Wally and Ginger returned to the trenches. Because our battalion had been so reduced in numbers we were attached to another unit of Royal Engineers. Two new lads were put with us to make up our unit of six: Terry Crow and Peter Parks. They were both from London, both in their early twenties, fresh out from training. Like all of us, they were trained-up telegraph operators.

In the trenches there was definitely a feeling that something big was about to happen. We could all tell that something was up. For one thing, there seemed to be more soldiers than before. Also, more trenches seemed to have sprung up in the time I'd been away, and they had been dug much nearer to the German lines. All those messages I'd taken and sent while I was at Base HQ, and all those conversations I'd overhead about the "Big Push", started to fall into place. Our Top Brass needed to get on and do something big to win this war, and soon.

Each time Charlie and I went out to repair cables or lay new ones, we were being sent further and further into No Man's Land, the patch of open ground between our front line and the German front line. We were putting more and more cables and telegraph points in the forward trenches, and more and more troops were being moved into them. Seven days passed, then two weeks, and we were still in the trenches, still working.

Then it started to rain. We'd been living with a steady drizzle for some time now, but this was different. This was heavy rain which made the mud we were in even more of a quagmire. Walking through it was like trying to walk through thick glue.

All the time the Germans were pounding at our trenches with their heavy artillery, as if they also knew that something big was about to take place and were doing their best to stop it happening.

At night the Germans sent up flares to light up No Man's Land so they could show up any surprise attack that might be launched. Charlie and I and the other Engineers sat in our dugout in the reserve trench and watched the night sky light up as each new flare went up from the German lines.

And all the time it kept on raining.

September 1917

One afternoon, just after the middle of September, even more troops filed along the reserve trench, heading for the Front. Charlie and I were in the trench at the time, trying to dig a reel of cable out of a shell-hole. As they passed I recognized one of them. It was my old friend, Jed Lowe from the Lonsdales.

I hailed him, and then looked further along the line of men, and sure enough I picked out the figure of Rob.

"Rob!" I called. He saw me, and stopped and shook my hand.

"Billy," he said. But this time I noticed there was no twinkle in his eyes, no smile on his face. His eyes looked deeper set in his face. He looked so much older than when I had last seen him, even though it had only been two months before.

I jerked my head towards the German lines.

"Looks like this could be it, at last," I said. "The final push."

"I hope so," he said. "Unless the rain stops it."

"Rain stops play," I said, and he almost smiled.

I looked along the line at the soldiers with Rob, and noticed that on many of them their badges and flashes were all different.

"The Lonsdales changed their badges?" I asked, trying to keep the conversation positive.

Rob grinned wryly. "Not many of us Lonsdales left now, Billy," he said. "I reckon just me and Jed Lowe and half a dozen others are all that's left. We're a combined battalion now. A mixture of us, added with some of the survivors from the Sussex, Middlesex and Hereford Regiments. We call ourselves the Allsorts."

"And how are things in the new unit?" I asked.

Rob shot a quick glance ahead, and then said quietly but angrily: "The men are great, but the new officers who've been sent out are awful. We're told what to do by idiots who don't know the first thing about it. They come out here as officers just because their dad owns a factory or something, and they haven't got a clue about how to mount an attack. We've lost more men because of the stupidity of some of our junior officers than because of German bullets."

"No talking along there!" barked a voice from ahead.

I looked towards the voice and saw a young man who could only have been about twenty himself with a small moustache doing its best to sprout from under his nose.

"Come on, men!" he snapped.

Rob rolled his eyes to show what he thought of his new officer. Then he and the bedraggled troops, with what few remained of the Lonsdale Battalion, trudged forward splish-splashing through the mud. As I watched him go my heart felt heavy. The Rob Matthews who was walking away from me wasn't the Rob I'd known all my life, a happy, positive, optimistic boy. Instead he was an angry and disillusioned young man.

That night, me, Charlie, Wally, Ginger, Terry and Peter tried to get some shut-eye in our dugout cave in our reserve trench. As always, we took turns to keep watch, just in case something happened that meant we had to swing into action. Usually we drew straws to see who took first watch, the one who drew the shortest straw taking it, but this time I volunteered. I didn't think I'd be able to sleep, anyway, my mind was full of what was about to happen. The Big Push that was coming. I thought of Rob and Jed and the remaining Lonsdales, waiting in the front-line trenches for the order to go over the top. They'd be getting their rum ration about now. The men in the front lines, the fighting units, were given a tot of rum each to "warm them up" just before the whistles went and they scaled the ladders and then ran forward to attack the enemy.

At 0200 I woke Wally and he took over on watch, and I crawled on to my bed and tried to get some sleep. I really didn't think I'd be able to sleep with all the thoughts that were in my head, but I suppose the tiredness got to me, because the next thing I remember was Charlie shaking me. It was 0430 hours.

"Time to get up," he said. "They're getting ready."

I scrambled out of our dugout and into the reserve trench. In the darkness I could hear the sounds of activity from the forward trenches: scaling ladders being put into place against the walls; the clicking of rifles being made ready.

"Not long now," said Ginger.

At 0540 our big guns opened up. The ground around us shook and I thought the trench might come down on top of us, despite all the timber holding it up. Even from our trench we saw that over the German lines the sky seemed to be on fire as shell after shell landed on the German positions and blew up.

As well as the heavy guns lobbing shells at the German lines, there was the chatter chatter chatter of our machine-guns opening up, pouring a stream of deadly lead towards the German Front. Then suddenly the machine-guns went quiet and there were the sounds of whistles from ahead of us, and the roar of men's voices as the Infantry went over the top of the trenches and hurled themselves at the German lines. As I huddled in the dugout I thought of Rob and Jed and the rest of the remaining Lonsdales out there in the mud and the infernal noise of No Man's Land, with the Germans firing at them.

The sounds of battle went on for what seemed like hours. Only at daybreak did the noise begin to die down. We waited in the dugout until noon, wondering what had happened. Had the attack succeeded? Were the Germans in retreat? Then Lieutenant Jackson appeared in the opening of the dugout.

"Right, men," he announced. "The attack has moved our position forward. This is where we come in. We have to run cables into what were the German bunkers so that we can keep our forward communication lines open, and we have to do it today, not tomorrow."

Charlie and I exchanged grins at this "we", which meant us poor ordinary soldiers. I'd never seen Lieutenant Jackson even hold a pick or a shovel except to hand it to one of us.

That afternoon we moved forward, laden down with rolls of cable and our picks and shovels. And, of course, our gas masks, just in case the Germans should launch a gas attack.

By mid-afternoon we were in what had been the German front-line trenches, running cables and setting up communication posts so that the officers at the Front could keep in touch with Base HQ. All along the trenches were dead German soldiers. Many of them were buried in mud-slides, with just their legs sticking out, or a hand, but now and then I came upon an upturned face. It was an appalling sight. The trouble was, after this time out in the trenches, I was getting hardened to it. That's one thing about war: the first time you see a dead body you shiver and shudder and you feel a bit sick. It's a shock. You can see yourself in that dead body. That's how I might look, you think to yourself. The next time it's still a shock, but not so much of one. Then after that, it's just another dead body, and the more you see, the less they affect you.

What struck me about these dead Germans, though, was how young so many of them looked. So many of them were just boys of about fourteen or fifteen, some even younger. Then it struck me that me and so many of the others on our side only *felt* old. I was just seventeen. So was Rob. Some of our soldiers were only fourteen or fifteen. We were still just boys.

We chose to set up the forward communication posts in what had been German dugouts. It seemed like a good idea because it saved making new ones. What surprised me was how well the German dugouts had been made. Unlike ours, which were just holes shored up with timber, the German dugouts were proper pillboxes, hidey-holes set in the ground made of concrete, with thick walls facing towards the Allied front line and on the sides. The back wall, though, was just a thin layer of cement. In the first one we went into we could see where it had fallen down in parts.

"Not very well built at the back," sniffed Terry. "Looks like they needed some good Tommy builders to come in and finish the job properly."

"Don't be an idiot," scoffed Ginger. "That's clever, that is. The back wall's thin because if the Hun had to retreat, like they have done now, then they don't have to use a lot of fire-power to punch a hole in it from their new positions, do they."

Terry looked at the hole and he gave a wry smile of admiration.

"Thinking two steps ahead!" he said. "You've got to hand it to 'em. They're clever beggars, and no mistake."

"Clever they may be, but it's us poor beggars who've got to reinforce that wall now," sighed Ginger. "More work for us!"

We spent the next week working knee-deep in mud, and sometimes waist-deep. As we worked, we heard rifle shooting as the snipers from both sides took pot-shots at each other. Then, without explanation, the Germans suddenly went quiet.

"Looks like we're winning, mates," said Wally, after the week was up. "I reckon the Huns must be building up to surrendering. We'll all be home for Christmas after all."

It was too much to hope for. Early the next morning a barrage of heavy artillery fire rained down on us. Shells going off, mud flying everywhere, the whole of our world going mad.

The Germans were launching their counter-attack.

We knew there was only one thing we could do if we were to have even a remote chance of staying alive. Retreat. The Germans knew precisely where to drop their shells to hit our positions because we were in their very own old trenches. As we struggled to make our way back through the water and mud, carrying as much of our equipment as we could manage, we found ourselves caught up with infantry units doing exactly the same thing.

We dived into dugouts, waiting a few minutes before squelching and sploshing through thick clinging mud to the next one. And all the time the German shells rained down around us. We kept our heads down and hoped the flying shrapnel wouldn't tear us to bits.

By nightfall we'd only managed to withdraw about 500 yards. The six of us had squeezed into yet another dugout and we'd been taking cover there for nearly an hour, with no sign of any let-up in the German bombardment.

"I can't stand this," grunted Ginger. "I'm going out to see if there's any way we can cut through to the reserve trench using some of the bomb-craters."

With that Ginger stepped outside, and promptly sank up to his waist in the mud.

"Just going for a quick swim, mates!" he laughed.

As we all started to laugh along with him there came an earth-shattering explosion from where he had been standing that hurled mud and smoke at us and poured more mud down on us from the ceiling of the dugout.

None of us could see because of the thick oily smoke. By force of habit, almost as soon as I started coughing I grabbed my gas mask and pulled it on over my face. But this was no gas attack. This was just smoke from a shell that had landed directly outside the dugout.

I felt the mud walls and roof of the dugout starting to cave in, and I grabbed Charlie and Wally by their sleeves and hauled them towards the entrance, and we stumbled out into the trench. Peter and Terry followed. We were just in time. Behind us the entrance to the dugout just collapsed, the whole wall of mud dropping down. If we'd still been in there we'd have been dead, buried under tons of mud.

I began to search around for Ginger in the hope that he'd survived the blast, that he might be just lying beneath a thin layer of mud, or under water. But I discovered, with a horror that made me retch, the first pieces of him, lying charred and still smoking in the mud.

Danny, Alf, and now Ginger. All dead. And I'm ashamed to admit that the next thought that struck me was: thank God it wasn't me.

For the next month we didn't leave the trenches. We just stayed there, living on what rations came up to us, and waiting for the orders to go forward and run more cables if our next attack succeeded. But it never did. We didn't move forward. And neither did the Germans. It was stalemate again.

"We're going to just die here like this in the mud," said Charlie one day. "All this time and no one's going anywhere. Not us, nor the Germans. All we do is go backwards and forwards and lose more and more men. I don't know why they don't just call it off."

"Who?" asked Wally.

"The top nobs from both sides," said Charlie. "They might as well play conkers and see who wins for all the point of this."

All the time I wondered how Rob was doing. What was it like for him in the fighting at the Front? Was he even still alive? Finally, in the second week of October, our unit were told that we were being sent back down the line to the Reserve Camp at Poperinghe. After almost eight weeks of nothing but mud and death, we were being relieved.

As soon as we got back to camp I grabbed myself a bath and changed my clothes, and then I set off in search of Rob. I wondered if his unit were back here, or if they were still at the Front.

I hurried towards tents where the Lonsdales and the rest of their makeshift unit were based, and one of the first faces I saw was good old Jed Lowe. My heart gave a leap of joy. If Jed was here then it meant that so was Rob.

"Jed!" I called.

He waved and hurried over towards me.

"Billy!" he said, and his face cracked into a sort of twisted grin. "It's good to see you're still alive."

"They can't keep us Carlisle blokes from popping up," I said, smiling. "Knock us down and we bounce up again." I looked towards the tents. "Where's Rob?" I asked. "Is he around?"

The grin vanished from Jed's face.

"Rob's dead, Billy," said Jed. "They shot him."

Even though the fear that it might happen had been in my thoughts for weeks now, to actually hear it said out loud hit me like a hammer blow. I could feel tears well up in my eyes, but I did my best to blink them away. It wouldn't be good for me to be seen crying, it wasn't manly. But ... Rob. Dead.

"Rotten Germans," I snarled, hoping the tremble in my voice wouldn't show.

Jed shook his head. "It weren't the Germans," he said. "It were our own side. A firing squad. They tied him to a post and shot him."

I stared at Jed, stunned. Rob shot by a firing squad? This I couldn't believe! I must have misheard. It was impossible! But the heavy gloom in Jed's voice told me it wasn't.

"It were a terrible thing," he said. "Terrible. Oughtn't to have been allowed to happen."

"But ... why?" I stammered.

"He wouldn't go," said Jed. "Weren't his fault. He'd been over the top more times than anyone. You know what Rob was like, nothing scared him. Like the rest of us, he'd seen his mates next to him cut in half by shrapnel, or blown to bits, or cut down by the Huns' machine-guns. I guess he just couldn't take it any more. We come to this attack and this junior officer – jumped-up little worm he was – ordered us over the top. Well it was obvious it was suicide. The Germans 'ad cut down the previous waves of men who'd gone over. Just mowed 'em down with their machine-guns like harvesting wheat.

"'I'm not going. Not this time,' said Rob. 'We're all going to get killed and there won't be one dead German at the end of it. It's stupid. I'm not going.' So the junior officer had him placed under arrest.

"They court-martialled him and sentenced him to be shot for desertion. Him and some other young kid, who was only fifteen. The men in the firing squad could hardly bear to look at them." Jed shook his head at the thought. "'T ain't right. They was only kids, really."

I walked around for the next two days in a daze. Rob dead. And shot by a firing squad from our own side! It was sickening. For Rob to be branded a coward and a deserter was unforgivable. He had been the bravest person I'd ever known. To me, the real cowards were the people who hid right back behind the fighting and gave the orders and put the death sentence on blokes like Rob.

Charlie tried to get me to talk about it, but at first I was so full of grief and anger that I didn't even want to think about what had happened to Rob. When I did finally talk to him about it, all my anger spilt out.

"They had no right to shoot him!" I said. "If he thought that the attack was pointless, then it was. Rob was no coward."

"Course he wasn't," said Charlie. "But he was working class, that was his real crime. If he'd been one of the toffs, or even a bit upper class, he'd have just been sent home to convalesce, nice and neat and tidy. If their class gets it it's called shell shock. It's only cowardice if it's our lot."

"I'd watch that talk, Charlie," muttered Wally. "Else they'll be saying you're one of them Bolsheviks like they got in Russia."

"Not me," said Charlie. "If you ask me, the Australians have got the right way of it. You don't see any class in their ranks."

Charlie was right. Whereas we could be punished if we didn't salute an officer properly, the Aussie privates didn't even call their commanding officers "sir", but called them by their first names. Our own commanders were shocked by the way the Australians acted and did their best to keep us away from them in case we tried to copy them.

To keep us in line the British commanders made sure that any breach of the rules, even the slightest, was heavily punished. Jed had told me about one of his outfit who was on leave and he'd had too much to drink, and when he got back to his billet he started singing and woke up his Sergeant.

Next morning he was up for orders before the Major and was charged with being drunk on active service. He got the maximum punishment, 28 days First Field Punishment, which meant he had to parade in full pack and go up and down the road at the double, watched by the Military Police. It was hard going because he had a full pack, tin helmet, all his stuff. Then, every morning and every night, he was spread-eagled and strapped by his wrists and ankles to the big wheel of one of the large guns for an hour. His pay was stopped straight away. What was worse, so was the allowance his wife got. I heard that his wife went to the Headquarters in London and asked why she wasn't getting her money. "Your husband's got himself in trouble," they told her, and there wasn't anything she could do about it.

Public punishments like this were done to make sure that the rest of us stayed in line and didn't disobey orders, if we didn't want to suffer the same fate. But, like Charlie said, these punishments only happened to ordinary soldiers, not the officers.

At the end of our seven days' rest at the reserve camp we went back to the Front. Back to the trenches and the mud, where life could change to death in just a second. Just in the time it took a bullet or a piece of shrapnel to fly through the air. I still couldn't get what had happened to Rob out of my mind. That could have been me. If I'd stayed in the infantry instead of being sent to join the Royal Engineers, that could have been me refusing to go over the top one last time. It could have been me tied to that post and shot by my own mates. I said as much to

Charlie on our last night at the camp, but Charlie just scowled and said, "No it couldn't. You're a survivor, Billy, like me. Just so long as the Huns don't shoot us or drop a bomb on us like they did poor Ginger, you and me'll get through this. Someone's got to."

Stalemate continued all through October, with neither side making much ground and staying stuck in their own trenches. Now and then there was an offensive which gained a few yards, and then a retreat where the few yards gained were lost again. And so were a few hundred more men.

Morale was going down on our side. We hoped it was going down among the Germans as well. At this rate none of us would be home for this Christmas, or the next one, or even the one after that.

The Top Brass back at Base HQ must have been aware of how low morale was sinking because we were told that a brigadier was coming out to see for himself how we were doing in the trenches at the Front.

"We're having fun," muttered Charlie sarcastically under his breath. "Better than Blackpool."

The next day the Brigadier arrived. He looked as if he'd just stepped out from his tailor's, with his clean uniform and his boots all shiny. His manner was very confident, very full of himself, as if this war was just a small inconvenience that was interfering with his time. The Brigadier had only been in our trench for about half an hour when suddenly the Germans launched a bombardment. It was as if they knew the Brigadier was visiting.

I flung myself against the wet wall of the trench, sinking into the muddy water and keeping my head down in the hope that my helmet would keep my head safe. There was an explosion, then mud and water poured down on us.

I looked round. The Brigadier had stayed on the duckboards and was just crouching down. There was no expression on his face whatsoever. He looked like a man lost in thought. Mud rained down on him and he just crouched there. More explosions were heard. The mud wall I was pressing into shook and I thought it was going to fall on me.

"I'd advise you to get into the wall, sir!" shouted a sergeant major at the Brigadier.

The Brigadier shook his head. "Can't ruin these boots, Sarn't Major." He shouted to make himself heard above the explosions. "If I'd known the Hun was going to do this I'd have worn my second-best pair."

There were more explosions and then the sound of whistling, and then shrapnel was flying across the top of the trench, broken sheets of metal, their edges sharp as knives. They sank into the mud above us. How none of us were killed, I don't know. A few pieces of shrapnel fell into the trench, hissing when the hot metal met the cold water, but luckily none of them hit us.

As soon as there was a break in the German bombardment, the Brigadier's aide-de-camp ushered him away, along the trench to somewhere a little safer to continue his inspection.

I heard later that further along the trench some men had been hit by shrapnel during the attack and been killed. One man had put his head above the top of the trench and a piece of shrapnel had taken his head clean off, helmet and all.

A few days after the Brigadier's visit word filtered down the line that another big assault was planned.

"Not again!" groaned Charlie. "Every time we do a Big Attack it ends up the same. We get 500 yards forward, then we come back, and things go on the same until the next Big Attack."

"They say this one's going to be different," said Terry. "Everything's being thrown at the Hun at the same time. Our boys, the Aussies, the Canadians, the French. Everybody going at once. They reckon we're going to take Passchendaele Ridge."

"I can't see the point," Charlie shrugged. "With all this shelling that's gone on, I bet there's nothing left of it. It'll just be another big hole in the ground."

"Yeah," chuckled Wally, "but it'll be our hole in the ground, not the Germans'. Ain't that what this war's about?"

We had confirmation of what Terry had heard the next day. We had a new sergeant, Sergeant Peters, and he assembled us in the mud outside our dugout.

"Right, men," he told us. "We're going to make a big advance and push the Hun right back to Germany where he belongs. It's going to be done with everything we've got: tanks, planes and men. The infantry are going over the top, but they'll be lost without us Engineers. Without us laying cable lines right under their noses, they won't know where they are or what's happening. They have to be able to keep in touch with Command at all times, is that clear?"

"Yes, Sarge," we responded.

"Right. For this offensive, you're being attached to specific units. Your job is to keep them in communication, whatever happens. Morgan. Stevens."

"Yes, sir!" Charlie and I said the same time.

"You're with 74th Brigade. Crow. Parks. You're with the 1st Battalion of the Hertfordshires." And so on down the list, as Sergeant Peters attached us to fighting units.

A sinking feeling came into my stomach. This was it. After all our time in the reserve trenches, now we were being pushed forward for this major assault. We were going over the top. This should have been my moment of glory, the one I'd dreamed about when I was back in Carlisle, but now, with all I'd seen of this war, so many dead and just stalemate after stalemate, it didn't seem so glorious after all.

0500 hours on 12 October found me and Charlie, each loaded down with rolls of cable and our tools, crouched in the darkness in a trench along with the men from the 74th Brigade of Guards.

Each Guardsman had his rifle ready, bayonet fixed. The Lieutenant in charge seemed a decent sort of bloke. He was young, but he didn't throw his weight about. He spoke quietly and his air of confidence passed around our group.

The rum ration appeared and was passed along the line, each man taking a swig.

"Deadens the pain if you get hit," winked one Guardsman to me.

"Only if you drink a whole bottle," cracked another.

At 0515 hours our big guns opened up, pouring shells down on the German lines just yards away from us.

The Germans retaliated with their own barrage, and soon the early-morning sky above our heads was filled with tracers of fire, and the earth both behind and ahead of us rocked with the sounds of explosions. Mud hurled up and came down on top of us in showers.

The Lieutenant came over to Charlie and me. "There's a German pillbox about a hundred yards ahead," he told us. "You Engineers come over with the third wave. We should have cleaned the pillbox out by the time you get there. That's where I want you to set up the first communication point."

"Right, sir," I said.

The Lieutenant headed back down the line, checking his watch.

0520. 0525. As the hands of my watch moved to 0530, we saw the Lieutenant put his whistle to his lips … and then he blew, the shrill blast barely heard beneath the sounds of the artillery barrage, but the movement of the soldiers around us told us it was time. The attack was on.

The first wave of Guards went up the scaling ladders and over the top, crouching low, firing their rifles as they went. I noticed that the Lieutenant had been the first one over. The second wave soon followed. I could hear the chatter chatter chatter of machine-guns from the

German lines, and the sound of our boys' rifles.

"OK, third wave!" said a voice.

Charlie and I looked at each other, then shook hands.

"Good luck, mate," said Charlie.

With that I grabbed the slippery rungs of the scaling ladder, and climbed up to the top of the trench, weighed down by the length of cable trailing behind me. This was surely hell on earth. Thick smoke hung over the mud. Dead and dying men were sprawled on the ground, some half in the mud, and the red lines of tracer fire kept coming. The distance we had to cover looked vast, even though it was only 100 yards or so. Already, many of the soldiers I had talked with in the trench lay on the ground, dead or dying.

"Come on!" yelled Charlie, and he began to run.

I joined him, moving as fast as I could with the mud dragging at my boots. Bullets smacked into the mud around me. It's amazing how fast you can move when your life is at stake. Now and then I felt myself stepping on a dead body and a couple of times I nearly lost my balance in the mud, but I put my head down, gritted my teeth and kept going.

As the Germans kept up their fire from their defensive positions I saw more soldiers around me stumble and then go down.

I neared the German lines and, through the smoke, saw the pillbox the Lieutenant had told us about, a concrete structure just visible sticking up from the mud. As I watched, one of our soldiers lobbed a grenade into the pillbox through one of the narrow openings, and then ducked away. There was the sound of a muffled explosion, and then smoke poured out from it, followed by the sound of screams as the Germans in the pillbox took the blast of the grenade. Then a couple of our soldiers dropped down into the German trench and I heard the sound of rifle fire.

Charlie and I reached the German trench and threw ourselves down into it. We were just in time. The spot where I'd been standing a second before erupted into a mass of flying wet clay as a German machine-gun poured its bullets into it.

Charlie and I dropped our rolls of cable and stood there, panting hard, trying to get our breath.

"Hurry up and get that line connected!" the Lieutenant shouted, then he charged forward, firing his pistol towards the German lines.

Charlie and I hurried inside the concrete pillbox. The three German soldiers inside were dead, their bodies lying twisted, their eyes still open.

"Better get them out first," I shouted.

We dragged the dead German soldiers out, and then set to work, hauling the cable in and setting up a telegraph point inside the pillbox. The Guards had moved on and were already attacking the next line of German defence, but the sound of rifle fire was so close we could tell that they were meeting very stiff opposition.

The Lieutenant appeared in the entrance to the pillbox just as we finished making the connections to the wire. "Are we in contact yet?" he demanded.

"Nearly, sir," said Charlie. "Just a minute more."

"Good man," said the Lieutenant. And with that he went out again to see how the forward troops were getting on.

In fact, that 100 yards was as far as we managed to advance that day. Or the next, come to that. The Germans poured everything they had down on to us, heavy shells, machine-guns, tracers, gas, but we just bunkered down and stayed where we were.

Charlie and I took it in turns to operate the telegraph-receiving key, while the other secured the line. On my stint at the key I started to get reports through from the other divisions on how they'd fared in the Big Attack, and I learnt that the Guards Division that Charlie and I were with had done well to get this far. Other units hadn't done so well. The main assault on what remained of the village of Poelcapelle on the Passchendaele Ridge by a joint force of British and Australians had been a disaster. The 2nd Australian and the British 49th and 66th Divisions had been all but wiped out in the attack.

The same story was repeated all along the line. Unit after unit had been wiped out, and only about 100 yards of ground gained in a few places, like ours.

Reports also came in about our tank offensives. Those great lumbering heavy machines had been unleashed, intended to force their way through the wire and right through the German lines. But tank after tank had got stuck in the mud, sinking so deep that their tracks couldn't haul them out. Bogged down like that, they'd been sitting targets for the German heavy guns.

It looked like the attempt to take Passchendaele had stalled.

The next day, the Germans launched a counter-offensive against our position. The machine-guns along our new trench top kept up a steady stream of fire, a constant barrage of noise that made it difficult for me to listen to the messages coming through the wires properly. All the time the German artillery kept up their attack on our positions – and still the rain came down.

November – December 1917

During the weeks that followed, we maintained our front-line position. The attacks from both sides kept on and the rain kept coming down. Men died and lay where they fell, or were wounded and were stretchered back to the dressing camps. The badly wounded got a "Blighty Ticket", which meant they would be sent back home.

Whatever High Command said about this war being over by Christmas and the Germans being defeated, in our trenches our belief that this war would ever be over began to fade.

And then, on 6 November, the news came over the telegraph wires that the Canadians had broken through the German lines and taken Passchendaele itself. The Germans were in retreat! The War was over!

Over the next week, I listened as the reports came in over the wires. The Canadian Corps had been the victors at Passchendaele, but had lost 16,500 men in the battle. Elsewhere along the line, our forces had pushed forward. There was now a new front line, just a few hundred yards further forward from the old front line. The Germans had moved back, but they were still there, just 100 yards or so away from our lines. The War was far from over – we were back at stalemate.

December finally came. The rain poured down as heavy as ever. The heavy guns kept up their barrage on both sides. The shooting from rifles and machine-guns continued from every infantry trench.

And then, one morning as dawn was coming up, Charlie and I came out of our pillbox and just stood there, listening, unable to believe our ears.

Silence.

Nothing. Not from our guns, nor the German guns. Not from any guns anywhere along the lines. Everything was quiet and still. It had even stopped raining at last!

"Maybe the War's over," I whispered, afraid to speak too loudly in case I disturbed the silence.

"No," said Charlie, also whispering, in awe at the stillness. "Do you know what day it is? It's Christmas Day."

We looked at one another as it sunk in. Charlie was right. Christmas Day.

"Happy Christmas," said Charlie. Then he looked around us, at the trench, the mud, and laughed. "We'd better get our Christmas dinner prepared," he grinned. "What'll it be? Roast turkey? Duck? Chicken? Christmas pud with custard?"

"No," I chuckled. "Let's have something really special today. Let's have tinned bully beef and biscuits."

And we both laughed.

A call from further along the trenches caught our attention. It was a Guardsman from the forward front trench.

"Hey, lads!" he called. "You should come along and hear what's happening up the Front!"

Intrigued, Charlie and me splashed our way through the mud along the reserve trench, and then made our way through the communication trench to the front line.

Some soldiers had climbed to the top and their heads were above the top of the trench, and they were straining their ears to listen to something. In the eerie silence, we could hear voices calling to us from the German trenches, drifting across the mud and barbed wire of No Man's Land.

"Hey, Tommy!" called a German voice. "Happy Christmas!"

The soldier at the top of the ladder nearest to us looked down at us, grinned, and said in surprise, "What d'you know? They're sending us Christmas greetings!"

"Well don't be a sourpuss, Jim!" said another soldier. "Send 'em back."

"Right," said Jim. He hauled himself higher up the ladder.

"Careful," warned another of the soldiers. "It might be a trick. Stick your head too far over the top and they might shoot it off."

"If they do you can stick some holly in it and put it on the table like a Christmas pudding," joked Jim. Then he called towards the German lines: "Hey, Fritz! Can you hear me?"

There was a pause, then the German soldier shouted back: "I hear you, Tommy!"

"Good!" shouted Jim. "Merry Christmas from all of us here!"

There was a pause, and then we heard more voices calling from the

German lines: "Merry Christmas to you!"

"Ask 'em what they're having for Christmas dinner," said another soldier.

"You ask 'em, Jack," said Jim. "I don't see why I should be doing all the shouting."

Jack climbed up another of the scaling ladders until he, too, had his head well above the top of the trench.

"Hey, Fritz!" he called. "What are you having for Christmas dinner?"

"We are having rat!" called back the German.

"Rat?" echoed Jack. "Is that all?"

"*Ja*, Tommy," came the German's reply. "But it is a very big fat rat. Lots of meat on it! What are you having?"

"Oh, the usual!" called Jack. "Roast beef. Roast potatoes. Gravy. Brussels sprouts." Then he laughed and added, "That's providing my butler gets here with it in time in my car!"

All us lads in the trench laughed, and we heard the Germans laugh too.

Suddenly we heard the noise of something coming through the air towards us from the German trenches.

"They're chucking something!" called Jim.

"Grenades!" yelled one soldier, and we all ducked.

Instead, something hit the top of the trench and lay there. Jack picked it up and showed it to us.

It was a small rock. Tied to it was a packet of German cigarettes.

"Happy Christmas, Tommy!" called the voice. "A present from us to you!"

We watched as Jack untied the packet of cigarettes. He took one, and then passed the packet down. "Here you are mates," he said. "A Christmas present from Kaiser Bill's men. Pass them around."

"We got to give them something back," said Charlie. "We can't just take them and leave it like that."

"You're right," I agreed. "But what?"

"I'm not giving them my tobacco," said one soldier firmly.

"Me, neither," said another.

There was much nodding of heads at this in general agreement.

"Come on, mates, we don't want to be seen to be mean," said Jim.

"How about chucking over a tin of bully beef?" suggested another soldier.

"What, and poison 'em for Christmas?" I said, and the others laughed.

"I've got a flask with some rum in it," said one soldier. "I've been saving up my rations. It's only a little flask."

"Sounds good to me," said Jack. "OK, Shorty, hand it up and I'll chuck it over."

Shorty rummaged around in his kit and produced a battered metal flask. He handed it up the ladder to Jack. "Here you are," he said. "But make sure you throw it right the way over. I don't want it ending up in the middle of No Man's Land and going to waste."

Jack held the flask in his hand, and then looked towards the German lines. I saw the look of doubt on his face. "I don't know," he said.

"Throwing a rock is one thing. It's hard to judge the weight of this, with the rum sloshing around inside it like that."

"I'll throw it," I offered.

Charlie gave me a doubtful look. "You reckon you can get it over there?" he asked.

"If a Hun can throw a rock, I can throw that the same distance," I said.

Jack came down the ladder and handed me the metal flask.

"OK," he said. "Over to you."

I climbed up the ladder. Although there was still no shooting, I couldn't stop myself from hesitating before I put my head over the top of the trench, it had become such a force of habit.

Then I hauled myself over the top and stood there, looking out over the expanse of clayey, potholed, bomb-shelled ground, strewn with barbed wire. Everyone and everything else was below ground level.

I looked towards the German lines. "Where are you, Fritz?" I called. "We've got a Christmas present for you!"

A head with a German helmet poked up from behind the lines, about 70 yards away. "Here, Tommy!" he called. And he waved his arm.

I held the flask in my hand and measured the distance to the German lines in my mind.

I pulled my arm back, crouched, and then shouted: "Merry Christmas, Fritz! Have a drink on us!"

And then I let fly, swinging my arm round as hard as I could and putting as much force as I could into my throw.

The metal flask sailed up into the air, glinting as it caught the light from the sun's early rays. Then it came down ... down ... and disappeared into the German trench.

We heard a loud cheer go up from the German lines, and then the German's head popped back into view again. He was holding the flask and he waved it at me.

"Thank you, Tommy!" he shouted. "We will drink your health today!"

I clambered down the ladder from the top of the trench, and the soldiers in the trench grinned broadly at me and clapped.

"With a throw like that, you ought to be playing cricket for England, lad," said Jim.

Just then a young lieutenant appeared from the reserve trench, accompanied by a sergeant. "What's all this noise going on!" he demanded.

"Just exchanging Christmas presents with Fritz, sir!" said Jack. "A packet of cigs for a flask of rum."

The Lieutenant didn't seem impressed.

He looked along the line at each of us, unsmiling, and then he said in clipped tones: "Fraternizing with the enemy is an offence liable to court martial. I'd stop it if you don't want to find yourself in serious trouble. Don't forget, tomorrow you'll be killing them again. And they'll be killing you."

With that he turned and headed back to the reserve trench. The Sergeant gave us a look that seemed to say "Sorry, blokes, nothing I can do about it." Then the Sergeant went after the Lieutenant.

Shorty looked down at the packet of German cigarettes that were now in his hand. There was one left in the packet. He took it out and put it to his lips.

"It's a present and it's Christmas," he said. "It's more than I got from any general in this army, so I'm keeping it."

And then, strangest of all, we heard the sound of singing coming from the German trenches.

"It's a carol," said Charlie. "They're singing 'Silent Night' in German."

It seemed so strange, being here in this place surrounded by so much death and destruction and misery, and hearing that beautiful sound carrying on the air, a song I'd known and sung ever since I was a child. I remembered Rob and me singing it when we were at junior school, every Christmas. I couldn't help it, but I found myself singing along with them, but in English. And Charlie joined in, and then Jack, and then we were all of us singing, English voices and German voices mixed together singing the same tune.

If I live to be a hundred, I'll never forget that special Christmas Day. No presents, no special dinner, nothing but men on opposing sides in a war joining together to sing just one carol.

Then it was over.

The rest of that day was strange. Still no bombs, no shooting, just me and my mates being kind of quiet together and thinking about our families back home. We wondered how they were, and if they were thinking of us out here. It struck me that I hadn't written a letter home for ages, not since I'd been at Base HQ. Mum would kill me when I got back home for not writing.

At midnight exactly, the big guns started up again, from both sides. Christmas was over. It was just as the Lieutenant had said: once again, we were killing them, and they were killing us. Four years on, and we were still at war.

Epilogue
January 1918 – June 1919

My war ended on 6 January 1918 just outside Passchendaele. I was hit by a German shell. Once again, I was lucky to be alive, but this time my left arm and left leg were smashed by shrapnel. At the Casualty Station they talked about amputating both my leg and my arm, but again I was lucky: the doctor who treated me insisted that he could reset them enough so that they would mend. I would always walk with a limp, and it would take time before I could use my left arm again, but at least I wouldn't lose them.

I was sent back home to England. First I went to a military hospital on the northern outskirts of London at a place called Mill Hill. There I wrote home to Mum and Dad and told them what had happened and that I was alive, and I'd be returning home as soon as I was able.

I also wrote the hardest letter I've ever had to write. This one was to Mrs Matthews, Rob's mum, telling her how sorry I was about what had happened to him, and not to believe the worst of him. I told her how Rob was the bravest soldier I'd known all the time I was out there, and that what had happened to him was wrong. She wrote back. It was just a short letter, but she never had been very good at reading and writing. It meant a lot to me that she managed to write back.

I went back home to Carlisle in June. I was able to walk, even though I used a stick to help me get about. I thought my mum would be angry when she saw me again and say "I told you so!" when she saw me with my stick, but when I knocked at our door and she opened it, she threw her arms around me and burst into tears.

By September of 1918 everyone reckoned the War was as good as over. The Germans were in retreat on all fronts and our side was pushing forward all the time. The end came in November 1918 when the Germans finally surrendered.

In June 1919, they put up a monument in Carlisle with the names of the local men who'd gone out to the War and died. The name of Robert Matthews wasn't on it. I went along to see the local Council with Mrs Matthews and asked that they put Rob's name on it, but this little official with a small moustache said to us: "We don't put the names of cowards on the same memorial as brave men." I got angry then and asked him which part of the War he'd fought in, knowing full well he'd stayed safely back in Carlisle the whole time, but Mrs Matthews asked me not to make a fuss, so I shut up and took her back home. But it didn't stop me feeling angry.

I still feel angry every time I pass that memorial, and one day, I swear, I'm going to make sure that Rob's name gets carved on that memorial. He deserves to be there, along with all the others who died out there in the mud of Flanders.

HISTORICAL NOTE

The roots of the First World War, which lasted from 1914 until 1918, can be traced back to the Franco-Prussian War of 1870–1871. During this war, France was defeated by Germany, and France's eastern provinces, Alsace and Lorraine, became part of a new and larger unified Germany. From that moment, Germany seemed determined to continue to expand and become the leading world power. Aware of Germany's intentions, other European nations – including Britain and Russia – began to prepare for war. For its part, France was determined to get Alsace-Lorraine back from Germany. Germany was aware of this, and also aware that it might also have to fight a war against the Russians who were military allies of France. The German strategy, developed by Count Alfred von Schlieffen in 1905, was that if war was declared, Germany would attack and defeat France first and then attack Russia.

The spark that ignited the War was the assassination of Archduke Franz Ferdinand of Austria and his wife in Sarajevo on 28 June 1914. As a result, Austria-Hungary declared war on Serbia. Two days later Czar Nicholas II put his Russian army in support of Serbia. Germany, acting in support of her ally, Austria-Hungary, demanded that Russia stand down. Russia refused and Germany declared war on

Russia.

Putting the von Schlieffen strategy into action, on August 2 Germany demanded from neutral Belgium the right of passage through its land to attack France. Belgium refused, and on August 4, German troops invaded Belgium.

Britain was bound by a treaty to guarantee Belgium's safety if Belgium was ever attacked. Britain was also aware that if the Channel ports fell to an enemy, then Britain was at risk from invasion. So on 4 August 1914 at 11pm (London time), Britain declared war on Germany.

The reason it became a World War rather than just a European War was because all the major European powers, including Britain, Germany and France, were Empires with colonies overseas. Britain's colonies spread as far as Australia and New Zealand, Canada and India. All these colonies then joined the War in support of their "home" country. So, for example, soldiers from British units stationed in Africa were in conflict with soldiers from German units also stationed there, and so fighting broke out between them, although not with the same intensity as in Europe. Many of the British colonies also sent troops to Europe to fight in the War.

More alliances were formed as other countries across the world took sides and got drawn into the War. In 1917 America, which had so far been neutral, entered the War on the side of the two main Allies, Britain and France, although the main body of their troops did not arrive in Europe until 1918.

It was on the Western Front, in the fields of Flanders in Belgium that most of the casualties occurred. The casualty figures for the battlefield conflict alone were:

France: 1,385,300 dead, 3,614,700 wounded
Germany: 1,808,545 dead, 4,247,143 wounded
British Empire: 947,023 dead, 2,313,558 wounded
USA: 115,660 dead, 210,216 wounded

Total: 4,256, 528 dead and 10,385,617 wounded
– making 14,642,145 casualties in all

To put this into perspective (from the British side): it meant that 12 per cent of the total number of British soldiers who served on the Western Front were killed (that's one soldier in every eight), while nearly 38 per cent were wounded. In other words, half of all the British soldiers who went to France became casualties of the war.

The muddy quagmires that were the battlefields of the Western Front, which themselves contributed so much to the deaths of so many, were the result of the heavy shells used by both sides. The fields of Flanders lay on non-absorbent clay, and over generations a network of drains had been constructed just beneath the surface of the fields, to drain rainwater from the fields into the sea. The bombing smashed these drains. With the water unable to escape, the fields soon turned to mud.

During the years of war on the Western Front the front line swung backwards and forwards from time to time, but there was little decisive change. Sometimes the Germans would make advances, and sometimes the Allies – with often just a few hundreds yards being gained by each side. The stalemate between both sides on the Western Front, which included the battle at Passchendaele, continued until August 1918 when the Allies made a major break-through of the German lines at Amiens. From that moment the German military machine began to crumble. During August and September, major advances by the Allies pushed the German forces further back. By October 1918 the German leaders were sending out peace-notes to the Western leaders.

The War finally ended on 11th November 1918. On that day the Armistice was signed. Two days before this it had been announced that the German Kaiser, Wilhelm II, had abdicated and had gone into exile, and a German Republic had been proclaimed.

The First World War was over.

However, for one German soldier who served in the trenches on the Somme, it was just the beginning. A British shell had hit the trench and killed most of the German soldiers in it. This particular soldier was lucky and he escaped with just minor injuries. His name was Adolf Hitler.

Christmas truces on the Western Front

On the first Christmas Day of the War, 25 December 1914, there was an unofficial truce between the ordinary German and British troops in the opposing trenches. They came out of their trenches and met in No Man's

Land, where they shook hands, wished one another a Happy Christmas, and exchanged souvenirs. Some even posed for photographs together.

Perhaps the most famous event of this 1914 Christmas truce was the football game between British soldiers and German soldiers played in No Man's Land.

After this truce of 1914, there were no further examples of such close fraternization between the men of both sides, although the other Christmas Days right up to the end of the war in 1918 were marked by a ceasefire by both sides, and an exchange of shouted greetings, and an occasional exchange of small gifts such as cigarettes.

TIMELINE

June 1914 Assassination of Archduke Franz Ferdinand at Sarajevo. Austria attacks Serbia.

July 1914 Austria and Hungary at war with Russia.

August 1914 Germany declares war on Russia and France and invades Belgium. Great Britain declares war on Germany.

September 1914 First trenches of the Western Front are dug.

December 1914 Unofficial Christmas truce declared by Western Front soldiers.

April 1915 Battles of Aisne and Ypres.

September 1915 Battle of Loos. Italy joins War on side of Allies. Austro-German invasion of Poland.

February 1916 The longest battle of the War, Verdun, begins. Neither side wins, but there are an estimated one million casualties.

July–November 1916 Battle of the Somme – about a million casualties, but little ground gained by Allies.

December 1916 David Lloyd George is elected Prime Minister of Great Britain. Battle of Verdun ends.

March 1917 Tsar Nicholas II of Russia abdicates. Germany launches first of five major offensives to try and win the war.

April 1917 USA declares war on Germany. Mutinies in French army begin.

June 1917 Battle of Messines – British explode nineteen mines under the ridge.

October 1917 Battle of Passchendaele. Russian workers revolt against the ruling classes – leads to Armistice between Russia and Germany.

March 1918 Treaty of Brest-Litovsk ends Russian participation in the War.

July 1918 Former Russian Tsar, Nicholas II and his family murdered by Bolshevik rebels.

August–September 1918 Allied offensive on Western Front forces German retreat.

November 1918 Allied-German armistice. German naval fleet surrenders. Kaiser Wilhelm II of Germany abdicates. Germany proclaimed a Republic.

June 1919 Treaty of Versailles signed between Allies and Germany.

July 1919 Cenotaph unveiled in London to commemorate the dead.